The Edge of Wonderlust

Kimber Guise

ISBN: 979-8-9994794-1-9

Cover design by Kimber Guise

*Printed in United States

Published by Guise Publishing House

First Edition

This is a work of fiction.

Names, characters, businesses, places, events, locales, and incidents are either the products of the author's imagination or used in a fictitious manner. Any resemblance to actual persons, living or dead, or actual events is purely coincidental.

Table of Contents

Chapter One:
Where the Ground Echoes

The air thickened again—but this time, it wasn't oppressive. It felt reverent. Like the land was holding its breath, waiting for her response.

Haylee's fingers trembled as she pulled her hand back from the stone. Sam steadied her, his touch grounding, his eyes searching her face as if trying to make sense of whatever she'd just experienced. She blinked, slowly, like someone waking from a deep trance.

Bella jumped down from the rock with a quick flick of her tail—mission complete. Josie let out a single sharp bark, not from fear, but more like a command or a signal. All clear, let's move.

Haylee looked around. The ridge hadn't changed—but everything had. The light now fell at a different angle across the stones. A subtle ringing in her ears began to fade, and the weight in her chest loosened. Something had shifted. She couldn't name it yet, but she could feel it in her bones.

A whisper of footsteps stirred behind them. She turned. No one was there.

Sam's voice broke the silence. "What now?"

She didn't hesitate. "We go back," she said quietly. "And we listen."

Bella led the descent, but slower this time. She didn't dart ahead—she paused often, glancing back to make sure they followed. Haylee felt it too, the difference. Something was now with her—not a presence exactly, but a purpose. A quiet sense of responsibility woven into her chest.

When they reached Bertha, Haylee opened her journal and began to write. She scribbled quickly, not bothering with neatness, only urgency—before the images faded, before doubt tried to steal them away.

She wrote what she saw. She wrote what she felt:
I thought I'd be afraid if something like this happened again.

But I'm not.

Bella led me to it. Josie confirmed it. Sam felt it too.

That's what made it real—not just some dreamy leftover from my imagination, but real enough to make us pause.

Real enough that Sam didn't even question it. He just stood by me.

Maybe I'm not just uncovering Aggie's path.

Maybe I'm walking into mine.

And for the first time… I'm not doing it alone.

And she underlined the final line:

"I think the Ridge gave me a piece of the Veil."

The Message Beyond

That night, long after the fire had faded to glowing embers and the others had fallen asleep, Haylee tossed beneath the covers, her forehead damp with sweat. The darkness behind her eyes rippled—then gave way to a familiar dreamscape.

She stood in a shifting field of shadow and mist—the same place she had seen before. Cold silence wrapped around her, broken only by the whisper of wind, the rustle of something just beyond sight.

Then he appeared.

Elliot.

Tall. Indistinct. More like a smudge in reality than a man. He turned his head toward her, eyes glowing faintly with an unnatural light.

But this time, something changed.

From the shadows behind him, another figure emerged.

Aggie.

She stepped forward—ethereal, but unmistakable. Her face was softer than Haylee remembered, worn by time but filled with clarity. She locked eyes with Haylee, and for the first time, she spoke directly.

"Haylee," Aggie said, her voice echoing like wind through canyon walls. *"You can't let Elliot get the medallion. But there's something you need to know."*

The air shimmered. Aggie stepped closer.

"Go to River Canyon. I have a storage building there. You'll find everything you need."

Then, as if sensing Elliot's focus shift fully toward her, Aggie placed a protective hand between them. Her final look was filled with urgency.

"Don't wait too long."

Haylee gasped in her sleep, her body drenched in sweat—but she didn't wake. Her limbs twitched. Her breath was shallow. She was trapped in the dream.

Sam stirred beside her, drawn instantly from sleep by the distressed look on her face. In a heartbeat, he was leaning over her, concern etched across every line of his expression.

"Haylee? Hey—wake up." He cupped her cheeks, gently shaking her. "It's just a dream. Come back."

Nothing. Her body remained stiff, eyes darting beneath closed lids.

"Haylee!"

He gripped her hand. "You're safe. You're with me."

And then, with a violent gasp, Haylee bolted upright—eyes wild, body trembling. Her breaths came fast and shallow.

Sam stared at her—alarmed, but relieved. He held her hand tighter.

"You're back. You're okay."

Haylee blinked away the fog of sleep. "It was the same dream… but different this time. Aggie spoke to me. She told me to go to River Canyon. There's something there. Something she left behind."

They sat in silence for a beat, the weight of her words settling between them. Sam's voice was quiet, but firm.

"Then that's where we go next."

Chapter Two:
The Weight of Morning

Haylee hadn't slept the rest of the night—not after that dream.

By first light, she was already awake, hunched over a paper map at the small table inside Bertha. Her finger traced the worn edge of a highway leading toward River Canyon. She plugged the coordinates into her phone's GPS just to be sure.

"Aggie, what's really going on?" she thought, not expecting an answer. But then she felt it—a faint tingling in her chest, soft and comforting, like warmth blooming from within.

She closed her eyes for a moment. The feeling lingered. A whisper of reassurance.

Just as she opened the RV door to let Josie out, the sound roused Sam. He sat up, rubbing his eyes.

"I'll take the first shift driving," Sam said, stretching. He watched Haylee quietly as she slipped on her boots and hoodie.

Haylee gave him a small nod before stepping outside, Josie trotting ahead into the crisp morning.

Sam grabbed his jacket and followed her.

"I don't think you should be going anywhere alone," he said gently, falling into step beside her.

Haylee didn't protest. After the festival—and especially after that dream—her nerves were still tight.

"I'm okay," she said, though her voice didn't quite match the words.

They walked in silence through the dewy grass, Josie sniffing every wildflower and patch of dirt with renewed enthusiasm.

5

Sam finally spoke. "Did you sleep at all?"

Haylee shook her head. "Not really."

"You want to talk about it?"

"Maybe when we're on the road," she replied, her voice distant. "I just... need to move."

Sam nodded. He understood that kind of restlessness.

Behind them, the campground was beginning to stir. Bella had taken up her usual sunbathing position in the RV's kitchen sink. They were all waiting—for a direction, for answers, for what came next.

And River Canyon was calling.

Before They Go

After breakfast, Haylee and Sam sat across from each other at the tiny dinette table, a half-drunk cup of coffee cooling between them.

"We should call Dad and Riles," Haylee said. "They need to know what happened at the ridge. And the dream."

Sam nodded. "They'll want to be there. If Aggie left something behind, it probably connects all of us."

Haylee pulled out her phone and found enough signal to place the call. She put it on speaker.

David answered quickly, his voice alert. "Haylee?"

"Yeah. We're okay," she said. "But something happened."

She and Sam took turns explaining—Bella's behavior, the ridge, the symbol on the stone, and the dream with Aggie's message.

There was a pause.

"You're heading to River Canyon?" David asked.

"We are," Haylee said. "Aggie said she has a storage unit there. She said it has answers."

Riles chimed in through the speaker, his voice sharp with concern. "Then we'll meet you there. Text us the location."

Haylee glanced at Sam. "We'll see you soon."

As the call ended, the weight in her chest eased slightly. They weren't going into this alone.

And whatever lay ahead in River Canyon—they would face it together.

Ink and Ash

Haylee sat cross-legged on the bed with Aggie's worn leather journals spread out around her. Sam poured two mugs of coffee and joined her, peering over her shoulder as she thumbed through a volume marked only with the letters **RC**.

"You think this one means River Canyon?" he asked, nudging his mug toward her.

Haylee nodded slowly. "That, or she had a secret recipe for red curry." She cracked a smile, but it didn't quite reach her eyes. "I think she left us more than just the dream."

They flipped through pages scrawled with thoughts, dates, half-sketched maps, and cryptic notations. Sam pointed to one entry near the middle:

Safe Storage. Unit 13. RC. Locked. Keep the key hidden where only trust will find it.

Beneath it was a short riddle:

When you open me I will reveal
What you need when you need it.
Beneath the velvet,
Past the seal—
The answer waits where silence feels.

Haylee read it aloud, then stared at the words. "It sounds like… a place."

"Or an object," Sam said. "Wait—'beneath the velvet'?"

Haylee's eyes widened. She turned toward the trunk under the bed—the one Aggie had always said was *for keepsakes*.

She dropped to her knees and opened it. A few old quilts were folded neatly on top, alongside a velvet pouch that held a compass and a few small stones.

But when she ran her fingers along the inside corners of the trunk, one patch of fabric felt slightly raised.

"Here." Her voice trembled. She pulled back the lining to reveal a glowing symbol etched faintly into the wood. As they watched, it pulsed softly—like it was breathing.

Tucked into a narrow slot just below the symbol was a single brass key, delicate and aged, tied with a purple thread.

Sam let out a low whistle. "Aggie didn't just hide things. She buried them in poetry."

Haylee held the key in her palm, suddenly aware of its weight. "This is it. This is the next step."

Sam placed his hand over hers. "We'll face it together."

She met his gaze, then looked down at the journal still open beside them.

Aggie had left them a trail. And now, piece by piece, it was starting to unfold.

Roadside Revelation

They were halfway to River Canyon when the sharp pop of a blown tire jolted everyone inside Bertha.

"Hang on!" Sam called, gripping the wheel as Bertha swerved slightly before he eased her to a steady stop on the side of the quiet, two-lane road.

Haylee was already unbuckling.

Sam joined her. "I'll grab the jack."

"Think it's the front driver's side," he muttered, stepping out to inspect. The road was deserted—nothing but dusty trees and wide sky in every direction. No danger of passing cars. Just stillness and heat.

Haylee slipped on her boots and clipped Josie's leash. "We'll stretch our legs," she said. "No sense in just standing around."

As Sam got to work changing the tire, Haylee wandered a short distance down the roadside, Josie sniffing every wildflower and sun-bleached rock. The air was still, but the moment felt oddly peaceful.

By the time she returned, the new tire was almost in place. Haylee ducked inside to make sandwiches—thick slices of bread with whatever she could find in Bertha's fridge. When she handed one to Sam, he took it with a grateful nod, eyes still fixed on the horizon.

Haylee's breath hitched. "So River Canyon—it's not just about answers anymore. It's about staying ahead of Elliot."

Sam nodded. "But whatever's waiting for us—Elliot wants it. Bad."

They ate in silence for a while after that, the quiet hum of the wind and distant bird calls their only company.

Haylee looked out at the road stretching ahead. It wasn't just a route on a map anymore.

It was a line between before and after.

"We're out of time. Elliot's not just looking for the medallion. He's getting stronger. If he gets what he wants, none of us will be able to stop him," Haylee added.

Because the road was only getting darker.

And River Canyon held more than just answers—it might hold the last chance they had.

Chapter Three:
Shadows in the Familiar

River Canyon was smaller than Haylee expected—a dusty, sun-soaked town nestled between red rock cliffs, with a single main street that looked like it hadn't changed in fifty years. But something about it felt... important. As if it had been waiting for them all along.

They didn't go to the storage facility right away. David and Riles hadn't arrived yet, and Sam insisted they wait.

"No sense stirring things up before we have backup," he'd said.

So, they wandered.

Haylee, Sam, and Josie stuck together, strolling past faded storefronts and signs that creaked in the breeze. A coffee shop, a bait and tackle store, a bakery that smelled like cinnamon and firewood. It could have been any town—except it wasn't.

Haylee paused in front of an antique shop. "I want to go in," she said softly. Sam gave a slight nod and followed her, Josie trotting ahead.

Inside, the air was musty and sweet, filled with old wood and worn leather. Every surface held treasures from a different era—mismatched clocks, postcards from vanished places, dusty records with cracked covers.

Josie sniffed along the base of a low shelf, tail flicking with interest. Haylee wandered between aisles, her fingertips grazing the tops of old books and rusted tools.

"I used to love places like this as a kid," she said. "Felt like stepping into a story someone forgot to finish."

Sam smiled, hands in his pockets. "Still kind of feels that way."

In the back of the shop, Josie gave a sharp bark and nosed at a wooden crate. Haylee crouched beside her and pried the lid open. Inside was a small, wrapped cloth bundle. Something within it pulsed faintly—like warmth stored up from another time.

She unwrapped it carefully.

A photograph.

Haylee sucked in a breath.

It was Aggie—young, vibrant, standing beside Bertha in what looked like a desert landscape. But behind her, half-caught in shadow, stood a man. Tall, sharp-eyed, too familiar.

Elliot.

Sam knelt beside her, scanning the photo. "Is that...?"

"Yeah," Haylee whispered.

They stared at it in silence. There was something haunting in the way he looked at Aggie—like he already knew she'd one day try to stop him.

"Why was this here?" Sam asked.

"I don't know," Haylee said, heart pounding. "But maybe this town has more answers than we thought."

Dust Behind and Ahead

The road to River Canyon stretched out like a ribbon of heat and silence. David kept one hand on the wheel, the other resting on the console, his fingers tapping a steady rhythm. Riles sat beside him, slouched low, arms crossed, eyes scanning the desert horizon like it might suddenly shift into something else.

"You sure about this?" Riles finally asked, voice low.

David gave a dry laugh. "I'm not sure about anything lately."

Riles huffed, running a hand through his hair. "No offense, but driving halfway across the state because Haylee had a dream? Even after what we've seen... it still feels like a stretch."

David didn't answer right away. The Jeep rumbled beneath them, steady as always, but the air inside felt thick with everything unsaid.

"Riles," David said finally, "I've spent a lot of time ignoring what I didn't understand. It didn't make it go away."

Silence.

Then Riles shifted, uncomfortable. "It's just—what if we're walking into something we're not ready for?"

David's eyes stayed on the road. "Then we'll face it. Together."

A long beat passed.

"You see that car back there?" Riles asked suddenly.

"What car?"

"Exactly." Riles sat up straighter. "There was a dark SUV two turns back. It was behind us for a while, but now it's just gone."

David glanced in the rearview mirror, jaw tightening. "You think we're being followed?"

"I don't know." Riles rubbed his temple. "Probably just jumpy."

"Or maybe not."

They drove in silence for a few more miles.

Riles broke it again, quieter this time. "So... the dream. You really think Aggie sent it?"

David didn't hesitate. "If anyone could reach across the veil, it's her."

Riles stared ahead, the weight of memory flickering across his features. "I just hope she knows what she's asking us to do."

David nodded slowly. "Me too."

As the canyon walls began to rise on the horizon, Riles exhaled. The town was close now—just a few more turns between them and whatever answers waited. Or whatever dangers.

A Quiet Arsenal

As they pulled into the small, quaint town, David and Riles decided to peel off toward the hardware store, muttering something about being prepared "for anything."

David pushed open the door, greeted by the soft chime of an old bell and the faint scent of sawdust. A man behind the counter looked up from a worn catalog and gave a polite nod.

"Need help finding anything?" the clerk asked, eyes scanning David in the same way David had once scanned Sam.

"Yeah," David replied, approaching the counter. "Rope, duct tape, heavy-duty flashlight, maybe some industrial locks… bolts, chain. That sort of thing."

The clerk raised an eyebrow but didn't question it. "Aisle four for most of that. Locks are in the glass case near the front. You stocking up for the apocalypse?"

Riles chuckled dryly. "Just trying to be prepared. You never know what kind of trouble the road can bring."

The clerk gave a tight-lipped smile and led them toward the aisle. As they filled the basket, he hovered nearby, glancing occasionally with veiled curiosity.

"Passing through?" the man finally asked.

"Yeah. Just visiting. Meeting someone."

The clerk gave a nod that said he'd heard enough—or maybe didn't want to hear more. David didn't push the conversation either. He paid in cash and thanked the man before heading out.

As they stepped into the dusty afternoon light, Riles' eyes scanned the street instinctively. Just in case. He didn't see anyone following—but the paranoia was no longer just a habit. It was survival.
David glanced toward the antique shop across the street where Haylee and Sam had gone.

"They're probably in that shop there," David said, pointing.

They crossed over, unaware of the discovery waiting inside.

"I'll put these in the Jeep," Riles replied, taking the bag from David.

Lost memories in the Attic

David stepped into the antique shop just as the bell above the door jingled, catching sight of Haylee and Sam near the back. They were standing close together beside a dusty display case, a shoebox-sized wooden crate between them.

"We found something," Haylee said as David approached. Her tone was careful but charged with emotion.

Inside, the shop owner was dusting off a shelf when she noticed the picture in Haylee's hand.

"That woman... she looks familiar," the shopkeeper said thoughtfully. "Is that Aggie?"

David perked up. "You knew Aggie?"

"Oh, everyone around here did," the woman said with a fond smile. "She was a regular when she passed through—always brought little trinkets to trade or stories to share. A real spirit, that one." Her expression softened. "She left a box here years ago. Told me she'd come back for it... but never did."

Haylee asked, eyes widening,
"You still have it?"

"Upstairs," the woman replied. "It's marked with her initials—'AH' and a year. 1989. If you'd like, I can show you."

A few minutes later, they followed the creaking stairs up to a second-floor storage area filled with old trunks and furniture draped in faded sheets. The shop owner led them to a modest wooden box tucked behind a cabinet. Stenciled in fading ink: **AH '89.**

"You're welcome to it," she said.

Back downstairs, they opened the box carefully. Inside were more photographs —Aggie and Elliot, younger, smiling, arm in arm. There were snapshots from various places across North America, some marked with dates and cryptic symbols. One photo showed them in Quebec, standing in front of a cathedral. Haylee didn't know Aggie spoke French—or Quebecois.

There were also postcards, some in English, but many scribbled in French, their messages indecipherable for now.

Haylee held one up, tracing the looping script with her finger. "We're missing something," she murmured. "I can feel it."

David and Sam exchanged glances, both sensing the shift.

They had found more than memories.

They had found the next thread to follow.

"It's him," she whispered. "That's Elliot."

The photos spanned years—deserts, forests, city streets. One had them standing in front of Bertha, though it looked much newer then. In the background, faint but unmistakable, was Elliot's figure watching the camera with an unsettling calm.

Sam flipped through the stack.

He handed Haylee a bundle of postcards, their edges worn but the handwriting still visible. The script was fluid and elegant—and entirely in French.

Sam shook his head. "We'll need a translator."

Haylee traced her fingers over one of the postmarks. It was dated from Montreal. "She was hiding so much… but this feels important."

She looked at David and Sam, heart pounding. "This—this feels like another trailhead."

David gave a firm nod. "Then we follow it."

Dust and Disclosure

They laid out the contents on the dinette table. Riles scanned the images, pausing at a photograph of Aggie and Elliot beside Bertha. His eyes narrowed.

"Damn," Riles muttered. "He really was there all along."

Haylee pointed to a stack of handwritten postcards. "Most of these are in French or Quebecois. We can't read them."

Riles didn't answer right away. He picked one up, scanned it, and sighed.

"I can read it," he said. "My ex-wife's from Montreal. We spoke it at home all the time."

David crossed his arms. "What does it say?"

Riles translated slowly, brows tightening as he went. "He's growing impatient. I've hidden what he wants. If anything happens to me, tell Haylee she must never let him have it. He cannot cross through fully—not without it."

Haylee swallowed hard. "The medallion."

Riles nodded. "Aggie was protecting you from more than just a man. She was keeping something ancient locked away. And Elliot... he's getting desperate." The air in the RV seemed heavier.

Haylee looked out the window, then back to Riles. "What do we do now?"

Riles's voice dropped low. "We go to that storage unit. And we do it together."

Chapter Four:
Secrets in Storage

They all stood outside a small, weather-worn storage facility on the edge of River Canyon. Rows of steel doors stretched down the gravel lot, each unit numbered in faded paint. Number 13 sat at the far end, half-hidden by a crooked juniper bush.

Sam unlocked the unit. It wasn't large, but inside the space was stacked floor to ceiling with dusty boxes.

They got to work. Box after box held old belongings—books, clothes, equipment—but nothing immediately helpful. After nearly two hours of digging through almost 70% of the boxes, Haylee pulled one off a high shelf and set it gently on the floor.

She opened it slowly.

Inside were more journals—and several envelopes marked with symbols Haylee recognized from her dreams. There were photographs tucked between the pages, some labeled with names, places, and years.

As she sifted through them, her hand froze.

One photo showed Aggie, heavily pregnant, standing beside Bertha. Elliot stood behind her, hands on her shoulders, smiling. Another showed her further along, standing alone—but in the background, Elliot could still be seen, watching.

Haylee's breath caught.

Sam squinted, confused. "Wait… who's the baby?"

Haylee hesitated. Her voice came out small, almost a whisper. "Me."

Sam's brows furrowed. "What?"

"I never told you," Haylee said, eyes still locked on the photo. "I only found out several months ago. Dad told me… Aggie was my biological mother."

Sam stepped closer, looking between the photo and Haylee, as if piecing together a puzzle he hadn't even known was missing. "You didn't think to tell me after everything we've seen?"

"I grew up thinking she was my aunt," Haylee said softly. "Dad and my mom raised me."

David stepped in gently. "She asked us to raise her... and to protect Haylee. Agnes said she couldn't give Haylee the life she deserved."

"We never questioned it. But I always suspected there was more."

Haylee turned over another photo. This one showed Aggie holding a swaddled newborn. Alone. No Elliot.

Aggie's familiar handwriting flowed across the back:
If you're reading this, Haylee, then the veil is thinning and Elliot is growing stronger. You must know the truth. I lied to him. I told him you were stillborn. I had to. I knew if he believed you lived, he would never stop searching. I gave you to David and his wife to protect you. It was the only way. He must never get the medallion, or you. You're the key. If he claims it and you, he will become fully physical again—immortal. And nothing will stop him. Not even me.

"I guess this was after she told him I didn't survive," she murmured.

Sam was quiet for a long moment. Then, finally, his voice broke through the silence. "He's your father."

Haylee gave a single, slow nod.

Riles looked between them, shaken. "This... changes everything."

Sam's jaw clenched as he stepped back, the weight of it settling in. "He's not just after the medallion. He's after you."

23

Haylee placed the photos back in the stack carefully. Her entire world had shifted in a moment—but deep down, she already knew. Somehow, she had always known.

"Then we need to stop him. For good."

Riles' voice was steady. "We need a plan."

A Father's Truth

Haylee and Sam slipped away from the others, stepping outside into the heat of the late afternoon. The door to the storage unit clanked shut behind them.

They walked until they reached a small grassy clearing behind the facility, far enough away that they could speak without being overheard. Sam sat on a short retaining wall, hands resting on his knees. Haylee stood nearby, arms crossed tightly across her chest.

"I had no idea," Sam finally said. "About Aggie. About you."

"I didn't even know myself until recently."

Sam looked up at her, his expression unreadable. "And Elliot... he's your—"

Haylee nodded, her eyes shining. "Yeah. He is."

Sam let out a breath, then stood. "That's a lot to carry."

Haylee's voice cracked. "It is. I don't even know who I am anymore. I used to think I was just... lost. Then I thought I was found. Now, I feel like I'm being rewritten."

Sam took her hand and pulled her gently into an embrace. She didn't resist.

"You're still you," he said softly. "Everything you've been through, everything you've survived—it made you who you are. This doesn't erase that."

Haylee buried her face in his chest, letting herself breathe. "It's just a lot."

"I know," he whispered. "But you're not alone. Not now."

They stood like that for a long moment, letting the weight of truth settle between them—without crushing them.

They had each other.

And that, for now, was enough.

Chapter Five:
Echoes in the Map

Back in Bertha, the group gathered around the small table, the last light of day filtering through the curtains. Haylee had spread out Aggie's journals and postcards again, sorting them by date and language.

She paused on one card covered in swirling, poetic script. "This one keeps coming up. It's addressed to a P.O. box in Montreal."

David raised a brow. "I didn't know Agnes ever lived in Canada."

"She did," Haylee replied. "A lot, apparently. There are references to Quebec, to places like Le Plateau and the Basilica in Montreal. It's everywhere in here."

Riles leaned over, squinting. "Let me see that one."

He scanned the postcard, then slowly began to translate. "La porte ne s'ouvrira que pour celle qui connaît les silences entre les lignes." He looked up. "The door will only open for the one who knows the silences between the lines."

Sam let out a slow breath. "Sounds like another riddle."

Riles pointed to the return address. "This one's not just poetic—it's coded. That address is fake. But the phrasing... I think it's a clue. Something only someone fluent in Quebecois would catch."

David looked impressed. "So what do you think it means?"

Riles tapped the edge of the card. "I think she was hiding something important in Montreal. And she left instructions only someone she trusted—or someone with the right eyes—could follow."

Haylee sat back, letting the weight of the moment settle. "Montreal... it's the next thread."

"But if Elliot's watching—" David began.

"We don't have a choice," Haylee interrupted softly. "He's getting stronger. And if she left something there to stop him, we have to find it."

Sam reached over, his voice low. "If he's truly your father… we need to be ready for whatever that means."

Haylee nodded, her eyes shining but resolute. "Then we go to Montreal. And we find what Aggie left behind."

Checkpoint: Passports and Plans

The next morning, gathered around Bertha's table with coffee mugs in hand, reality set in.

"We need passports," Haylee said, her finger resting on the Montreal coordinates on Aggie's map. "We can't just roll across the border."

Riles exhaled. "I haven't had a valid one since my military days."

David nodded. "Same. Mine expired a long time ago."

Haylee glanced at Sam, who shook his head. "Nope. Never needed one. Not until now."

They all exchanged a look. Six weeks. That's how long expedited processing would take—if everything went smoothly.

"Well," Haylee said, trying to sound optimistic, "we've got time to plan."

They decided to return to the cabin for the wait. It felt like the only grounded place left. Somewhere quiet enough to regroup—and dig deeper.

Back at the cabin, they unpacked the journals, boxes, and photos from the storage unit, creating a war-room of sorts across the dining table and couch. Aggie's scrawled notes were pieced together like a jigsaw puzzle—timelines forming, connections surfacing.

Haylee spent her days studying the postcards and symbols, decoding as much as she could. Riles continued to translate the French ones, occasionally chuckling at Aggie's choice of slang or cursing softly when he hit something cryptic.

Sam compiled a list of supplies they might need for the next leg of the journey. David paced often, unsettled but determined to be useful.

.

At night, they talked by the fire. About Montreal. About what Elliot might want. About who Aggie really was.

And every day, they grew more certain: this wasn't just a detour.

It was the path

C'est Ici, Bon

The next morning, Haylee bounced between Aggie's journals and the dusty volumes in the hidden library. Her fingers moved with purpose, trailing over handwritten notes, symbols, and faded maps.

She flipped open a worn leather-bound journal to a page she hadn't noticed before. In Aggie's familiar script was a note:
"There is power in crossing. There is danger in staying. The Veil is not just a boundary—it's a choice."

Haylee frowned. That phrase had come up before. In another book, or maybe during the dream.

Riles entered with a mug of coffee and glanced over her shoulder. "C'est ici, bon," he said.

Haylee blinked. "What?"

He smiled. "It means 'It's here, good.' Like… you found it. You're in the right place."

She let the words settle, and they felt right. The page, the phrase, the energy of it all—it was pointing to something just beneath the surface.

She flipped to another marked page and found a symbol she hadn't seen before, etched beside the swirl-circle of the medallion. This one looked like two mirrored crescents—almost like a portal.

"What's this?" she asked. "*Le creusement.*"

Riles leaned in. "Aggie wrote something about 'the deepening.' That might be connected to the Veil. Like… *C'est pas juste d'le traverser—faut qu't'y entres, qu't'y fasses partie. Va plus loin qu'avant.*"

He glanced at her. "You don't just cross it. You merge with it. Go deeper than before."

Haylee's pulse quickened. "So the medallion isn't just a key—it's a conduit."

Riles nodded. "That's what it looks like."

Haylee traced her finger along the mirrored crescents. "Then I need to understand both sides—this world and the one behind the Veil. Before he does."

And she knew, deep in her bones, that Montreal wasn't just a place—it was the next crossing.

Stamped and Waiting

Time had passed faster than they thought. David had asked his neighbor Tom to look out for the passports in the mail for him and Haylee, and Mike did the same for Sam. Riles got a text from a buddy cop that he had a secret package at the station waiting for him.

David and Riles exchanged a look. David finally said, "We'll take care of it. Haylee, you and Sam stay here at the cabin. Keep going through the journals and anything else that might help."

"Where do we go first?" Riles asked.

David rubbed his jaw. "Haylee's and my stuff is in Ashland. For you two..." He paused, thinking. "You said you were living in Silver Ridge, right? That desert town in New Mexico?"

Riles nodded.

"Then we'll loop down that way after Ashland. Grab everything in one trip."

As the Jeep rumbled down the dirt road a short while later, Haylee stood outside Bertha, arms crossed, her gaze fixed on the winding ridge until the dust finally settled. The wind tugged gently at her hoodie, as if nudging her toward something yet unseen.

Sam joined her, holding two mugs of coffee. "They'll be gone a week, give or take."

Haylee accepted the mug with a quiet "Thanks," still watching the road. "Feels strange... after everything, it's just us again."

Sam sipped his coffee. "In the meantime, we've got work to do."

She smiled faintly. "You're right. We've got journals, boxes, and breadcrumbs that lead to Montreal."

Sam nudged her shoulder. "Then let's dig in. Who knows what's waiting in those pages?"

Haylee looked toward the cabin, something kindling behind her eyes. "Let's find out."

The drive back to Ashland felt different this time—quieter, heavier. David focused on the road while Riles scrolled through his phone, checking for updates from his buddy at the station.

Just outside the city limits, a soft ping broke the silence.

Riles glanced over. "Something?"

David frowned. "Ray. Finally."

The message was short:
"Need to disappear. Safe spot? Somewhere off-grid. Not hurt. Just watched."

David's grip on the wheel tightened. "He's alive."

Riles leaned over, sighing. "And on the run. We can't just leave him hanging."

"No. We won't."

They picked up the first set of passports from Tom, David's neighbor, who handed them over without question. Then, before heading south toward Silver Ridge, they made a quick detour—down familiar streets, until they reached a dusty turnout where Ray was waiting.

He looked tired. Worn at the edges.

"You came," he said, sliding into the back seat of the Jeep.

"We said we would," David answered.

But none of them noticed the unremarkable sedan that pulled out from behind a gas station across the street. Tinted windows. No plates.

By the time they were heading toward Silver Ridge, the dust was rising again—this time from more than just the desert wind.

Chapter Six:
Crossing Lines

The miles stretched quiet between them, the only sound the low hum of tires on pavement and the occasional rattle of gear in the back. David kept his eyes on the road while Riles scanned the rearview mirror for the third time in twenty minutes.

"You expecting someone?" David asked, not looking over.

"Don't know," Riles muttered. "Just a feeling."

A dark sedan pulled onto the road a few cars back. Riles narrowed his eyes. "Same car from town."

"You sure?"

"Not yet. But getting there."

Ray slumped in the backseat. "They've been watching me for weeks. I don't know who they're working for—could be Elliot, could be someone else. But the minute I started digging into old records—stuff about Aggie, and the medallion —they showed up. I had to vanish."

David clenched the wheel. "So you went dark."

"I didn't know who to trust. Until now."

The sedan didn't follow them onto the state road heading toward Silver Ridge. For now, they had breathing room.

"What's the next step on the trail?"

"Montreal. Agnes left clues for Haylee there, and we're going to find out what they are very soon," Riles replied.

Ray leaned forward. "I still have my passport. So, if you're going to Montreal… I'll go with you. I'm done hiding."

Riles looked over his shoulder. "You sure about that?"

Ray nodded. "If what Haylee found is real—and I believe it is—we can't let Elliot get there first."

David didn't speak for a moment. Then: "Alright. One more seat in the Jeep."

They turned off the main road and headed toward a run-down stretch of town where Ray had been holed up. The place was a converted storage shed behind a closed repair shop—barely noticeable from the road. Ray hopped out and jogged inside to grab a duffel bag, a few essentials, and his passport tucked into a box beneath loose floorboards.

Riles waited near the Jeep, eyes sweeping the area. "We shouldn't stay long."

David nodded. "Let's keep the engine running."

Just as Ray locked the door behind him, headlights turned the corner. A black sedan slowed as it passed—windows tinted, unreadable.

Riles moved instinctively, hand near the small of his back. David stepped slightly in front of Ray as he returned to the vehicle.

The sedan didn't stop. It coasted by, slow enough to be intentional.

"Same car," Riles muttered. "That's confirmation."

"They're watching," Ray said quietly, throwing his bag in the back. "But they're not ready to move. Yet."

David slid behind the wheel. "Then let's not give them a reason."

They pulled away, the Jeep kicking up a cloud of dust behind them as the sedan turned at the next block and disappeared into the distance.

As they drove on toward Silver Ridge in silence, the weight of their new alliance settled in. Lines had been crossed. Secrets spilled. And now, someone was watching.

The road ahead would demand more from each of them than they'd ever imagined.

Off the Record

Silver Ridge hadn't changed much since Riles last drove its sun-bleached roads—dusty storefronts, power lines humming in the heat, and that ever-present feeling of waiting for something to happen.

They pulled up to Mike's café just past noon. The smell of fresh coffee and grilled onions wafted out as the bell above the door jingled.

Mike looked up from the counter and grinned. "Well, look what the desert dragged in."

Riles clapped him on the shoulder. "Thanks for holding the mail."

Mike ducked behind the counter and came up with a padded envelope. "Sam's passport came two days ago. Figured someone'd swing by eventually."

"Going somewhere?" Mike asked.

"Montreal," David said.

Mike let out a whistle. "Wow, that's not just up the road."

Ray settled into a booth by the window while Riles accepted the envelope. As they took a breath over a round of coffees, Riles checked his phone.

A new message blinked on the screen from Det. Buten:
"Don't come to the station. Someone's been asking about you—didn't like the vibe. Meet me at the old warehouse by the tracks. You know the one. Come alone."

Riles read it twice before pocketing the phone.

David noticed. "Something wrong?"

Riles stood. "Buten says someone came looking for me. I need to meet him at an old warehouse."

Ray sat up straighter. "Want backup?"

Riles shook his head. "No. He said come alone."

David's jaw clenched. "You sure about this?"

"No," Riles said. "But if someone's sniffing around the precinct, I need to know who—and why."

He grabbed his keys and headed for the door.

"Text us when you get there," David called after him.

Riles raised a hand in acknowledgment as he disappeared into the heat.

Back inside the café, David and Ray sat in uneasy silence, nursing cold drinks and watching the road through the dusty front window.

Something about this trip was shifting.

And they weren't alone on the trail anymore.

Threads Between Worlds

Riles pulled into the alley behind the old warehouse just after sunset. The structure looked abandoned, its corrugated siding rusted and dented, windows long since boarded up. But he knew this place—locals used to call it "The Trackshed." A place where things once moved and disappeared.

He parked the Jeep and stepped out cautiously, checking his surroundings. The air was still, except for the faint creak of metal in the wind.

Inside, the warehouse was dim and cavernous. Faint shafts of light pierced gaps in the roof. Riles moved quietly through the dust, eyes scanning.

A figure emerged from the shadows.

"Buten," Riles said, relaxing only slightly. "This is some real cloak-and-dagger shit."

"Didn't want to say more over text," the detective replied, glancing behind him. "Someone's been asking questions about you—real subtle-like. Suits. No names."

"Elliot?"

Buten shook his head. "Could be. Could be feds. Or worse. They weren't local."

Riles nodded grimly. "You bring it?"

Buten reached into his coat and pulled out a thick envelope. "Everything I could find on Agnes Hensen. Plus some old maps she had copied from the archives— marked up, circled. Half of it I couldn't make sense of. But she was into something deep."

He added, "And your passport."

Riles took it, then looked Buten square in the eye. "Thanks."

"Watch your back, Riles. They're getting close."

Between the Pages

Meanwhile, back at the cabin, Haylee stood at the small desk tucked into the corner, sorting through a stack of envelopes that had been jammed between the pages of a thick green binder. Most were yellowed with age, addressed to aliases she didn't recognize—*Margot L., Rose C., E. Anselm*—but all bore Aggie's distinct handwriting.

She opened one and unfolded a faded letter written on paper that crackled like dry leaves. The ink was splotchy, rushed. But the urgency came through:

If you're reading this, something's been triggered. I never finished the ritual. I didn't have time. But the lock isn't complete without the third element—the tether, the bloodline, the voice. You'll know when it calls. Just don't answer too late.

Haylee stared at the words, chilled. "She knew," she whispered. "She knew this was coming back around."

Sam glanced up from the couch where he'd been organizing maps from the storage unit. "What do you mean, 'third element'?"

"I think it's me," she said, holding out the letter. "The bloodline. Elliot has the power. Aggie had the knowledge. But I'm… the tether."

Sam stood slowly. "So if he gets to you and the medallion—"

"He finishes what she stopped," Haylee said, finishing the thought.

Just then, Bella stirred from her nap and leapt from the window, tail swishing as she padded toward the wall behind the woodstove. She let out a single low *mrrrrow* and pawed at the floor.

"Bella?" Haylee asked, kneeling.

Together, she and Sam pulled aside the corner rug. Beneath it, hidden under a loose floorboard, was a cloth-wrapped parcel no bigger than a journal.

Inside: a thin, black-bound book with no title. When Haylee opened it, only the first page had writing:

What's hidden in one world must be remembered in another.

Sam looked over her shoulder. "That... doesn't sound like Aggie's usual tone."

"No," Haylee said, fingers tracing the edge of the page. "It sounds older."

Whisper Ridge Remembered

That night, Haylee dreamed she stepped outside with Bella tucked beneath her arm. The air held a cool bite, crisp and whispering with the weight of something unfinished.

She wandered up to the ridge—Whisper Ridge, as they'd called it. The place where she had seen the figure.

She didn't know why she came. Only that it called her.

Bella slipped from her arms and moved ahead, body low and alert. The wind shifted. A hush rolled over the land like breath held too long.

And there it was.

A flicker.

A figure.

Not close, but not far either—standing at the edge of where the land dropped into shadow. It didn't move. It didn't speak. It simply *was*.

Haylee's breath caught. The edges of it shimmered like heat rising off stone. She felt Bella press against her leg.

"Who are you?" she whispered.

The figure didn't answer.

But something inside her stirred, ancient and aching. A memory that wasn't hers. A thread pulled tight.

She blinked—and it was gone.

Only the wind remained, curling through the canyon like a forgotten lullaby.

Haylee wrapped her arms around herself. Whether it was Elliot, Aggie, or something else entirely—she wasn't sure.

But whatever it was… it knew her.

And it was waiting.

Haylee awoke with a start.

Chapter Seven:
Returning Currents

Riles made his way back to the café. The neon **OPEN** sign buzzed faintly in the window, casting a glow against the dusty glass. Inside, Mike was wiping down the counter while Ray and David nursed mugs of late-day coffee.

David stood as soon as Riles entered. "What did you find?"

Riles dropped the envelope on the table with a quiet thud. "Answers. Or at least more of the map."

The room stilled.

Ray leaned forward, eyes sharp. "Anything actionable?"

"Some. Enough to know we're running out of time."

Outside, the wind picked up, carrying the scent of sagebrush and the low hum of something shifting. Threads were starting to weave together.

Mike, sensing the weight in the room, stepped out from behind the counter and tossed Riles a set of keys. "You boys look like you could use a place to crash. Sam's apartment behind the café is still empty—water's on, beds are made. Nothing fancy, but you can clean up, catch some sleep."

Riles gave him a grateful nod. "That'd be perfect. Thanks, Mike."

"You're like family," Mike said simply. "Besides, something tells me you're going to need your strength."

The three men headed to the apartment in silence, the envelope tucked under Riles' arm like a thread waiting to be unraveled.

Night Below the Neon

Each man carried more weight than just the day's dust and heat. The apartment was small but clean—two bedrooms, a futon in the living room, and the faint aroma of stale coffee clinging to the walls.

There were clean towels, a few bottles of water in the fridge.

David dropped his bag in the smaller bedroom and closed the door halfway. Riles claimed the master without saying much, setting the envelope down on the nightstand like it was made of glass. Ray grabbed the futon, tossing his jacket over the back of a nearby chair before kicking off his boots.

For a while, the only sound was the groan of pipes as someone turned on the shower, and the soft murmur of traffic two floors below. The neon sign buzzed faintly outside the window, casting a pink glow against the far wall.

They didn't sleep much—but it was better than the Jeep.

Eventually, the night folded around them. The city exhaled, unaware of the threads being pulled above it. And in the quiet, each of them tried—unsuccessfully—to outrun the shadows they carried.

David sent a quick text to Haylee:

"Got the passports. Staying at Sam's old place tonight. We'll head back first thing in the morning."

He didn't expect a reply right away, but just knowing the message was out there gave him something to anchor to. The road was long—and growing stranger by the day—but they weren't traveling it alone anymore.

And by morning, the trail to Montreal would call again.

Morning Holds Us Gently

Haylee woke to soft sunlight pouring through the cabin window, Bella curled at her feet and the scent of pine drifting in from outside. She blinked at her phone and smiled as the message came into focus.

She exhaled, relief warming her chest. "They're safe," she murmured.

Sam stirred beside her, one arm draped lazily across his chest. "Hmm?"

She nudged him with a smile. "My dad. They've got the passports. They stayed at your old place in Silver Ridge."

Sam rubbed the sleep from his eyes.

Haylee nodded. "He said they're heading back first thing today."

Bertha sat parked just outside the cabin, her windows catching the morning sun like golden mirrors. The air buzzed faintly with the sound of waking birds and wind in the trees.

"Want to run into town?" Sam asked, already swinging his legs out of bed. "We can grab something for dinner tonight."

Haylee stretched, then sat up with a contented sigh. "Yeah. Let's make it a good one. They'll probably be hungry."

"Think the little market's open?"

"Only one way to find out."

They dressed, gathered a list, and stepped out into the crisp morning. The cabin, for all its silence, felt briefly like a home—temporary, yes, but full of memory and meaning.

Together, they walked toward Bertha, the kind of quiet only found in earned moments wrapping around them like morning light.

Chapter Eight:
Shadows Before Sunrise

At 5:30 a.m., the world was still wrapped in silver-blue quiet, the kind that made every sound feel louder than it should. Riles stood outside the apartment, leaning against the railing as he sipped a cup of lukewarm coffee. The neon glow from the café sign was dimmer now, flickering faintly in the early light.

Mike stepped out, letting the screen door shut gently behind him.

"You're up early," he said, scratching his head.

"Never really slept," Riles replied, eyes scanning the horizon like it might give something away.

Mike followed his gaze. "Didn't want to say anything last night, but after you boys turned in, I saw a black SUV hovering around the café. Slow, like they were casing the place."

Riles tensed but didn't flinch.

"Thanks," Riles said, gripping the mug a little tighter. "Had a feeling we were being followed. After we stopped at Ray's storage container—it wasn't a guess anymore."

Mike offered a firm pat to his shoulder. "You've always trusted your gut. Don't stop now."

Riles gave a small nod, then turned back toward the apartment. "Appreciate the heads-up."

Inside, the place was quiet. David had just stepped out of the bathroom, towel slung over his shoulder, rubbing condensation off the mirror.

"All yours," he said, catching Riles' eye.

Riles headed in with a nod, setting his mug on the counter as he passed. Behind him, David got dressed and moved around the kitchen quietly, careful not to wake Ray, who was still knocked out on the futon, breathing heavy and slack-jawed.

Riles re-emerged fifteen minutes later, damp hair combed back, clean shirt clinging to his shoulders.

He glanced toward the futon. "Should we wake him?"

David shook his head. "Let him sleep. He looks like he needs it."

They gave Ray another half hour before Riles finally crouched beside him and gave a gentle shake.

"Hey man, we gotta get going. Grab your shower and we'll pack the Jeep."

Ray groaned, sitting up with a squint. "Yeah, yeah. I'm up."

"I want to stop by the café to grab some breakfast to-go," Riles added. "Mike's cooking smells like it could wake the dead."

Ray chuckled, rubbing his eyes. "That might be the only reason I'm moving."

Riles offered a tired smirk, then turned back to finish packing the last of their gear.

Outside, the sky was beginning to soften—shadows stretching, but not yet gone. And somewhere just out of sight, the watchers were likely doing the same.

Sweet Enough to Keep

The morning sun had climbed higher, warming the mountain air as Haylee and Sam pulled into the small town market just after eight. It wasn't crowded—just a few locals grabbing coffee and chatting over folding newspapers. A soft bell chimed as they stepped inside.

Haylee reached for a basket, brushing Sam's hand as he did the same. They both paused, fingers tangling for a beat too long.

"Sorry," Sam chuckled, clearing his throat.

Haylee smiled, a little pink in her cheeks. "You take it."

"No, no—you got here first."

Their hands hovered awkwardly for another second before Haylee laughed and snatched the basket. "We're off to a great start."

Sam grinned, brushing his hand through his hair. "This is what peak coordination looks like."

They moved through the aisles, gathering what they needed: vegetables, bread, a few snacks. When they reached the produce section, Haylee reached for a small carton of strawberries just as Sam did.

Again, their hands touched.

"Seriously?" she laughed.

Sam lifted both palms like a surrender. "Okay, now I'm just trying to be cute." Haylee arched a brow, amused. "Well... it's working."

For a second, it felt like everything else faded—the chaos, the danger, even Elliot. It was just them. A shared smile. The lightness they'd nearly forgotten they were allowed to feel.

They paid at the counter and stepped back outside into the crisp mountain morning, a gentle breeze rustling the trees lining the road.

"Hey," Sam said, nodding toward a nearby overlook with a faded picnic table nestled in the shade. "You want to eat now? Before the world throws something else at us?"

Haylee glanced at the bags in her hand and smiled. "Yeah. Let's do it."

They spread out a simple lunch—cheese, bread, fruit, a bit of chocolate Sam had tossed into the basket at the last second. The view stretched wide in front of them—layers of green hills tumbling into one another under the morning sun.

Haylee leaned back on her hands. "It's strange… how this can feel like something we get to keep. Even with everything going on."

Sam nodded. "That's because we do. Maybe not forever, but this moment? Yeah. It's ours."

She looked at him then, really looked, and saw the quiet worry tucked behind his easy smile. He was still holding space for her, still giving her room to breathe— but she also knew he hadn't stopped loving her for a second.

She nudged his knee with hers. "Thanks for being patient."

"Thanks for not running," he replied softly.

Their fingers brushed again, slower this time, and neither of them pulled away. The road would come calling soon.

But for now, this sweetness—this moment—was enough to keep.

Beneath the Quiet

Haylee and Sam returned to Bertha for a bit of stillness before heading back to the cabin. Haylee had just slid the brown paper bag onto the counter when Bella leapt up onto the dashboard and let out a sharp, low mrrrrow.

Sam turned. "That was... pointed."

Haylee watched as Bella paced in a tight circle, tail flicking with tension. Then the cat stopped, crouched low, and pawed at the small cabinet near the passenger seat—one Haylee rarely opened.

"She's doing it again," Haylee whispered.

Sam stepped aside as Haylee knelt to open the cabinet. Inside, behind a mess of old travel brochures and faded maps, was something she hadn't noticed before—a shallow panel in the back wall, slightly askew.

Carefully, she tugged at the edge.

With a soft click, the panel gave way to a hidden compartment.

Tucked inside was a faded velvet pouch, no larger than her palm. Her fingers tingled as she pulled it out. Inside: a smooth, iridescent stone etched with the same swirl-circle symbol from the medallion, and a thin strip of parchment. Haylee unrolled it, heart racing.

Light it when the Veil stirs. It will show the unseen path.

Haylee met Sam's gaze. "Bertha's hiding secrets again."

He crouched beside her, voice low. "It's like she's been waiting for the right moment."

Bella gave a satisfied flick of her tail and leapt down.

Haylee met Sam's gaze. "Bertha's hiding secrets again."

He crouched beside her, voice low. "It's like she's been waiting for the right moment."

Bella gave a satisfied flick of her tail and leapt down.

"Thanks, Bells," Haylee murmured.

They drove back to the cabin in quiet wonder. The sun had shifted by the time they arrived, casting long beams through the trees. The stillness there felt different now—charged, not heavy.

In the kitchen, they moved together easily. Haylee chopped vegetables while Sam seasoned the meat. Bella curled up in the patch of sun by the window. Josie dozed nearby, head resting on her paws.

No tension. No rush. Just the steady rhythm of making something together. At one point, they both reached for the same tomato. Their hands brushed, and they froze—then laughed like kids caught in something they hadn't meant to say out loud.

Sam looked at her, his expression soft. "You okay?"

Haylee nodded. "Yeah. This… this helps."

They carried their meal out to the front steps just before sunset, letting the breeze wrap around them as they sat in easy silence.

The night would bring the Jeep crew home, and with them, another turn in the story.

But for now, beneath the quiet, the threads between worlds pulsed gently— undisturbed, for just a little longer.

Chapter Nine:
Objects in Mirror

The road home stretched long and winding, the sky painted in fading streaks of orange and deepening blue. The last glow of sunset clung to the horizon, while the first stars blinked to life overhead. The hum of the Jeep was steady, headlights casting long shadows through the trees.

David drove with quiet focus, his grip firm on the wheel. His eyes flicked to the rearview mirror more often than usual.

"You good?" Riles asked from the passenger seat.

David gave a small nod. "Just a feeling."

Ray stirred in the backseat, stretching. "That SUV again?"

"Haven't seen it since Canyon Creek," Riles said, glancing behind them. "But I wouldn't be surprised if they're still tailing us—just farther back this time." David reached for his phone at a stop sign near a quiet highway turnoff. He typed out a quick message to Haylee:

"Almost there. Should reach the cabin by 9:45. Jeep crew intact. See you soon."

He hit send, then set the phone aside with a tight exhale.

Back on the road, the air thickened with that strange stillness that only comes at the edge of night—too quiet, too watchful.

That's when it happened.

A pair of headlights crested behind them—bright, fast, and unmistakably familiar.

Ray leaned forward. "That's them."

Riles turned in his seat. "Too aggressive for locals."

The SUV surged forward, gaining fast. It weaved side to side, then pulled even with the Jeep.

David stayed steady, not speeding, not slowing. Just watching.

The black vehicle hovered close. Too close. Then it veered suddenly—edging into their lane, trying to force them toward the guardrail.

"Hold on!" David shouted, swerving slightly to avoid contact.

"Brake!" Ray called from the back.

David tapped the brakes just enough to drop behind. The SUV sped forward, cut sharply in front of them, then gunned it—vanishing around the bend. Silence fell in the Jeep, broken only by the sound of tires crunching gravel as they coasted back into their lane.

"You okay?" Riles asked, turning toward Ray.

Ray nodded, though his knuckles were white against the seat. "They weren't trying to kill us."

"No," David muttered. "Just make a point."

They rode the rest of the way in silence, every shadow along the trees looking just a little too still.

Ahead, the trees thinned and the familiar outline of the cabin came into view— porch lights glowing soft against the gathering dark. A warm welcome at the end of a jagged road.

And this time, they weren't arriving empty-handed.

The last stretch of highway wound into gravel and pine as the Jeep crested the final ridge, headlights cutting through the dusk.

The sun had just slipped behind the trees, leaving the sky awash in soft indigo and the faint glow of a rising moon.

Dust kicked up behind them in a familiar cloud as they rolled up the long drive to the cabin.

Inside, Haylee and Sam had just finished setting out the last of the dinner plates on the front porch table. Bertha's windows gleamed in the low light, and the scent of roasted vegetables and grilled meat lingered in the air.

Josie barked once and bounded toward the porch railing, tail wagging like mad. "Looks like they're here," Sam said, wiping his hands on a towel.

Haylee stepped onto the porch just in time to see the Jeep pull to a halt, gravel crunching beneath the tires. The doors swung open, and David stepped out first, followed by Riles—and then someone she hadn't expected.

"Ray?" Haylee's voice rose in disbelief.

Ray stepped out of the backseat, lifting a hand in a casual wave and flashing a tired grin. "Surprise."

David gave her a sheepish smile. "We picked up an extra on the way."

Haylee blinked. "Well, okay then."

"Hope we didn't miss dinner," Riles added, stretching as he looked toward the warmly lit cabin.

"Not at all," Sam said, clapping him on the back as they all headed to the table. "We've been waiting."

"He's with us now," Riles said. "Long story. One we'll tell over dinner."

Sam stepped forward, nodding toward Ray with cautious welcome, then met David's eyes. "Everything okay?"

"More or less," David said. "But we've got things to talk about."

Haylee smiled despite herself. "Well, dinner's ready. So I'd say you got here just in time."

They grabbed their bags and followed the scent of food toward the porch. Riles muttered something about it beating fast food. Ray looked surprised but grateful. No one mentioned the black SUV just yet.

That could wait.

Not Alone at the Table

Dinner had been warming on the stove when the Jeep crew rolled in, and now the meal stretched before them like a quiet offering—bowls passed, glasses filled, conversation flickering between bites. The soft glow of the overhead light cast warm shadows across the table, and the cabin walls seemed to breathe a little easier with everyone home.

Josie sat patiently between Haylee and Sam, ears perked and eyes hopeful, waiting for something delicious to fall in her favor. Bella perched on the porch railing, her tail flicking in slow, steady rhythm.

"So," Riles said, nudging a piece of cornbread across his plate. "Before things got a little... reckless on the highway, I picked up this from Buten." He tapped the thick envelope sitting on the counter behind him. "Full of stuff on Aggie—maps, notes, even copies of old archive requests. We haven't had a chance to go through it yet."

Ray wiped his mouth with a napkin. "And I guess since I'm officially here now... I owe you the story."

Everyone quieted as he recounted how he'd been on the run—ever since he started digging into the wrong set of records. "That black SUV," he said, voice low. "It was there at the storage unit. Just watching. I didn't think much of it at first, but by the time we left Silver Ridge... they were tailing us. Tonight they got too close."

Sam leaned forward. "But how did they know where you were?"

"I don't kno—" Ray started, but Riles suddenly stood up, chair scraping loudly against the floor.

"Wait." His tone had shifted.

He grabbed his phone and bolted off the porch. A beat passed before David and Sam followed.

The beam from Riles' flashlight cut through the dark as he dropped to the ground beside the Jeep. He swept the light slowly underneath—until he stopped.

"Son of a bitch," he muttered.

There, clinging to the underside of the Jeep's frame, was a small black device— no larger than a deck of cards, its surface blinking faintly with a red light.

"A tracker," David said flatly.

"They must've put it on while we were sleeping in Sam's old place," Riles said, his voice thick with frustration. "I should've checked. Mike told me he saw a black SUV hovering near the café after we left."

Riles ripped it from the frame and smashed it. He stood, brushing dust from his jeans, eyes dark. "I thought I was being smart. Guess not smart enough."

The mood had shifted. Bella stretched, tail twitching.

Haylee glanced toward the door, pulse picking up. "So what does that mean?"

"It means," Riles said, stepping back in, "they've been watching longer than we thought."

The Invisible Passenger

"If they got to Bertha, what made me think the Jeep was safe?" he muttered, pacing.

David leaned back, arms crossed. "No need to beat yourself up over this."

"Yeah," Ray added. "We were so beat no one thought of it. We were lucky they didn't just follow us right out of the city."

Riles didn't argue. He just rubbed the back of his neck and exhaled slowly. Haylee spoke up, her voice a little tighter than she meant. "Do you think they'll try to come here?"

Everyone paused.

Sam echoed the question. "Would they really try?"

David's gaze darkened. "I don't know, but we'd better be prepared in case they do."

Without another word, Riles nodded at Ray. "Come on. Let me show you what we've got in place."

The two men stepped outside, disappearing into the trees behind the cabin. Riles pointed out the trip wires, the concealed cameras, the reinforced fencing hidden behind bramble and brush. "And we've got bear traps placed around the perimeter. Not a lot—but enough to slow anyone down."

Ray gave a low whistle. "Shit. You were expecting trouble."

"Just didn't expect it this soon."

Ray looked back toward the glowing cabin windows. "I'll take first watch, if you don't mind. I don't plan to sleep tonight."

Riles gave a tired smile. "Sounds like a plan. We need to keep eyes on the drive in case they try anything."

Back inside, David turned to Haylee and Sam. "You two should stay in the cabin tonight instead of Bertha."

Haylee opened her mouth to protest, but David cut in gently. "I'd feel better knowing you weren't out there while the rest of us are in here."

Sam and Haylee exchanged a glance, then nodded.

Together, they slipped out to Bertha and gathered what they needed—sleeping bag, pillows, extra blankets. Bertha's familiar scent of pine and old leather clung to the fabric as they returned to the cabin.

Everyone picked their spots carefully. Riles took the creaky armchair by the front door. David claimed the sagging couch, already half-asleep. Sam and Haylee laid out their sleeping bag near the hidden room, their backs to the wall.

Bella settled on the windowsill like a watchful gargoyle, tail twitching softly. Josie, ever loyal, curled beside Ray, who stood silently by the kitchen window.

He could see the Jeep and Bertha from his post—dark silhouettes under a sliver of moonlight. If anyone came down the winding drive, even without headlights, he'd know. The motion sensors would flash at the faintest shift in the air.

And tonight, that was enough to keep them all on edge.

Sleep came slow, if at all. But for now, they were safe.

And they would be ready.

The Longest Watch

As the night grew more still, the cabin felt more like a prison than a sanctuary. Riles relieved Ray after four hours. David took the next watch.

When Sam stirred to get up, Haylee looked over at the others, then whispered, "They got this. Stay with me."

Sam sat back down, wrapping an arm around her. Bella lay at their feet, on guard. Josie curled beside whoever was on watch.

Sam kissed Haylee's forehead and whispered, "We're going to be alright."

She smiled at him, and they drifted back to sleep together.

As dawn crept in, Riles sighed with relief that nothing had happened during the night. But how long would that last, he wondered.

David was first to wake. He slapped Riles lightly on the shoulder and told him to take a rest as he began making coffee for everyone. David glanced over at Haylee and Sam. He smiled, glad to know she had someone willing to be there for her in a way he never was.

David was about to take Josie out for a stroll when Sam and Haylee offered. He didn't argue. They grabbed their jackets and the leash and headed out the back door.

Ray was just waking up when David glanced out the window. He thought he saw movement.

He shoved Riles' arm with his foot. "What, man? I just dozed off for a minute," Riles replied.

"Get up. I think I saw something."

Riles jumped up and threw open the door, gun drawn. Just in the distance, a deer and a fawn moved through the woods.

They spotted Riles and took off running in the opposite direction.

He lowered his weapon and stepped back inside.

Chapter Ten:
Plans and Papers

Haylee and Sam came back in to find everyone sitting around the table looking frazzled, half-finished mugs of coffee scattered in front of them. The tension in the room was thick enough to feel—like static waiting for a spark.

Sam was the first to break the silence. "What happened?"

"We were lucky last night," Riles said, rubbing his temples. "But I have a feeling we're all wound up too tight."

Ray leaned forward, arms on the table. "That SUV... it didn't just tail us. It played with us. Like it was testing how far we'd go without reacting."

"We need to make plans to go to Montreal," David added. "And soon."

Haylee sat down beside Sam, her brows knit with worry. "How soon?"

David glanced at the others before answering. "A couple of days, max. We can't sit on this any longer. Whatever Elliot's after, he's not far behind."

Sam nodded, glancing at Haylee. "Yeah, I was thinking the same thing after the tracker on the Jeep."

The room fell into a heavy pause. Then they began laying out the pieces.

They agreed that Haylee, Sam, and David would drive Bertha over the border—she blended in better and would draw less attention—while Riles and Ray would take the Jeep, a day behind, in case they were still being tracked.

Haylee, already scrolling through her phone, stopped mid-swipe. "If we're going to Canada, I need to get paperwork for Bella and Josie. They won't let us cross the border without proof of vaccinations and a health certificate."

"I'll make the arrangements with my vet friend in Oregon," David offered. "She's helped me before—no questions, no fuss. I'll call her today."

They looked at the calendar. Tomorrow was Thursday.

"We'll take the girls that morning," Sam said. "Make it a quick trip."

"That gives us tomorrow to gather what we need," David replied. "Provisions, backups, everything."

Riles tapped a pen on the table. "Remember, we can't take fruits, vegetables, or meat across the border. So we stick to what we'll eat on the way—sandwich meats, bread, canned stuff, dry goods."

"Smart," Ray added. "And if anything goes sideways at the border, we'll need to have stories straight. Just a road trip, nothing more."

They all nodded in agreement, the weight of unspoken things pressing down on them.

For a moment, there was quiet. Bella hopped up onto the windowsill, tail curling around her paws, while Josie wandered over and lay between Haylee and Sam's feet with a sigh.

Haylee reached down to stroke Josie's head, grounding herself in the familiar. "It's really happening," she said softly.

"It is," Sam answered. "But we're not walking into this blind. We've got each other."

The plan wasn't perfect. It wasn't even complete. But it gave them something to hold onto.

The threads were tightening, pulling them toward Montreal. Toward answers. Toward something none of them could name.

But they were moving.

And that mattered.

The Final Piece (for Now)

The group spent the rest of the day preparing the cabin for departure and packing up Bertha. Once Haylee and Sam left for Oregon, they'd swing back through only to pick up David on the way to Montreal. Everything had to be ready to go at a moment's notice—just in case.

Haylee stepped into the hidden room one last time to see if there was anything else she could use. The ping in her head was strong but not unbearable now. While waiting for the passports to arrive, she had tested her will by entering the hidden room daily, training herself to withstand the sensation. At first, it was overwhelming. But the more time she spent there, the more she learned to sit with it.

Alongside the journals and photographs they'd gathered from the storage unit, she and Sam had mapped out a trail of clues leading into Quebec. Aggie had hidden many details in Quebecois, and thanks to Riles' translations, Haylee was finally beginning to understand.

Bella wandered into the room and began pawing at a shelf. Haylee didn't notice until Bella let out a loud, drawn-out meeeowww.

She turned just in time to see a book fall to the floor. It looked oddly clean, untouched by the dust that coated the others.

Haylee crouched and picked it up. Instantly, a strong ping filled her head and a wave of something surged through her chest.

"C'est ici, bon," she whispered. Riles had taught her that phrase—for when she found something meant for her.

The ping lingered, but the wave pulsed in and out like a tide. Inside the book was a map of Whisper Ridge, notes on Montreal, spell recipes, and a short message:

*If you find this, Haylee, it's getting to be a close call. I've prepared things in advance for you. You need to find **Jean-Paul and Mireille Bouchard** at **Le Fil du Monde**, their mystical shop. They'll help you. Be safe, my dear Hummingbird. I love you.*

Haylee let out a breath she hadn't realized she was holding.

Just then, Sam stepped through the doorway.

He pointed. "What's that?"

Haylee jumped slightly, then smiled, glancing down at Bella. "She found it. It's another piece of the puzzle."

Her tone shifted, steady and clear. "We need to get everyone together. Something's come up."

Beyond the Cabin Door

Later that afternoon, the group gathered around as Haylee laid the newly discovered book on the table. The weight of its contents felt like it anchored the room.

"There's more," she said, flipping through the pages. "Maps, notes in Quebecois, spellwork—things Aggie must have prepared in case I ever made it this far."

Ray leaned in. "Wait… where did you find this?"

Haylee hesitated, then looked toward Sam. He nodded.

She gestured toward the wall. "There's something we haven't shown you yet." They led Ray into the hidden room.

As the false panel slid open and the narrow entry revealed itself, Ray stepped back slightly. "You're kidding me."

"Come on," Sam said with a smirk.

Ray followed them into the space, eyes widening as he took in the shelves upon shelves of books, journals, artifacts, and weathered bundles of parchment.

"From the outside, this place looks like a one-room cabin," Ray muttered. "How the hell—"

"Magic. Architecture. Aggie," Haylee said. "Maybe all three."

Ray laughed under his breath. "Yeah. That tracks."

He walked slowly around the room, trailing a finger along the spines. "This… this is a treasure trove. We could spend years in here."

Haylee nodded. "And we might need to, eventually. But for now—we have a direction."

Sam added, "Aggie left a message in the book. Told Haylee to find Jean-Paul and Mireille Bouchard. They run a mystical shop in Montreal."

Ray let out a low whistle. "Guess it's time we really start packing."

Outside, the light was starting to fade.

But inside the hidden room, something had already begun to stir.

They weren't just following a trail anymore.

They were stepping into something much older—and it had been waiting.

Before the Veil Opens

That night, the fire crackled softly in the pit behind the cabin. They sat around it without much ceremony—just warmth, flickering shadows, and a silence that felt full, not empty.

Sam leaned closer to the flames, poking the embers with a stick. "Feels like the quiet before a storm."

Riles looked over, brow furrowed. "It is. We're heading into something none of us fully understand. I keep thinking—what if we're wrong? What if this is bigger than any of us can handle?"

Ray, seated beside Josie, took a swig from a flask. "It is bigger than us. But we're here anyway."

David gave a slow nod. "Aggie knew this would fall to Haylee. And Haylee's not alone."

Haylee looked across the fire at Sam, who was already watching her. She gave a small smile.

Later, she and Sam stepped away from the fire, walking through the trees in comfortable silence. The moon was thin, the air cool.

"You've been quieter lately," Sam said gently.

Haylee hesitated. "There's just... so much. Every day something new unravels. I feel like I'm trying to remember a dream I didn't know I had."

Sam reached for her hand. "I miss you," he said. "Not the version that's lost in the Veil or magic or whatever this is. Just... you."

She stopped walking, turned to face him. "I'm still here."

He kissed her forehead. "I know. I just needed to hear you say it."

They stood there for a moment, foreheads touching, letting the wind carry the weight for a little while.

Back at the fire, Riles threw another log into the flames. The sparks rose, vanishing into the dark like scattered thoughts.

By morning, the path to Oregon would open.

And the real journey would begin.

Chapter Eleven:
The Oregon Thread

Sam, Haylee, Bella, and Josie piled into Bertha just after sunrise, the RV rumbling softly as it idled outside the cabin. David handed Haylee a small folded slip of paper.

"The vet's name is Dr. Shubs," he said. "Tell her I said hello. She owes me a favor."

Haylee smiled, tucking the note into the glove compartment. "Thanks, Dad. We'll be back Saturday, give or take."

David nodded, his expression tight. He tried to mask it, but Ray caught the worry in his eyes before he could look away.

"It'll be alright, man," Ray said, resting a hand on David's shoulder. "They'll be back by Saturday."

David exhaled slowly. "Yeah. I know."

Riles slapped Ray on the back. "Come on. Let's make good use of the time. We've got shopping to do."

With that, Riles and Ray hopped into the Jeep, gravel crunching beneath the tires as they backed down the winding drive. Bertha rolled out behind them, turning east toward Oregon, dust swirling in her wake.

David stood alone for a moment longer, watching until both vehicles disappeared around the bend. Then he turned back to the cabin, rolling up his sleeves.

There was still work to do. Everything had to be ready. Just in case.

Between Stops and Stillness

Haylee took the first shift behind the wheel, the sun climbing higher as Bertha rumbled down the two-lane road. Josie lay sprawled between her and Sam, snoring lightly. Bella was curled up in her favorite spot—the small sink just above the lower cabinets, her tail flicking occasionally in her sleep.

It wasn't a long trip, but their appointment with Dr. Shubs wasn't until 5:00 p.m. —after hours, for privacy. That gave them plenty of time to take it slow.

They stopped mid-morning at a truck stop just off the highway. Haylee pulled into a shaded spot while Sam stretched, arms over his head, before hopping down to pump gas. Josie sniffed the air eagerly as soon as the door creaked open.

"Even though this is a quick trip," Sam said as they stepped into the convenience store, "I'm glad we're alone."

Haylee smiled, reaching for his hand as they passed the snack aisle. "Me too."

She meant it. Through all the chaos, they were finding their rhythm again. And in that moment, it mattered more than anything.

They grabbed sandwiches, fruit, and a couple of bottled drinks, then stepped outside to let Josie stretch her legs. She darted between them, tail wagging, as if she could feel the lightness between them too.

Back in Bertha, they parked near a grassy patch and took their time eating. The breeze was soft. The day still young.

For just a little while, the road felt kind again.

Errands and Undercurrents

Riles pushed the cart through the narrow aisles of the Mountain Creek grocery store, grabbing cans of soup, bread, and enough sandwich fixings to last them through the border crossing. Ray trailed behind, tossing in a few bottles of water and jerky packs.

"You think the food in Montreal as good as what we have in the states?" Ray asked, scanning a shelf of granola bars.

Riles smirked. "Different coast, different magic. But Quebec takes its food seriously."

They moved in a rhythm, checking off items on the list Haylee had scribbled out before leaving that morning. But beneath the surface of the errand, there was tension—unspoken but thick.

Near the checkout line, Ray leaned against the cart. "You ever think about just... not doing this? Turning around, heading somewhere quiet, and forgetting all of it?"

Riles didn't answer right away. He loaded a few last items onto the conveyor belt, then met Ray's eyes. "Yeah. All the time. But forgetting doesn't stop what's coming. It just leaves someone else to face it alone."

Ray nodded slowly. "Just feels like we've been pulled into something too big for us. Like we're standing too close to a storm we don't understand."

Riles gave a half-smile. "Probably are. But I figure if the world's gonna twist itself inside out, I'd rather be with people who give a damn. Even if they're a little strange."

Ray chuckled. "Yeah. Strange but solid. I'll take it."

By the time they got back to the cabin, the sun had dropped lower in the sky. David was outside stacking firewood, the steady rhythm of the axe splitting wood echoing off the trees.

He looked up as the Jeep pulled in, giving a short wave. Riles cut the engine and stepped out, grabbing a few bags from the back.

"Anything weird while we were gone?" he asked.

David shook his head. "Just a quiet day. You guys get everything?"

"Yeah. Enough to keep us fed through the drive and a couple of days into Canada."

Ray joined them with an armful of supplies. "You know, for people lying low, we eat pretty well."

David cracked a grin. "Gotta keep morale up."

Inside, the cabin already felt a little emptier without Bertha parked out front. But the supplies were set on the counter, the firewood stacked high, and the trail ahead was slowly taking shape.

Even in the quiet, the current beneath it all kept humming—low and steady, pulling them forward.

When the Fire Fades

After unloading the groceries, the three men moved through the cabin with a kind of quiet efficiency—each one lost in thought but glad for the normalcy of the task.

Later, with the sun setting in streaks of amber through the trees, they sat outside on the porch steps, the fire pit crackling in front of them. David nursed a cup of coffee while Riles flicked a stick into the flames. Ray leaned back against the railing, arms crossed over his chest.

"Hard to believe this place was ever peaceful," Ray muttered, watching the smoke curl upward.

"It was," David said. "Long time ago. Before everything got tangled up in Veil lore and secrets."

"You regret coming back here?" Riles asked without looking over.

David took a long sip. "No. Just... wish I'd done it sooner. Maybe I could've helped Aggie. Or kept Haylee out of this mess."

Ray tilted his head. "She's in it either way. But she's not alone."

That settled over them for a moment like dust.

"You think she's ready for what's coming?" Riles finally asked.

David didn't answer at first. He watched the trees sway in the last light. "I think she has to be."

Papers and Pawprints

The late afternoon sun stretched low across the pavement as Haylee parked
Bertha beside a quiet brick building with a weathered sign: **Cedar Pines Animal
Clinic**. A pine tree carved into the wooden post swung gently in the breeze.
"This is the place," Haylee said, glancing at the name David had scrawled on the
back of a receipt. "Ask for Dr. Shubs."

Josie jumped down first, tail wagging as if she were heading into a park instead
of a vet's office. Bella, as usual, took more convincing. Sam coaxed her from the
sink with soft words and a well-timed treat.

The clinic's interior was cozy and smelled faintly of cedar and antiseptic. A
receptionist greeted them with a warm smile and gestured toward the clipboard.
"David said to tell Dr. Shubs hello," Haylee added as she filled in the paperwork.

"Of course," the woman nodded. "She'll be happy to hear that. She's just
finishing up with another patient."

They didn't wait long. A tall woman with silver-streaked hair and kind eyes
appeared at the door, wiping her hands on a towel.

"David Hensen's daughter, I assume," she said with a gentle grin. "He always
said you'd come through here one day."

Haylee blinked. "He did?"

Dr. Shubs didn't elaborate. Instead, she crouched to greet Josie, who offered her
paw without being asked. "Well-mannered. Let's get you both checked out."

The exam room was quiet except for the soft murmurs between vet and animal.
Bella submitted with regal disdain, while Josie enjoyed the attention. Dr. Shubs
administered updated shots, scanned their chips, and filled out the international
travel forms with practiced ease.

Dr. Shubs handed her an extra slip of paper. "And if you need anything while you're in Canada—anything—you call this number. Friend of mine in Quebec. Just in case."

Sam raised an eyebrow. "Just in case?"

The vet gave them a knowing look. "Things have a way of showing up when you least expect them. And from what I gather… your road has a few of those." Back in Bertha, the sun dipped behind the pines as they buckled in. Bella resumed her post in the sink, Josie curled between them again.

Haylee looked at the papers in her hand and the number written in neat block letters at the bottom.

Just in case.

Unmarked Trails

With the girls' paperwork safely tucked into the folder, Bella on the dash and Josie snoozing in her bed behind the passenger seat, Haylee leaned back against the headrest. The road ahead wound through towering trees, the scent of pine thick in the air as twilight crept in.

"Any campgrounds nearby?" Sam asked, glancing at the fuel gauge.

Haylee tapped her phone. "There's one about twenty minutes from here, tucked in the woods near an old artists' village. Says it has hookups and fire rings. Sounds quiet."

"Perfect," Sam said, his hand finding hers on the console.

They pulled into a rustic clearing just as the last of the sun dipped behind the hills. A carved wooden sign welcomed them: **Whispering Pines Camp & Arts Co-op.** Beyond the check-in booth sat a modest gift shop glowing with string lights.

After settling into a shady site, Haylee grabbed her wallet and stepped into the little shop while Sam started hooking up Bertha. The smell of herbs and old books drifted through the air.

"Bonjour, chérie," came a voice from behind a counter lined with quartz crystals and painted wood carvings. An older woman with salt-and-pepper braids and a velvet wrap looked up from her open journal. Her eyes—one green, one cloudy blue—landed on Haylee with eerie familiarity.

"You're Aggie's girl," she said.

Haylee froze. "Excuse me?"

The woman smiled gently. "You walk with her shadows around your shoulders. I knew her long ago—before she crossed the border for good."

Haylee stepped closer. "Do you know what happened to her?"

"She left threads behind. Some shouldn't be pulled too soon, mon cœur." The woman closed her journal and slipped it into a drawer. "But if the stone hums, and the cat follows the wind... then maybe the Veil is stirring again."

Haylee swallowed. "What does that mean?"

The woman didn't answer. Instead, she reached under the counter and handed her a bundle wrapped in indigo cloth. "Something she left behind found its way here. It waited for you."

Inside was a folded slip of handmade paper. In Aggie's familiar script:

You're closer than you think. Trust the ones who guard the quiet places.

Haylee stared at the note, her pulse quickening.

Back at the campsite, Sam looked up as she returned. "Everything okay?"

Haylee nodded slowly, her hand still wrapped around the bundle. "Yeah... I think we just found something we didn't know we were looking for."

As the night settled in and the crickets began their song, something about the campground felt older than the trees around it. Bella stayed close. Josie curled tight.

Tomorrow would bring another mystery.

But tonight, they were somewhere *meant*.

Where the Thread Tugs

By morning, the crisp air carried a dampness that promised rain, and soft pine needles clung to Bertha's steps. Haylee moved about the RV quietly while Sam took Josie out for a short walk before breakfast. Bella had been perched on the windowsill, alert and twitching her tail since dawn.

Haylee was just refilling the kettle when she realized Bella wasn't in her spot. "Bella?" she called, scanning the cabin. "Where'd you go, girl?"

She stepped outside barefoot, heart already tight. "Sam?" she called out. No answer.

She walked toward the trees lining the back of the campground. There was a slight path—barely worn, more animal than human—but something pulled her feet to it. A nudge. A thread.

Twenty yards in, she found Sam crouched low, whistling for Josie. "She took off after something, but I didn't see what."

Haylee's eyes scanned the woods, until a flash of silver-gray darted through the brush. "Bella!"

The cat didn't stop. She moved with eerie intent, as though tracking something unseen. Haylee and Sam followed quickly behind, deeper into the trees.

Just when Haylee was about to break into a run, Bella stopped beside a moss-covered rock at the base of a crooked pine. She pawed at something just beneath its edge.

Haylee knelt and gently brushed away a layer of leaves. Beneath them was a small, smooth stone—painted with the same swirl-circle sigil from the medallion and the grimoire. Next to it, carved into the bark of the pine, was another symbol—one she'd seen in Aggie's notes. A directional rune. A pointer.

Haylee sat back on her heels, the air thick around her. "She led us here," she whispered.

Sam stood over her shoulder, brow furrowed. "That mark—it's the same as on the grimoire's chapter about portals."

Just then, Josie bounded into view, tongue lolling out, tail wagging wildly. She plopped down next to Bella, as if they'd both simply gone on a shared morning stroll.

Haylee shook her head with a quiet smile. "I don't think they were lost. I think they were trying to show us something."

She picked up the stone and tucked it into her pocket. Bella brushed against her leg before trotting ahead, clearly ready to go.

Back at Bertha, Haylee cleaned the pine needles off her feet and looked toward the campground shop. Something in her gut urged her to say goodbye.

Inside, the Québecoise woman was behind the counter again, sipping from a mug.

"Your cat is very old," she said without turning. "Older than her body."

Haylee blinked. "What do you mean?"

"Some animals are just companions," the woman said. "Others… are watchers. Guardians. That one has seen the other side before."

Haylee touched the velvet pouch inside her coat. "I think she's showing me how to see it, too."

The woman nodded. "It will come in layers. You see one thing, then another. But soon, they will begin to overlap."

Haylee hesitated, then offered the painted stone. "Do you know what this means?"

The woman took the stone gently, studied it, then returned it. "It's not meant for me. But yes… I've seen it. That's Aggie's mark for crossing safely. When you see it again, follow."

A gust of wind stirred the chimes outside the door.

Haylee smiled softly. "Merci."

The woman smiled back. "De rien, petite lumière."

Chapter Twelve:
Of Stone and Sight

Bertha rested in a shaded gravel lot of a quiet Oregon campground by early evening. the place felt like a small pocket of stillness tucked between pine trees and dusky hills.

Josie snored softly on the floor while Bella curled in the sink, her tail flicking. Sam dozed on the small bed with a blanket draped across his lap.

Haylee sat at the tiny dinette, the velvet pouch and the grimoire spread open before her. The book's pages seemed to shimmer faintly in the low cabin light, as if waiting.

She ran her fingers over the smooth stone, the one etched with the swirling medallion mark. Her pulse quickened.

She whispered the words written in Aggie's spidery handwriting:

"Light it when the Veil stirs. It will show the unseen path."

Haylee took a slow breath, then lit the small candle beside her. She held the stone just above the flame.

A sudden shimmer rippled across the RV—like heat rising off pavement. The candlelight bent unnaturally, casting strange shadows.

For a moment, Haylee felt her breath catch in her throat. Her vision blurred, then shifted.

She wasn't in Bertha anymore.

The trees around her were taller, impossibly ancient. The air shimmered, thick with the scent of moss and something older than time. In the clearing ahead stood Aggie, younger, dressed in flowing layers Haylee had never seen before.

"Haylee," Aggie said softly. "You're closer than you think. But remember—not all doors lead forward. Some bring you back to what must be undone."

Then the vision blinked out. The candle sputtered. Bertha returned.

Haylee gasped and gripped the table.

A knock at the door made her jump.

It was the woman from the campground shop—the Québecoise. Her hair was pinned up, and her eyes held knowing.

"Forgive me, I saw the shimmer. The air bent. You used something from the other side."

Haylee hesitated. "You felt that?"

The woman nodded. "I've known your aunt. Long ago. She bought chalk from me once, when she needed to mark a boundary not meant to be crossed." Haylee's heart skipped. "Aggie?"

The woman stepped inside gently. Her gaze fell to the grimoire.

"May I?" she asked.

Haylee nodded.

The woman ran a hand over the page. "This is old. Very old. But it listens. And it will listen to you. Just don't let it speak too loudly when you're alone."

Haylee swallowed hard. "How do I know what to trust?"

"Magic isn't just about trust," the woman said, "it's about respect. And listening more than you ask."

She looked down at the stone.

87

"Use this again only when the wind feels wrong. You'll know."

With a kind smile, the woman turned to leave. "Bon courage, petite lumière."

Haylee closed the door gently behind her, heart still pounding.

Sam stirred on the bed, rubbing his eyes. "Did something happen?"

Haylee looked at him, then at Bella—who now sat upright, eyes locked on the velvet pouch.

"Yeah," Haylee whispered. "Something's waking up."

It Knows You're Coming

They left the campground just after 9:00 a.m., Bertha humming steadily beneath them as the early morning mist burned off the Oregon roads. Josie was curled at Sam's feet, Bella nestled on the bed—watchful, but calm.

Haylee had sent the text to David before they left:
"All good. Leaving now—should be back late afternoon. Be ready for an early start Sunday."

A calm sort of anticipation settled over her, but it didn't last.

Around midday, they pulled off at a rest stop tucked against a stretch of towering pines. The lot was mostly empty—just a rusted sedan, an old RV, and a man standing at the edge of the tree line, staring into nothing.

Haylee climbed down from the RV to stretch her legs while Sam filled Bertha's tank.

As she passed the vending machines, the man turned. His eyes met hers, sharp and clouded, like smoke on glass.

"You shouldn't be wearing that," he said.

Haylee froze. "What?"

"The medallion. The mark," he said, voice low but certain. "You're walking straight into the place she tried to escape."

A chill crawled up her spine. "Who are you?"

But the man didn't answer. He turned and disappeared into the trees.

Sam jogged over, sensing something was off. "Everything okay?"

Haylee's eyes scanned the tree line, heart pounding. "I... don't know. Someone just—warned me. Said I shouldn't be wearing this."

She touched the necklace at her throat, where the medallion now pulsed faintly warm.

Sam's brow furrowed. "What did he look like?"

"Older. Weathered. But—he knew. About Aggie. About where we're going."

They both looked toward the forest, but there was nothing there now.

Haylee exhaled slowly. "Let's just go."

Back in Bertha, the mood had changed. Bella crouched low in the sink, alert. Even Josie had stopped snoring.

Something was shifting.

Lines on the Map

David stood by the cabin's small dining table, a large paper map spread out beneath a few mugs and a half-eaten protein bar. He looked down at his phone, then to Riles and Ray.

"Haylee just texted. They're staying one more night. Said they'll be back late afternoon tomorrow so we can leave first thing Sunday morning."

"Sunday," Riles repeated, tracing a finger from the Oregon mountains to a tiny black dot labeled Montreal. "That's a hell of a drive."

Ray leaned in, eyes scanning the path they'd penciled out in red. "How long you think it'll take us? Four, five days?"

David nodded. "At least four if we push. Five if we want to keep it safe."

"Safe sounds better," Riles muttered. "Especially with whoever's still tracking us."

They had mapped the route carefully:

- I-80 E (Nevada → Utah → Wyoming)

- I-90 E / I-94 E (Wyoming → South Dakota → Wisconsin)

- US-131 / I-69 / I-75 S (through Michigan)

- I-80 / I-90 E (into Ohio)

- I-86 → I-88 → I-87 N (New York → Vermont)

- VT-104 N → I-89 N to the Highgate Springs–St. Armand/Philipsburg Border Crossing into Québec

Estimated Time & Distance

Total Driving Distance:
~2,700–2,900 miles (4,345–4,667 km), depending on exact turns and bypasses.

Daily Travel Plan (realistic for the Jeep crew with stops):
- Day 1: NV → Western WY (~500 mi)

- Day 2: WY → SD → MN/WI (~500 mi)

- Day 3: MN/WI → MI → OH (~550 mi)

- Day 4: OH → PA → Eastern NY (~500 mi)

- Day 5: NY → VT → Montreal (~350 mi)

Total Trip: ~5 Days

Even just tracing the path made it feel more real. Riles tapped the corner of the map. "So, once Haylee and Sam get back tomorrow, we pack, sleep, and you, Haylee and Sam leave at first light?"

David folded the edge of the map and nodded. "Exactly. No later than six."

Ray leaned back in the chair. "And Riles and I head out Monday?"

"Right. You'll follow the same route, but give us a day's head start."

Ray nodded. "Guess this is it, then. One last deep breath."

David gave a quiet smile. "Before the real crossing begins."

Chapter Thirteen:
Embers in the Quiet

The sky above the Oregon campground faded into deep velvet, stars flickering like scattered ash. Haylee and Sam sat side by side near the fire pit, their legs brushing under a shared blanket. Josie lay curled at their feet, twitching in some dreamy chase, while Bella rested on a nearby stump, eyes half-lidded but alert.

The flames crackled and hissed as Sam poked a fresh log into the embers. He handed Haylee a steaming mug of tea, their fingers lingering a moment longer than needed.

"Thanks," she said, voice soft.

He smiled. "Didn't think we'd find peace like this again—not after everything."

Haylee sipped slowly, letting the warmth seep into her. "It's weird how the quiet feels different now. Not empty. Just... full of what's coming."

Sam looked at her, then past her to the woods. "Do you ever wish we could just stay here? Build something without the next thing pulling at us?"

She didn't answer right away. The weight of his question lingered in the air.

"Sometimes. But then I think... that's not what Aggie set in motion. That's not what any of this has been about."

He nodded, gaze returning to the fire. "You're changing, you know."

"I feel it," she whispered. "Like something in me is waking up."

They sat in silence for a while, the kind only shared by people who didn't need to fill the space between them. Haylee reached out, lacing her fingers with his.

"Thank you for staying," she said.

"Always," he replied.

Behind them, Bertha stood like a quiet guardian under the starlit trees. Tomorrow they would return to the cabin, gather David, and cross into the unknown. But for tonight, all they had to do was hold onto each other, and the fragile stillness that burned like an ember between them.

Morning Before the Miles

The first golden rays of sun stretched over the horizon, casting long shadows across the quiet campground. Haylee stirred beneath the blanket, the cool morning air brushing against her skin. Sam blinked awake beside her, a sleepy smile tugging at the corners of his mouth.

Josie yawned, stretching before hopping off the sleeping mat, tail wagging as she trotted to the edge of the clearing. Bella perched on the RV steps, already awake and watching the sky with eerie stillness.

They moved slowly, savoring the gentle hush of early light. Haylee and Sam packed up their things, folding the blanket and securing their small breakfast stash. Josie danced at their heels, eager for her morning walk.

They strolled one last time through the trees behind the campground, the world still wrapped in soft silence. Sam reached down to squeeze Haylee's hand, and she looked up at him, smiling.

"You feel like home," she said.

His hand tightened slightly. "So do you."

By 8:45 a.m., they were packed and ready. Bertha rumbled to life, and as the RV pulled out of the campground, the dust kicked up behind them glowed in the morning sun. Vermont—and the Veil—waited.

But first, the cabin. And the journey forward, together.

Lines in the Dust

David rose with the first light, his nerves wound tight like the cords of his duffel. He paced the cabin floor, checking his phone again and again, waiting for Haylee's message.

"You better sit down or you'll wear a hole in the floor," Riles commented, stretching as he sat up from his sleeping bag.

The days since Haylee and Sam left had been uneventful, but none of them had let their guard down. The silence around the cabin wasn't comforting—it was tense, a calm before something they couldn't name.

Ray was still snoozing on the couch until the scent of fresh-brewed coffee drifted across the room. He groaned and rolled over, finally blinking awake.

David handed him a chipped mug without a word, then turned to double-check the gear by the door. With the map and his bag already packed, he was ready for anything. "Got your gear squared away?" Riles asked, peering into the half-packed cooler.

Ray and Riles still had to load their provisions and pack the cooler for the long trip ahead. David would have the relative comfort of Bertha; Riles and Ray would be roughing it in the Jeep.

"Almost. Just need to grab ice and top off the water jugs," Ray replied, stifling a yawn.

Their plan was set: David would leave with Haylee and Sam in Bertha Sunday morning, while Ray and Riles would follow the next day. They'd meet on the Canadian side of the Highgate Springs–St. Armand/Philipsburg border crossing, at the duty-free shop located at 3 Route 133 in Philipsburg.

The Road Knows More

Haylee and Sam made one last stop before reaching the cabin, pulling into a quiet roadside turnout for coffee and fuel. The sky was beginning to haze with the weight of late afternoon sun, and the shadows on the pavement stretched long beside Bertha.

Inside the RV, Haylee's phone buzzed. She glanced down, expecting a reply from David—but it wasn't a saved number.

Unknown number:

"You think you know what you're doing, but you don't, little girl."

The message made her stomach lurch. It was condescending, yes—but something colder lurked beneath it. A chill traced up her arms as she locked the screen.

Sam caught the expression on her face. "Another one?"

Haylee nodded and showed him the message.

He didn't say anything at first. Just reached over and gave her hand a gentle squeeze. "Good thing we're heading out tomorrow. Putting some miles between us and this place."

She looked back at him and managed a small smile, her grip tightening in return. Back on the road, the trees gave way to open stretches of golden grass and wide, rolling curves. Haylee kept one hand on the wheel and the other rested lightly on her thigh, fingers drumming out a quiet rhythm.

She glanced in the rearview mirror, catching a glimpse of Bella snoozing in the sink and Josie curled against the side of the passenger seat.

She'd never been further east than Utah before.

The road ahead was unfamiliar. But in that uncertainty was something else too: possibility.

And maybe, just maybe, the road knew more than she did.

The Last Quiet Fire

Bertha pulled onto the gravel drive leading to the cabin, tires crunching softly beneath her weight. It had been a long couple of days, and the thought of a warm meal and one more quiet night in the mountains brought a surprising wave of comfort.

Riles was out on the porch when he saw them coming. He turned and called into the cabin, "They're back!"

David and Ray stepped out just as Bertha came to a stop, their faces easing into smiles. Bella leapt onto the dashboard and pressed her nose to the glass.

The reunion was warm, with Josie bounding ahead as soon as the RV door swung open. There were hugs, soft words, and the kind of laughter that came not from humor, but relief.

Sam grabbed a few things from Bertha for the night, and David stowed his own gear into the RV's cargo compartment. The group made their way into the cabin, where the table had been cleared for dinner.

They shared a simple meal—nothing fancy, just hearty and warm. The kind of food that filled more than just stomachs.

Afterward, they drifted outside, drawn to the firepit like moths to its glow. The flames danced as the sky deepened into a violet dusk, stars beginning to blink into view above the treetops.

They sat in a loose circle. No one said much at first. But in the quiet, their shared presence said enough.

It was their last night together before the road would split them into separate paths. Tomorrow would bring motion again. Miles. Maps. Uncertainty.

But tonight was still.

And it was theirs.

Chapter Fourteen:
First Light, Second Sight

5:00 a.m. came earlier than expected for Sam, Haylee, and David. They moved quietly around the cabin, the chill of morning lingering in the air as they packed the RV's fridge with supplies. Riles brewed a final pot of coffee while Ray handed out plates for a simple breakfast—eggs, toast, and whatever fruit was still fresh.

There was a quiet weight to the morning, but it wasn't heavy. It was reflective. Intentional.

After loading the last of the bags, Sam and Haylee gathered Josie and Bella, ushering them gently into Bertha. Josie hopped up between the front seats, tail thumping lazily as she settled into her spot. Bella immediately made her way to the bed in the back, curling into a warm patch of sunlight already spilling through the window.

David took the first driving shift, hands steady on the wheel as he guided Bertha onto the gravel road. Sam rode shotgun, folding the map one last time and tucking it into the center console.

Haylee sat on the bed with a blanket around her shoulders, grimoire open in her lap. The road ahead curved gently into gold-lit pine and aspen, and the hum of the tires on pavement was strangely grounding.

She'd felt it before—the pulse, the ping, the almost-audible pull when the grimoire had something for her. It was more than just reading now. It was connection.

The book was full of cryptic messages scribbled in the margins—some in English, some in French, some in a looping script she didn't yet recognize. Still, she pressed on.

A name flashed in her mind like it had been waiting for the right moment. ***Jean-Paul and Mireille Bouchard. Le Fil du Monde.***

Signs in the Sage

Bertha rolled into a quiet fuel stop just outside central Utah a few hours into the drive. It looked like any other rustic highway gas station—sun-bleached signs, a gravel parking lot, a distant mountain range hovering like a faded painting on the horizon—but something in the air made Haylee pause as they pulled in.

The wind carried more than dust. It carried weight.

While David filled the tank and Sam popped the hood to check for anything unusual, Haylee clipped Josie's leash and walked her toward a patch of tall grass on the edge of the lot. She moved slowly, senses more heightened than usual. Colors felt sharper. Sounds more layered. It wasn't overwhelming—just... deeper. Like the world had tuned itself up a key.

Josie tugged toward the tall grass, nose twitching with interest. Haylee followed, expecting to find a discarded sandwich wrapper or maybe a rabbit trail. Instead, nestled in the green was a snake—curled and coiled, but not striking. Its copper-toned body shimmered under the rising sun.

Haylee stiffened, instinctively tugging Josie back, but something about the snake's eyes made her freeze. It didn't feel threatening. It felt... aware.

The snake lifted its head, not in warning, but like it recognized her.

Her heart pounded, but she didn't move. "Hello."

"This is ridiculous," she whispered to herself. "Talking to a snake?"

Then again—why not? She spoke to Bella. She swore Josie understood every word. Maybe this wasn't so different.

"Hello, snake," she said softly.

The creature didn't slither away. It loosened its stance, tongue flickering briefly, and simply watched her.

Josie gave a bark, sharp and unsure, but Haylee laid a calming hand on her.

"We'll leave you be now," she said gently.

The creature didn't slither away. It seemed to regard her quietly, unmoving. Then, slowly, it began to ease back into the grass. But it didn't leave immediately. It paused—turned slightly—as if giving her a silent nod.

A moment of strange reverence passed between them. Then it vanished.

Haylee backed away gently, guiding Josie with her, not speaking until they were safely back near Bertha.

As Sam approached with a bottle of water, he caught the look on her face. "You okay?"

Haylee nodded, glancing once more toward the grass.

"Yeah," she said, still breathless. "Just... Utah saying hello."

Chapter Fifteen:
The Watchers Who Stay

Back at the cabin, the morning passed slowly but deliberately.

Riles and Ray moved like men on a mission—checking sensors, walking the perimeter, inspecting every nook where trouble might slip through. They reset a few of the bear traps, replaced batteries in motion lights, and cleared brush from the western fence line.

Ray pulled a heavy black case from the back of the Jeep. Inside were two compact trail cameras—high-resolution, night-vision capable, and discreet enough to miss unless you were looking for them.

"Didn't think we'd need these anytime soon," he muttered, attaching one to a thick pine near the front gate. "But I've got them linked to my phone. Anything moves out here, I'll know."

Riles nodded, adjusting one of the older motion sensors he'd rigged months back. "Won't stop 'em, but it'll slow 'em."

Together they swept the cabin one last time, checking locks, signal boosters, and the solar panels on the roof. It wasn't paranoia—it was precaution. With everyone hitting the road, the place would be vulnerable.

Or so they thought.

Cover Stories and Contingencies

With the perimeter sweep done and the last camera feed checked, Ray and Riles finally made their way back inside the cabin. Riles tossed a few pieces of kindling into the wood stove, letting the gentle crackle fill the quiet room. Ray sat at the small kitchen table, phone in hand, flipping through the camera app. Everything looked still—for now.

"We should go over it again," Riles said, nodding toward the envelope of printed documents on the counter.

Ray didn't argue. He closed the app and reached for the papers, spreading them across the table like a makeshift mission briefing.

"The story's simple," Riles began. "I'm visiting my ex-wife Madeline over some lingering property issues from our divorce. You're tagging along for a fishing trip up in British Columbia."

Ray nodded slowly. "They're going to be looking for red flags, you know. Two former military guys crossing into Canada last minute? That could light something up."

"Which is why we've built the story carefully," Riles replied. "We've known each other for years—old military buddies reconnecting. You've been staying at my place out West, and we're driving together since you wanted to head toward BC while I settle some stuff with my ex."

Ray leaned back in his chair. "Close enough to the truth to make it believable."

"Exactly," Riles said. "We're not acting. Just... trimming the details."

He tapped a forged rental agreement with a Quebec address. "Madeline agreed to say I'm staying at her apartment if border patrol calls. She's headed out of town anyway, but she'll answer if they push."

"And your name's still on the lease?" Ray asked.

"Technically, yeah. She never took me off." Riles paused, rubbing the back of his neck. "One of the few favors she's willing to do, so I can come and go as I please."

"We act like we've got nothing to hide," he continued. "No rushing. No stammering. Just a couple of guys making conversation at customs."

Ray nodded. "Yeah. Just gotta hope they buy it."

"They will," Riles said, more certain than he felt. "We've taken the steps. All we can do now is run the play."

He tucked the documents back into the envelope and slid it into his duffel. Ray grabbed two beers from the small fridge and handed one over.

"To smooth border crossings," Ray said with a tired grin.

Riles raised his bottle. "And convincing lies."

They clinked bottles and sat in silence for a moment. The fire popped gently in the stove. The faint sound of a raven called from deeper in the woods.

Everything looked quiet on the outside.

But they both knew better.

Before the Asphalt Calls

They double-checked their gear one last time—flashlights, extra batteries, flares, backup water, and enough dried meals to last them a week. Riles went over the cooler contents, making sure nothing would spoil too quickly. Ray checked their duffels, zipping and unzipping compartments like a man on autopilot.

The fire in the stove had burned low, just a quiet orange glow beneath the grate. Riles let it die, closing the iron door with finality.

"Alarm's set for 3:15," Ray muttered, glancing at his watch even though he knew the time. "We good?"

"We're good," Riles said, more to the room than to Ray.

The two men slept in shifts, but neither truly rested. When the alarm finally buzzed in the dark, they moved with practiced calm. Quiet footsteps, whispered reminders. The Jeep came alive with their gear—the duffels, the cooler, their shared thermos of strong coffee. By the time they stepped out to lock up the cabin, the sky was still heavy with stars, just a whisper of light on the eastern ridge.

Ray turned to glance back at the porch. "We really did everything we could."

Riles nodded. "If something happens, it won't be because we weren't ready."

The air shifted—cool and weightless, like a held breath. Not ominous, just... expectant. As if the land itself acknowledged their departure.

They climbed into the Jeep without another word. Ray took the first shift behind the wheel, his eyes steady on the winding road ahead. Riles folded the map over his knee, tracing their route east.

The miles unfolded in silence at first, just the hum of tires and the low static of the radio. But something crawled beneath Ray's skin the farther they got from the cabin. A nagging feeling, an itch he couldn't quite place.

Chapter Sixteen:
In the Wake of Wheels

They stopped again just outside Rock Springs, Wyoming, stretching their legs in the chilled late-morning air. Sam filled the tank while David let Josie roam the nearby grass patch. Bella stayed curled up on the dash like royalty.

Haylee prepped a quick lunch—sandwiches, chips, and a couple of sodas—careful not to spill mustard as Bertha gently rocked in the wind. David checked the map again, always calculating. He wasn't obsessed with the clock, just cautious of too many unknowns stacked together.

They found a quiet place to park for the night at a visitor center along I-80. Nothing unusual. A few big rigs hummed in the distance, and scattered RVs dotted the lot. Sam and Haylee turned in early, needing rest from more than just the road. They needed distance—space to breathe.

David stayed up. He brewed a single pot of coffee and watched without being asked. He sat outside for a while, listening to the night shift of bugs and tires and time. With a mug of coffee in hand, he stayed outside a little longer than usual, scanning the parking lot from the folding chair just outside Bertha's door. The air held a silence that wasn't quite comforting, but not alarming either—just still.

He knew they were being followed. Maybe not today, maybe not this stretch of road. But somewhere out there, threads were pulling tighter. Haylee and Sam needed rest more than they knew, and David was determined to give them just a few more hours of peace.

Tomorrow, Ray and Riles would hit the road too. And they'd all be one step closer to the crossing.

That meant they needed a story.

David turned it over in his mind like a well-worn coin. Riles had his cover—an ex-wife and leftover paperwork. But David knew they'd need more than just a good story. They'd need trust in one another... and luck.

But for now, the coffee was hot and the stars were steady overhead.

The morning broke slowly over the Rock Springs horizon, casting gold and lavender hues across the open Wyoming sky. Bertha sat quietly beside the pumps as Josie sniffed the edge of the parking lot, nose twitching with curiosity. Haylee stood nearby, stretching out the tension in her shoulders while the crisp air kissed her cheeks.

David topped off the fuel tank while Sam went inside to grab waters and snacks. It had only been a day since they'd left the cabin, but the road already felt long, coiling eastward like a question still waiting to be answered.

They would need to pick up the pace if they wanted to get to Montreal in 4 days. Back in the RV, Haylee jumped into the passenger seat. When Sam returned, he slid into the driver's seat with a grateful sigh, brushing her hand as he passed. David gave a quick thumbs-up and climbed onto the couch to rest.

Bella leapt up to the dash, settling in for her usual front-row nap, while Josie disappeared to the couch with David.

Inside, Haylee flipped absently through the grimoire, her thoughts drifting to Jean-Paul and Mireille Bouchard, and the cryptic footnotes she'd found scribbled in the margins. She didn't yet understand what was calling her forward—but something was.

Shifting Stories and Shared Smiles

David stirred in his sleep as the tires hummed against the pavement. Sam kept his eyes on the road, hands steady on the wheel as Bertha rolled through the early afternoon stretch of Wyoming.

They needed to keep moving. If they were going to make Montreal in the allotted time, every hour counted. Sam had decided they would drive in shifts, only stopping for fuel, quick meals, and letting Josie out. It wasn't the most comfortable strategy, but it was the most efficient.

Earlier, David had mentioned the need for a believable story at the border. Sam and Haylee had talked it over during lunch and come up with something simple —but effective. They would pose as a newly engaged couple, with Haylee's father joining them on the trip as a generous pre-wedding gift.

It wasn't a lie. Not really.

The idea had made them both blush, especially when Sam joked about needing to find a ring if they were going to sell it. Haylee had laughed, but something about the thought settled into her chest like a soft ember—warm and strange. Not uncomfortable. Just... surprising.

The story gave them a frame, a shared purpose. Something more than just running from or toward something. It gave them a reason to belong to each other in a way that even this journey hadn't fully defined yet.

Haylee had already booked a site at Camping Mont-Saint-Anne, a wooded campground just outside Quebec City in Beaupré. They would stay there for three weeks, plenty of time to find Jean-Paul and Mireille Bouchard and sort out what came next. If there was anything she had learned in the past few months, it was that the road always brought answers, even if not the ones she expected.

Bertha rolled on. Josie shifted on the couch beside David, her paws twitching as she dreamed. Bella stretched in a sunbeam along the dash. Sam glanced over at Haylee, who had turned her gaze to the horizon.

"You think they'll believe it?" he asked.

Haylee smiled, the blush still faint on her cheeks. "Let's just say... it wouldn't be the worst story we've told."

Sam chuckled and gave her hand a quick squeeze before turning back to the road.

Ahead, the highway unspooled like a ribbon leading toward something that felt a lot like fate.

Jokes Like Truth, Rings Like Magic

As the miles stretched on, the weight of everything began to loosen for Haylee. The road offered more than stories to share—it brought a sense of peace and calm over her. It had been her saving grace in the beginning of all this. She hadn't realized how much she needed the open road until she was back on it.

With the journey east, she felt secure knowing that although what lay ahead was uncertain, she wasn't alone. Her heart had fully opened to Sam, and every mile seemed to strengthen the bond between them.

Somewhere between long thoughts and a half-empty soda can, Haylee spotted a billboard for an antique shop: *The Pickett Fence* in Chamberlain, South Dakota. The ad showed faded lettering, dancing cacti, and the promise of "vintage treasures and timeless finds." She pulled off the exit.

David, stirred from sleep, squinted at the clock. "What's going on? Where are we?"

"We're in South Dakota, Dad," Haylee replied, adjusting her grip on the wheel. From the back of the RV, Sam shouted over a bump in the road. "Whoa, take it easy there, babe. I nearly fell off the can."

David blinked. "Are we needing fuel already?"

"Nope," Haylee said with a grin. "I just saw something that might be useful."

As they pulled into the antique shop parking lot, Haylee realized it was bigger than she'd imagined—almost like a barn-sized maze of nostalgia. She asked a staff member at the entrance where to find the jewelry section.

"Go down until you see the dancing cacti, then turn right. You can't miss it—lots of cases along the wall," the man said.

Haylee and Sam headed left. David asked about tools and wandered off with a nod. They all agreed to meet back at the RV by 2:00 p.m. for lunch.

The place was a labyrinth of knickknacks and doodads—aisles of oddities stretching farther than expected. Sam found a cowboy hat and placed it on his head with a dramatic tip. Haylee snorted, trying to contain her laughter, but the sound escaped, drawing a disapproving glare from a seasoned shopper. They didn't care. They were having fun.

Haylee picked up a $3 apron that read: "A happy camper is a firepit and a warm meal." She held it up with a proud grin and tucked it under her arm.

Finally, they reached the jewelry section. The cases sparkled under fluorescent lights, showcasing everything from gaudy brooches to delicate rings. Haylee's eyes landed on an obsidian brooch shaped like a raven, its eyes amber, mysterious. It reminded her of Aggie. The price tag read $200—more than she wanted to spend—but it still warmed her to think of her.

Sam, meanwhile, was scanning the ring cases. He didn't know gemstones, but he trusted his gut. One ring caught his eye—a simple silver band with a diamond and a black stone, balanced in tone and energy. It felt right.

When Haylee reached his side and saw it, a grin bloomed across her face. Sam saw it and knew—it was the one.

Without missing a beat, he dropped to one knee with a theatrical flourish. "Miss Haylee, you've made every mile better just by being beside me… Will you marry me and keep making this journey with me—".

Haylee laughed and nodded. "Yes! Yes, I will!"

The woman behind the counter clapped her hands over her heart. "Well, that's just the sweetest thing I've seen all day." She gave them 30% off without hesitation.

They left the shop a little lighter in spirit and with a makeshift engagement ring tucked safely into Sam's coat pocket—one more piece of magic wrapped in a joke, and maybe, just maybe, something more.

David had a small box of tools and a new pair of work gloves. After a little more wandering through rows of dusty treasures, they all met back at the RV just before 2:00. Haylee modeled her new apron as she set out sandwiches, chips, and iced tea for lunch. Sam set the ring aside quietly, and neither he nor Haylee said a word about it to David. But David wasn't oblivious—he could read the air between them.

He watched the easy way they moved around each other, the way Sam always reached for the heavy things first and the way Haylee seemed to light up near him. David had had his doubts in the beginning. But over time, Sam had proven himself—again and again.

After lunch, Sam took Josie for a quick walk around the edge of the lot. David climbed into the driver's seat and started the engine. Haylee cleaned up the small kitchen and joined them up front, sliding into the dinette with her journals and postcards.

Sam unfolded the map beside her and traced their route with a fingertip. "If we keep taking shifts like this," he said, "we can make it to Ann Arbor by noon tomorrow."

Haylee nodded, already picturing the next stretch of road.

Bertha rumbled to life. The engine hummed, the wind shifted, and the wheels rolled forward again.

Chapter Seventeen:
A Wrench in the Road

Riles had the wheel steady in his hands as the late summer dusk settled around them. The Jeep hummed down the stretch of highway just outside Casper, Wyoming. Ray had nodded off about twenty minutes earlier, slumped against the passenger door with one boot braced on the dash. The silence was calming, broken only by the low rumble of the tires and a distant country station whispering through the speakers.

Then the headlights appeared.

Bright. Close. Too close.

Riles narrowed his eyes and adjusted the rearview mirror. A black SUV. He eased up slightly on the gas to let them pass.

It didn't.

Instead, it lurched forward, tailgating with erratic movements. The distance between their bumpers closed and reopened like a threat. Riles tapped the brake lightly, hoping to send a message. The SUV backed off briefly—then surged forward again.

"What the hell?" Riles muttered.

Ray stirred. "Something wrong?"

Riles didn't answer immediately. The SUV dropped back again, just far enough to be out of range—but not out of mind.

"We're being followed," Riles said flatly.

That got Ray's attention. He sat up, stretching his arms before glancing behind them. "Same one from before?"

"Pretty sure."

They drove in silence for another mile or two. Then the Jeep gave a sudden jolt. A loud clunk echoed beneath them, and the dash lit up like a Christmas tree.

"No, no, no—" Riles said under his breath, steering toward the next exit.

The SUV didn't follow this time. It disappeared into the twilight like a shadow dissolving into dusk.

Steam hissed from under the hood as they rolled into the nearest gas station parking lot. Riles popped the hood and was greeted by a sharp waft of burning rubber and hot metal.

"Well," Ray said, grimacing. "That's not good."

A quick call to roadside assistance confirmed it—something had cracked or snapped. They'd need a tow and a mechanic to look it over. Nothing that couldn't be fixed, but they weren't going anywhere tonight.

Riles texted David:

"Minor issue with the Jeep. Staying in Casper tonight, will update you in the morning."

Ray booked them a room at a small motel; *Roadside View Inn*, a few miles down from the shop. It was a no-frills place with mustard-colored curtains and a humming mini-fridge. But the door locked, and the beds were clean.

They hauled in their duffel bags, and settled in. Riles kept his phone on the nightstand, checking it more often than he admitted to.

"Think that SUV had something to do with it?" Ray asked from across the room, sitting on his bed with a map unfolded in his lap.

Riles exhaled slowly. "Wouldn't be the first time someone wanted to slow us down."

Ray nodded. "Still. We'll get back on the road soon."

"Yeah," Riles said, though his eyes stayed fixed on the window. "Just a wrench in the road."

David's phone buzzed softly on the counter near the stovetop as Bertha hummed down the darkened highway. He reached for it, squinting at the message from Riles.

"Jeep's out of commission," he said aloud. "They're stuck in Casper for the night."

Haylee looked up from where she'd been perched at the dinette table, notebook in her lap and pen dangling from her fingers. "What happened?"

David read the message again. "Said it was a minor issue—didn't say exactly what. They're at a motel. He'll update in the morning."

Sam, who had been driving since sunset, glanced in the rearview mirror. "Do you think it's that black SUV again?"

Haylee's brows furrowed. "We haven't seen it in a while, but... maybe. I don't know. But now it's in my head, and I hate that."

She stood up and stretched. Josie, curled up beside David on the couch, shifted but didn't wake. Bella was a warm ball of fur tucked neatly into the kitchen sink.

Bertha rolled along just outside Rochester, Minnesota. The clock on the dash blinked 12:57 AM.

"Let's pull over soon," David suggested. "Stretch. Maybe grab something to eat." Sam nodded. "There's a rest stop coming up in a few miles."

Ten minutes later, they parked under a flickering light near a small, sleepy rest area. Haylee clipped Josie's leash and stepped out into the crisp air. Sam went inside to grab coffee, and David stayed back to check the route.

They regrouped by the passenger door. Sam handed her a steaming cup. "Fuel for the co-pilot."

Haylee smiled and took a sip. "Strong enough to wake the dead. Thank you."

She slid into the passenger seat while Sam buckled in behind the wheel. David moved to the couch and settled back in, keeping his phone close.

As Bertha rumbled back onto the road, Haylee glanced toward the mirror. Empty. Still, her stomach twisted.

"Maybe we just need to stay sharp," she murmured.

Sam reached over and squeezed her knee gently. "We will."

The road stretched out like a ribbon under the stars, and Bertha carried them quietly forward—watchful, waiting, and wide awake.

Not Just Wood and Nails

Ray stirred around midnight, unable to sleep. He grabbed his phone and opened the security camera app connected to the cabin. A fresh ping had lit up his notifications.

The footage was grainy at first, bathed in moonlight. Then movement.

Four figures crept into frame, approaching the cabin with silent caution and clear intent. Each moved like they had a job to do. Their dark clothing blended into the forest, but the camera picked up the shimmer of metal tools.

"What the hell..." Ray whispered, sitting up straighter.

The first man circled around the east side of the cabin—and yelped. He dropped like a stone, clutching his leg. The camera caught the unmistakable clank of steel: a bear trap, well-hidden in the brush.

"Ouch," Ray muttered, a little impressed.

The second man moved toward the front steps—then was blasted with a burst of light from the security lights. But this was no ordinary light. It flared with a force that knocked him back and sent his tool skittering into the trees.

The third man reached for the front door handle—only to scream and yank his hand back, shaking it in pain. The metal had seared him like it had been sitting in fire.

Seeing this, the fourth guy tried a different approach. He hurled a rock at the nearest window, shattering it on impact.

Or so he thought.

The glass shimmered, vibrated—and then reformed itself, whole and untouched.

All four men froze. Then, without a word, they gathered themselves—limping, stumbling, clutching bruises—and bolted back into the trees.

Ray stared at the screen. "Holy shit!"

He restarted the footage and played it again. This time, he turned up the volume. Riles stirred, groaning. "What is it?"

"You need to see this," Ray said, grinning. "The cabin has... defenses."

Riles blinked sleep from his eyes and sat up. They watched the footage together in stunned silence.

"Well," Riles said, rubbing his jaw. "I guess we don't need to worry about the cabin anymore."

They each took a turn staying awake to keep watch, but there was an odd sense of peace now. Like something—someone—was watching over them. Even from miles away.

Chapter Eighteen:
Too Quiet, Too Easy

The highway signs were spaced wide apart, the road empty enough to feel almost serene. The quiet was a little too perfect.

Haylee set her notebook aside and reached behind her to pat Josie's head. The dog yawned and blinked up at her. Bella was curled contentedly in the sink, as always, queen of the counter.

Then her phone buzzed in her hand.

Unknown number.

"You can run, but we'll find you."

Her stomach dropped.

She read it twice. Then a third time. Her hand clenched the phone.

Sam saw her face. "Haylee? What is it?"

She turned the screen to him. His expression darkened.

David looked back from the driver's seat, having heard enough to know something was wrong. "Is it that number again?"

Haylee nodded. "Yeah. We're not as invisible as we thought."

David exhaled sharply. "Okay. We stay alert. We stick together. And we don't panic."

Sam put a steady hand on Haylee's shoulder. "We'll be fine. Whatever this is, it doesn't get to win."

She took a breath and gave a small nod, then climbed into the passenger seat. Sam took the wheel, setting his coffee in the holder beside him. The road was quiet again, but the mood had changed. Awareness sharpened.

David climbed onto the couch with Josie beside him. Bella stirred in the sink but didn't wake.

Haylee sat quietly next to Sam, watching the night unfold around them. Her heart beat a little faster than usual.

Too quiet, too easy. Not anymore.

Exit Ahead

By the end of day three, the road had blurred into a patchwork of cracked asphalt and glowing signs. They'd made steady progress, passing through Ohio and Pennsylvania before finally crossing into New York. Now, as night settled in, Bertha rolled into the outskirts of Jamestown.

Sam tapped the GPS screen, then glanced at the old road atlas open across his lap. "We're not far now. Maybe eight hours to the border at Highgate Springs, give or take."

David nodded, stretching his arms above his head from the co-pilot seat. "We should stop for the night. I saw a diner sign off the last exit. I say we grab some food, walk the dog, and catch a few hours of sleep."

They pulled into the cracked parking lot of a twenty-four-hour diner with neon letters buzzing above the entrance. Sam parked Bertha in the back corner, to be more or less out of sight.

Sam hopped out with Josie, who immediately trotted to the patch of grass near the fence like she'd been holding it since Syracuse. David popped the hood and checked Bertha's fluids and belts by flashlight.

Haylee stepped out and leaned against the RV's side, the cool night air washing over her. The humidity had eased slightly, and a soft breeze tugged at the edge of her flannel shirt. Somewhere nearby, a cicada trilled. The diner smelled of pancakes and old coffee.

She watched the sky, stars just barely peeking through the gaps in the streetlights. Sometime tomorrow, they'd cross into Canada. Just one more checkpoint, one more version of the truth to rehearse and carry across the line.

The plan was solid. The story was consistent. But Haylee knew—once they crossed over, things would change.

Not just the scenery. Not just the pace.

Everything.

David joined her, wiping his hands on a rag. "Bertha's good. She'll get us there."

Haylee gave a quiet smile. "She always does."

Sam returned with Josie, her tongue hanging out happily. "This place smells like heaven. You ready to eat?"

"Definitely," Haylee said.

They made their way into the diner, the bell over the door jingling as they stepped inside. Vinyl booths, chipped mugs, and a waitress who looked like she'd been working night shifts since the '80s—it was perfect.

For a few minutes, things were normal. Syrup on the table. Coffee refills without asking. Laughter from the kitchen. Even Bella had settled into a loaf shape on the front dash, her little body silhouetted in the windshield like a fuzzy guardian.

Haylee sipped her tea, watching the steam rise.

One more day.

One more push.

And then... the unknown.

But for now, they were here.

Something Old, Something True

The Bertha crew settled in for the night, full bellies and warm hearts guiding them to sleep. Josie curled up at the foot of the couch beside David, who snored gently beneath a worn blanket. Bella perched on the dash in the soft wash of moonlight, her green eyes half-closed but always watching. In the back, Sam and Haylee drifted off in each other's arms, the kind of peaceful sleep that only comes after long roads, hard truths, and unexpected healing.

Morning came gently, casting golden light through the trees and filtering across Bertha's windows like a quiet blessing. Haylee stirred to the scent of pine and warmth, her body wrapped around Sam's, the hum of safety still wrapped around them.

Sam was already awake.

"Hey," he whispered, brushing her cheek with the back of his hand. "Want to take Josie for a walk? Let your dad sleep in?"

Haylee nodded, stretching slowly. Josie thumped her tail from the foot of the couch, already alert and ready.

They stepped out into the stillness, the morning air crisp and kissed with dew. The sun was just starting to rise, casting long shadows that danced through the trees. They walked for a while in easy silence, Josie trotting ahead, nose to the earth, leash loosely in Sam's hand.

"I've been thinking about this," Sam said, his voice almost shy as he slowed to a stop. "I know it was kinda corny in the moment, but..."

He reached into the pocket of his jacket and pulled something out.

Haylee's breath caught.

There, nestled in his palm, was the ring from the antique shop—the one he'd once held out in jest, a playful moment now echoing with something deeper.

Sam dropped to one knee. This time, it was different.

"Haylee," he began, voice steady. "I never told you this, but I fell for you back at the café. All those walks to the pond, Josie getting sprayed by that skunk… even the quiet days, when we didn't say much at all. I loved all of it."

He looked up at her, eyes full of quiet certainty.

"This journey with you has shown me that, with each passing day, there's nothing I want more than to spend the rest of my life walking beside you—wherever the road leads, whatever that looks like. Would you make me the happiest I've ever been and continue this life's journey… together?"

For a heartbeat, Haylee just stood there, stunned. But in her heart, the answer had already bloomed. It had been growing with every mile, every moment. She felt it in her bones.

Tears welled in her eyes as she dropped to her knees in front of him.

"Yes, Sam," she whispered, voice trembling. "Yes."

He slipped the ring onto her finger, and they kissed, the forest their witness.

And as if on cue, Josie circled them with the leash, tangling them both in a moment of canine intuition and comic timing.

They laughed, wrapped up in each other and the leash, unable to move but not needing to. Josie plopped down in front of them, her tongue lolling, tail wagging, clearly proud of her work.

They stayed there for a while—entwined in laughter, in love, in the glow of something true.

They walked back to Bertha in a soft glow—arms wrapped around each other, the weight of the moment still humming in their chests. The trees rustled gently above them, a whispering chorus to what had just unfolded. With every step, Haylee kept glancing at her hand, watching the antique ring catch the rising light like a promise.

The air was cool and quiet, the kind of quiet that settles over the world before it truly wakes. Birds hadn't yet started their songs, and the only sound was the light crunch of gravel beneath their boots and Josie's cheerful sniffing as she trotted ahead, leash now firmly under control.

Bertha greeted them like an old friend—warm lights glowing low from the street lights above, Bella still curled up on the dash, tail twitching in a dream. They eased the door open, stepping in carefully, trying not to disturb the peace inside.

But it was short-lived.

David stirred from the couch, blinking groggily as he sat up and rubbed his eyes. "What time is it?" he asked, voice rough with sleep.

"About 4:30," Haylee replied, trying not to sound too chipper.

He groaned slightly, stretching out a kink in his back. "Why are we up this early again?"

"Because there's a 24-hour diner and I'm craving burnt toast and pancakes," she said with a small grin. "Want to grab breakfast before we hit the road again?"

David blinked at her, then nodded slowly. "Yeah. Yeah, actually that sounds good."

Within minutes, the trio was up and dressed, layering flannel over t-shirts and brushing hair with quick fingers. Sam grabbed their travel mugs and gave Haylee's hand a quick squeeze before she slipped the ring into the sleeve of her jacket, just in case.

The diner was nestled between two gas stations, its neon sign flickering against the early dawn sky like a sleepy beacon.

127

Inside, the scent of strong coffee and crispy bacon welcomed them like an old friend. A waitress with kind eyes and tired feet gave them a smile as she led them to a booth by the window.

They slid into the red vinyl seats, the table sticky with syrup rings and stories told long before them. Their order came quickly—bacon, over-medium eggs, slightly burnt toast, and pancakes stacked high.

They ate mostly in silence, the comforting kind. The clink of forks and the soft hum of the old jukebox were the only sounds filling the space. But every now and then, Haylee and Sam's eyes would meet across their mugs, full of unspoken words and secret grins.

David, still yawning between bites of pancake, didn't notice the way Haylee cradled her left hand close or the sparkle just barely peeking from her cuff. The secret was still theirs—for now. Wrapped in warmth, caffeine, and the quiet knowing that something had shifted between them forever.

For the Story

Sam took the first driving shift while David navigated from the passenger seat. Haylee spread the journals and postcards out along the dinette table, sorting through the pieces like a puzzle just about to make sense.

"Getting close," she whispered to herself. "But to what?"

Her eyes drifted to the ring, and she caught herself smiling. She never thought she'd get married. She had been with Jake for ten years, and he never liked talking about the future—or marriage. But why not? She deserved to be happy. And Sam made her happy in so many ways. He was there for her in the chaos, showing up for her in ways Jake never had. Honestly, there was no comparison.

She shook the thought of Jake from her mind. That chapter was closed. She was finally happy with her found family, and nothing was going to take that from her.

Up front, she could hear the muffled conversation between Sam and David. Something about making sure their story was solid.

Then Sam called back from the wheel. "Hey babe, will you get the ring out of my jacket pocket and go ahead and put it on? So we don't forget the most important detail of our story."

Without hesitation, Haylee stood from the dinette and made her way to Sam's jacket hanging by the door. She reached into the pocket, found the ring box, and opened it slowly—letting the soft *click* of it snapping shut carry just far enough.

She with the ring on her finger, pausing to admire it with a quiet smile before walking up to the front to show David.

"Isn't it pretty?" she asked, trying to keep the excitement from bubbling over in her voice.

David looked down at her hand, then up at her face. What she didn't realize was that her face had already given her away. She was glowing.

But David kept it cool.

"Oh yeah, that's real nice," he said, giving a slight nod. "That should do... for the story."

Chapter Nineteen:
This Ain't the Ritz

The morning came with a start.

A loud backfire cracked through the stillness like a gunshot, jolting both Riles and Ray awake. Ray nearly fell off the edge of the narrow twin bed, arms flailing as he tried to catch himself. Across the room, Riles shot upright, his hand already on the gun beneath his pillow.

"What the hell was that?" he barked, scanning the room with wide eyes.

Ray stumbled to the window, pulling back the dusty curtain just in time to see an old red Ford pickup chugging out of the parking lot. The truck backfired again, then sputtered its way down the street.

"Just a truck misfiring," Ray said, scratching the back of his neck with a yawn.

"Oh good," Riles muttered, lowering the gun and swinging his legs over the edge of the bed. "For a second there, I thought I was gonna have to shoot up the place."

He stammered his way to the kitchenette in boxer shorts and a wrinkled t-shirt, opening random cabinets like something better than instant coffee might magically appear.

"Want some coffee?" he called over his shoulder as Ray headed into the bathroom.

"Nah, I'll get something later. But you go ahead," Ray replied as he turned on the shower, steam already clouding the tiny mirror.

Inside the bathroom, Ray caught a glimpse of himself and grimaced. He ran a hand over the stubble across his jaw. He needed a shave—desperately—but decided it could wait another day or two.

In the kitchenette, Riles found a rusted little coffee pot and half a jar of instant crystals. The chipped mug on the counter had a faint coffee ring and a small crack near the bottom, but he'd seen worse in his time. Probably drank worse, too.

The morning moved slowly, each man eventually taking his turn in the shower and pulling himself together. Riles, always the early riser, called the mechanic as soon as the shop opened.

"Well, it's what you thought it was," the man said on the other end. "Blown seal on the transfer case. I don't get many Jeep Wranglers out here, so I'll have to order the part. Should be in by late tomorrow afternoon."

"Alright," Riles said. "Go ahead and order it. Call me when it's done."

He ended the call and turned to Ray, who was sitting on the edge of the bed, pulling on his boots.

"It's the transfer case," Riles reported. "Part should be in tomorrow, and it's an easy fix. We should be back on the road by 7:00 p.m."

Ray let out a sigh and stood, stretching his back. "Well, alright then. What do we do in the meantime? Sit around here and twiddle our damn thumbs?"

Riles smirked. "No way in hell. We'll go grab something to eat and check out the town. I'm not staying in this shithole a minute longer than I have to."

Ray gave a chuckle, grabbing his jacket. "Yeah, this ain't the Ritz."

Horses, Hopes, and Half-Decent Coffee

With nothing but time on their hands and a beat-up motel room that smelled faintly of mildew and old takeout, Riles and Ray found themselves scanning the motel lobby for something—anything—to do in Casper.

A corkboard cluttered with local flyers and sun-bleached brochures offered a few options: a community theater play from last weekend, a petting zoo open Saturdays only, and then—there it was.

High Stakes Palace.

Ray plucked the glossy brochure from the rack and read aloud with a mock announcer voice: *"Win huge playing horse racing terminals at the High Stakes Palace. Full off-track betting with live simulcast horse and dog racing from tracks across the U.S. and Las Vegas-style electronic gaming."*

He looked up. "So… fake horses, fake dogs, and real money?"

Riles shrugged. "Hell, it's better than twiddling our thumbs."

They grabbed breakfast first—a real diner this time, not the motel's sad excuse for coffee and vending machine muffins. The waitress poured them two mugs of dark roast that didn't taste like cardboard, and that was enough to call it a win. Afterward, they called a cab and rode across town toward the glowing sign of the *High Stakes Palace.*

Casper, as they quickly learned, was more of a family-oriented town. Not much to do if you were stranded for twenty-four hours without kids or a plan. But tucked off a nondescript side road, the High Stakes Palace was its own little world. Booze, betting, blinking machines—it wasn't Vegas, but it'd do.

Inside, the lights were low and tinted in amber. Flat screens covered the walls, broadcasting races from across the country—Florida, California, Kentucky. A woman cheered softly at her terminal as a virtual greyhound zipped across the digital track. The machines buzzed with near-misses and last-second wins. An older man in a cowboy hat nursed a whiskey at 10:00 a.m. like it was no big thing.

Ray looked around and gave a low whistle. "Well, this place is... something."

Riles cracked a grin. "Yeah, like the ghost of a casino hooked up with a gas station."

They took up a corner booth to get the lay of the land before throwing any money down. Ray watched a replay of a quarter horse race in Arkansas while Riles sipped on what passed for a Jack and Coke. After a few minutes, they found an open pair of terminals and fed in a few bills—just enough to keep it interesting.

They didn't expect to win big. It wasn't about that.

It was about passing time with a little distraction, maybe a little luck, in a place where no one knew their names or why they were in town.

Outside, the wind carried dust down the quiet streets of Casper. Inside, the air hummed with artificial noise and the low murmur of hope that maybe, just maybe, the next ticket would hit.

Chapter Twenty:
Where the Path Opens

They were just pulling into Adirondack Park, New York when Haylee spotted a weathered wooden sign at the edge of the parkway:

Outdoor Fun for Everyone: Walking Paths

"Let's stop for a bit," she said, tapping the window. "Josie could use a good walk —and honestly, so could we."

David glanced in the rearview mirror and nodded. "Yeah, let's take a breather. I'll stay here with Bertha and stretch out. You two go enjoy."

Haylee smiled and reached for the small daypack in the back. She and Sam filled it with water bottles, snacks, and a pouch of Josie's favorite treats. Josie, already panting with excitement, let out a single bark as if she knew exactly what was happening.

They crossed into the walking path, a gentle trail that wound through soft trees and wildflowers, eventually wrapping around a glistening pond framed by weeping willows. The sun sat warm overhead, casting gold over the water's surface. It felt like stepping into a postcard—or maybe a memory not yet made. They didn't talk much as they walked, and they didn't need to. The quiet between them was full of something stronger than silence.

Eventually, they found a bench facing the pond and sat down. Sam took Haylee's hand in his and glanced down at the ring on her finger. He didn't say anything. Neither did she.

Birds dipped and skimmed the water, wings flashing in the light. A pair of kids on the far side of the pond giggled as they raced remote-controlled boats, the tiny engines humming across the surface. Josie lay at their feet, content and still, her eyes tracking the birds like she was trying to memorize every movement.

It felt like something out of a movie—too peaceful, too perfect to be real. But it was.

Haylee leaned her head onto Sam's shoulder and exhaled a long, slow breath. The kind of breath you only release when you realize just how long you've been holding it in.

For once, the road wasn't demanding. The mystery could wait. The hurt was quiet.

This moment was just theirs—untangled, unhurried, and whole.

Haylee felt like this was the perfect time to break out the snacks and water. The air was warm but not too hot, and the scenic pond shimmered with light that seemed to slow everything down. It was the kind of place that invited you to linger.

She unzipped the backpack and pulled out two apples and a small bag of trail mix, along with their water bottles. The soft rattle of the treat pouch immediately caught Josie's attention. Her ears perked up, head tilting in curiosity as she sat up with hopeful eyes.

"You always know the sound of that bag," Haylee chuckled, tossing her a treat. Sam grabbed one of the apples. The crunch echoed slightly in the quiet space around them, the pond still and glimmering in the afternoon light. They both drank from their water bottles, the coolness grounding them even more in the moment.

It wasn't extravagant. Just a bench, a pond, a dog dozing happily at their feet. But it was peaceful. Real, tangible peace. And they needed it more than they realized. Haylee leaned back, letting the sun kiss her face while Sam rested his elbow on the back of the bench, hand loosely cradling her shoulder. Josie, satisfied with her snack, let out a content sigh and stretched across the grass in front of them.

Back in Bertha, David sat in the front passenger seat with his phone balanced on one knee. He tapped in the name of the border crossing and scrolled through the map. **Highgate Springs—** the only 24-hour border crossing into Canada near their route. Just under two and a half hours away.

The time read 3:50 p.m.

He sent Haylee a quick text:
"We are about 2 1/2 hours from the border. We can leave when you get back."

Back at the pond, Haylee's phone buzzed on the bench beside her. The sharp vibration broke the silence like a tiny alarm. She and Sam both flinched slightly —funny how quickly even peace can be interrupted.

Haylee glanced at the screen. "It's from my dad."

Sam watched her closely.

She read the message aloud. "He says we're only two and a half hours from the border. We can leave when we get back."

For a beat, they both just sat there, quiet. The weight of what was ahead— crossing into another country, stepping further into the unknown—settled gently over the moment like a soft shadow.

Sam slid his arm around her and pulled her close. "I want this moment to never end," he murmured, pressing a kiss to her forehead.

Haylee closed her eyes and leaned into him. "I know. Me either."

She looked down at Josie, now fully stretched out in the grass, her chest rising and falling in a deep, peaceful rhythm. "I think Josie's content here too."

They stayed for just a few more minutes, clinging to the stillness before the next stretch of road pulled them forward.

Chapter Twenty-One:
No Turning Back

An hour later, Haylee, Sam, and Josie made their way back to Bertha. The sun was beginning to dip toward the horizon, casting a golden wash across the parking lot. When they opened the RV door, David was just finishing a bag of chips. Bella stretched lazily across the dash, bathed in the warm, amber light. Josie bounded inside first and leapt onto the couch with a contented sigh, curling up like she'd never left.

"I'll take the next shift driving," Haylee offered, already climbing into the captain's seat.

Neither Sam nor David argued. Sam slid into the passenger seat, and David settled next to Josie, patting her side as she closed her eyes again.

The drive toward the Canadian border wasn't quite what they had expected—though truthfully, none of them had any clear expectations to begin with. None had been to Canada before. David's military years had taken him overseas, mostly to Germany and Japan, while Sam and Haylee had never traveled out of the country at all.

The border crossing at Highgate Springs buzzed with movement. A steady stream of vehicles flowed in both directions—RVs, pickup trucks, semis, even a polished silver Airstream glinting in the fading light. Despite the activity, the lines moved quickly. A few vehicles were pulled off to the side for additional inspection, and as they edged closer, Sam and Haylee exchanged a glance.

They watched a border agent climb into a nearby Class A motorhome. Sam didn't say anything, but he reached down to unclip Josie's collar and gently coaxed her into her travel crate. Bella, already tucked behind the dash curtain, was lured into hers with a soft treat.

By the time they were four vehicles away, Sam had retrieved the large manila envelope from the glove box—inside were their passports, along with vet records and vaccination certificates for both animals.

They waited in line for just over 25 minutes.

When it was their turn, Haylee eased Bertha up to the booth and handed over the documents to the border officer. He was middle-aged, with tired eyes but a kind smile.

"What's your business in Canada?" he asked, looking over the paperwork.

"We're on our way to Camping Mont-Sainte-Anne," Haylee answered. "My dad's treating us to an early wedding gift—he paid for a three-week stay."

She held up her hand slightly, the antique engagement ring catching the evening light.

The officer smiled. "Do you have any fruits, vegetables, or meats aboard?"

"No, sir."

"Well alright then," he replied, handing back the documents. "Enjoy your camping experience—and congratulations on your upcoming nuptials."

"Thank you," Haylee said with a grateful smile.

As Bertha rolled through the gate and into Canada, all three of them let out a collective breath.

"That wasn't so hard," Sam said, laughing softly.

Haylee smiled as she kept her eyes on the road ahead.

No turning back now.

Clear to Proceed

They had barely made it a few hundred feet past the border checkpoint when an officer stepped into the roadway and motioned for them to pull over into a designated parking area.

"What the fuck?" Sam muttered under his breath, tension tightening his grip on the armrest.

"It's just routine," David said calmly, though his eyes narrowed as he scanned the approaching officer.

Haylee followed the directions and eased Bertha into the marked space, killing the engine.

As she and Sam were preparing to step out of the cab, a sharp knock at the RV door startled them all. Josie gave a single low ruff from her crate, then laid back down as if she sensed something off.

David opened the door slowly. "Hello, officer."

The border agent gave him a once-over before speaking. "I need all of you and the animals to vacate the RV. Now."

They didn't hesitate. Sam and David lifted Josie's crate carefully while Haylee grabbed Bella's, along with the manila envelope containing all the documents. They were led across the lot to a half-covered shack labeled *Secondary Inspection Waiting Area*—a sparse shelter with a plastic bench and a metal ashtray bolted to the ground.

They waited.

A few moments passed before a second officer appeared, this time with a drug-sniffing dog at his side. The dog was focused, tail rigid, posture alert. The first officer gestured toward Bertha, and the pair moved in without a word.

Haylee exchanged a wide-eyed look with Sam. David clenched his jaw but stayed quiet.

Forty-five long minutes passed.

Finally, the officer with the dog exited the RV, followed by the first officer. He waved them over.

"You're free to go," he said simply. "Enjoy your stay here in Canada."

David stepped forward. "Can I ask what this was all about, sir?"

The officer paused, then replied, "We received an anonymous tip about an RV matching this description—supposedly transporting narcotics from the States. Looks like it was a false claim."

Without another word, he returned to his post.

David opened Bertha's door—and froze.

The place had been turned upside down.

Cabinets stood open, contents strewn across the floor. The fridge had been emptied and left ajar. The trunk storage under the bed had been pulled out completely, with clothes and gear dumped around it in disarray.

Haylee sighed, walking over the scattered mess to gently set Bella's crate on the dinette bench. Sam and David brought Josie back to the couch and opened her crate. She immediately curled up in her usual spot, as if reclaiming her territory.

"Let's just make a walking path for now," David said. "We'll clean up once we're settled."

He pulled out his phone. "There's a full-service truck stop about twenty miles from here in Saint-Jean-sur-Richelieu. Showers, food, parking. That okay with you two?"

Haylee nodded. "Sounds perfect."

Josie was already snoozing on the couch again, unbothered. Bella stretched and hopped up to the dash, settling herself in the glow of the late-day sun.

Haylee restarted the engine and eased Bertha back onto the road, their path forward rumpled but intact.

No one spoke for a while. There was no need.

They were still together. Still rolling.

And for now, that was enough.

Chapter Twenty-Two:
Whiskey and War Stories

The neon buzz of the High Stakes Palace faded behind them as Riles and Ray stepped out into the dry Wyoming evening, pockets heavier with winnings and no immediate plans until the mechanic opened shop in the morning. The sun sat low in the sky, casting long shadows across the cracked parking lot as they flagged down another cab.

"Somewhere with a good steak," Riles muttered, sliding into the back seat.

Ray nodded. "And a stiff drink."

The cab dropped them off at a local favorite, Big Iron Steakhouse, a rustic spot known for its oversized portions and predictable menu. Inside, the air was thick with the smell of char-grilled meat, buttered vegetables, and the hum of a half-dozen TVs competing for attention—hockey, football, soccer, and even tennis lit up the walls like a shrine to sports fandom.

They claimed a booth near the back, dark and semi-private, and placed their orders without much deliberation—two sirloin steak dinners, thick steak fries, steamed carrots and broccoli. Riles went with a 7 and 7, and Ray raised his glass of Jim Beam and Coke as their drinks arrived.

"To unexpected detours," Ray toasted.

Riles smirked and clinked glasses. "And not getting blown up by morning."

Conversation flowed in easy currents, weaving between harmless banter and war-born reflections. Ray shared tales from his time in technical forces—base work, surveillance ops, long stretches overseas. Riles' stories ran darker, edges jagged from time spent in the trenches: Korea, Iraq, Afghanistan.

Neither of them glorified it, but they spoke with the kind of unspoken understanding that only came from surviving it. The kind of talk that needed whiskey to land soft.

They lingered over dinner longer than they should've, ordering a final round after Ray talked Riles into dessert. Riles rolled his eyes but relented, ordering the triple chocolate cake while Ray went all in with the dessert sampler: cheesecake, apple pie, and a slice of Riles' chocolate monstrosity.

Belly full and head buzzing, Riles wiped his mouth and exhaled through a grin. "This is how they get you. You survive three deployments just to die of a sugar coma in a Wyoming steakhouse."

Ray chuckled, easing back in the booth. "Not the worst way to go."

They sauntered out of the restaurant under a navy sky, the streets quieter now as twilight pressed its hands across the city. The walk back to the motel was slow and meandering, filled with half-laughed stories and the comfortable silence of shared fatigue.

As they approached the Roadside View Inn, a black SUV pulled out of the lot, headlights off. It was barely noticeable, but Riles caught a glimpse. He stilled.

"You see that?"

Ray squinted, swaying slightly. "What?"

"Black SUV. No lights. Just pulled out."

They both stood frozen for a second too long. Neither of them could say for sure what they saw—or if they saw it at all.

"Could've been anyone," Ray offered cautiously.

"Could've," Riles said, voice flat. "But I'm not betting on it."

Fortunately, their Jeep was still in the shop, and no one at the motel had seen them arrive.

Riles had checked in under an alias, one he hadn't used since his special ops days: *Lieutenant Mark Sharp*. Just enough history behind it to make it convincing, just enough distance from his real name to keep him off anyone's radar.

As they entered the small, dingy room, the tension faded a little, giving way to the quiet hum of the motel fridge and the weight of exhaustion.

"You think we'll make it to the border in one piece?" Ray asked, pulling off his boots.

"We've made it this far," Riles replied, settling into his bed. "Just gotta keep our heads low a little longer."

And with that, the two soldiers-turned-shadow-men let the static from the muted TV lull them toward a restless sleep.

Grease, Guns and Getaways

The next morning was not kind.

Ray was the first to stir, dragging himself into the tiny kitchenette of the motel room and fumbling with the battered coffee maker. The result smelled more like regret than caffeine, but it was hot and it was something. Riles groaned from the bed, shielding his eyes from the muted light spilling in through the faded curtain.

"Mornin', sunshine," Ray called over his shoulder. "How you feelin'?"

Riles sat up slowly, hands pressed to his temples. "Turn down the damn TV, my head's splitting."

Ray laughed. "TV's not even on, man."

"Then where the hell's all this noise coming from?" Riles mumbled, dragging himself upright.

Ray shrugged, sipping the scorched coffee like it was a delicacy. "All I know is, I slept harder than that mattress. Head's a little foggy, but I'm alright."

Riles winced at the sunlight as he cracked open the curtain. "It's 1:15? Shit, we slept half the day away."

"Guess we needed it," Ray said. "Part for the Jeep ain't comin' till late afternoon anyway. Might as well get some grub."

Cleaned up and marginally more human after showers, the two headed back to the same steakhouse from the night before. There was comfort in the routine—comfort in the grease and booze and predictability of menus laminated and stained by a hundred other hands.

This time, Riles ordered a spicy Bloody Mary with his sirloin steak—extra Tabasco, of course. Ray, true to form, went big: the lunch special quadruple bypass burger with three slices of American cheese, a mountain of steak fries, a side of coleslaw, and a fresh Jim Beam and Coke.

"For a little guy, you sure put away food like it's your damn job," Riles muttered, eyes wide at Ray's plate.

Ray just grinned. "Gotta keep my strength up. Never know when we'll have to outrun another black SUV."

They didn't talk much during the meal, the quiet filled with the muted roar of the sports games overhead. Hockey, football, tennis—none of it really registered, just background noise while their minds chewed on more than food.

At 3:49, Riles' phone buzzed. The mechanic.

"We got lucky," Riles said after ending the call. "Part came in early. Jeep'll be ready by 5:30."

They lingered over dessert this time—Riles indulged in another thick slice of chocolate cake while Ray devoured what looked like a mountain of fried ice cream.

By 4:45, they were standing outside the auto shop. And there she was—the Jeep, fixed up and parked like a loyal dog waiting for its master.

Riles' chest tightened slightly. "Damn, I missed this thing."

He paid the bill without flinching. Practicality always won, and there was no price too steep for getting back on the road. They took the Jeep back to the motel and began packing their bags.

Ray was loading the last duffel when he stopped mid-motion.
"Psst. Riles. Three o'clock."

Riles followed his gaze with a low crouch, hand instinctively drifting toward the weapon he kept concealed beneath his jacket.

147

The black SUV was back—creeping around the edge of the parking lot like a shadow that didn't belong in daylight.

"Shit," Riles whispered. "You think they saw us?"

"Hard to say," Ray muttered, keeping behind the open Jeep door.

Their room was on the far end of the building and the motel was unusually full today, which offered them decent cover. The SUV slowed as it neared them, the windows dark enough to hide whoever was inside. Riles held his breath and his grip on the weapon tightened.

Then—tires squealed. The SUV peeled out of the lot in a rush of burned rubber and vanishing bravado.

"They didn't want it today," Riles said, exhaling as he straightened up.

"Which means they might want it tomorrow," Ray replied, tossing the last bag into the Jeep. "Let's get outta here while the gettin's good."

They pulled onto the interstate within five minutes, dust still hanging in the air behind them. Ray tapped out a quick message to David.

Hey, we're headed out sooner than expected—and with good reason. How did you do at the border?

David's reply came almost instantly.

Just get your asses here. We'll talk then.

Riles smirked. "Classic David."

Ray chuckled, leaning back in the passenger seat. "Never change."

They didn't know what was waiting up ahead—but they knew damn well it was better than what was lurking behind them.

Chapter Twenty-Three:
A Bit of Truth with Mustard

After clearing the final inspection at the Canadian border, Haylee, Sam, and David made their way to Saint-Jean-sur-Richelieu. While Bertha technically had a decent shower setup, they didn't want to fill the grey tank just yet—especially with several miles ahead. So they all headed inside the truck stop for a proper rinse.

Sam and Haylee shared a stall, taking their time beneath the hot water. Sam made her laugh by puffing a ridiculous dollop of shampoo on top of his head like a mohawk. For a moment, they were just two people laughing in a shower, young and weightless again, forgetting—if only briefly—the pressure that surrounded them.

David took his time in his own stall. He propped his phone up and played a mix of oldies, letting the music fill the space while the steaming water washed over him. There was something about it—this moment of privacy, of normalcy—that let a weight fall off his shoulders. It wasn't just about getting clean. It was about catching his breath.

Clean and somewhat recharged, the trio made their way to the food counter. They had run out of sandwich meat just in time to cross the border, so truck stop food felt like a minor luxury compared to stale bread, mustard, and cheese. They picked up their meals and brought them back to Bertha.

Sam volunteered to take Josie for a walk while Haylee set up their "feast." David helped stow things away, then lingered beside her.

"You handled the border crossing and the second inspection really well," he said. "I'm proud of you."

Haylee paused, setting down a packet of ketchup. "Yeah, well… we had a great story and plan. But inside, I was screaming. I couldn't wait to get back to Bertha. I don't even know what to call the feeling—it was like a pull. Like I had to be near her." She exhaled a breath she didn't realize she'd been holding.

"And what's with that anonymous tip? Drugs? Nobody knows where we are. Who would do that?"

"I don't know," David said, his voice tight. "But if I had to guess? Elliot. Or someone doing his dirty work. Hopefully, now that we're across the border, his reach won't stretch up here."

Just then, Sam returned, panting slightly, with Josie in tow.

"She saw a goose," he said between breaths, "and decided to chase it. But it turned on us. We ended up being the ones running."

Josie dropped onto the floor with a dramatic thud.

They all sat to eat, the truck stop's version of hot meals warm in their hands. The silence stretched comfortably between them—until David's phone buzzed. He glanced down. "Ray says they got the Jeep early. They're back on the road. Sounds like they ran into a little trouble." He tapped out a quick reply and set the phone aside.

"I was just telling Haylee how proud I was of her for the border story," he added.

Sam smiled. "She did great. The story worked."

He gave her a sheepish grin, glancing sideways. She caught his look and smiled back.

David raised a brow, amused. "The truth will set you free, you know."

Haylee and Sam froze, mid-bite.

"What do you mean, Dad?" Haylee asked cautiously.

David chuckled. "How slow do you think I am?"

The two exchanged a glance—somewhere between sheepish and shy.

"So… when were you going to tell me that Sam actually proposed?" he asked, casually polishing off the last bite of his food.

"Buh—uh…" Haylee stammered, blushing.

"It happened so fast," Sam said, rubbing the back of his neck. "We didn't really think about telling you until all this was behind us."

"I'm not upset," David said, softening. "It just would've been nice to be in on the moment."

They sat in silence again, the kind that wasn't awkward, just full of unspoken things. Eventually, David stretched out on the couch with Josie curled up beside him, already snoring. Bella lay on the dash, basking in a sunbeam.

Haylee and Sam retreated to the bed, curling up without a word. There was nothing they needed to say. For now, they were simply content to be.

Sleepless in Saint-Jean

David snored like a freight train, sprawled across the couch with Josie curled up beside him, just as loud in her own way. Meanwhile, sleep evaded Haylee and Sam. The truck stop buzzed with movement—semis groaned, diesel engines coughed, and horns blared as two trucks nearly collided at the pumps. Sam jumped up to check the window.

"Just a near miss. No one's hurt, just irritated," he whispered, easing back into bed. "Can't wait till we get to the campground. Feels a little too exposed here."

Haylee yawned in agreement. "Yeah... feels like the air itself is shifting."

They tried to doze again, but by 11:00 p.m., all three of them were wide awake. The unease wasn't from the caffeine or the chaos—it was the anticipation.

Camping Mont-Saint-Anne was just over three hours away, but there was no point leaving in the dark. Instead, they moved Bertha further into the parking lot, away from the brighter lights and engine noise, and started mapping out their next leg.

"We've got check-in at 1:00 p.m., so we've got time to stop along the way if anything catches our eye," David said, tapping his phone screen as he zoomed in on the route. "Wouldn't hurt to find a decent trail for Josie either."

"Yeah," Haylee replied. "She could use a long walk. We all could."

Suddenly, a knock at the door.

Everyone stiffened. Sam moved to peek out the window and saw a middle-aged couple grinning up at them like they were long-lost friends.

He cracked the door.

"Hi," he said cautiously.

"Well hey there!" the woman chirped. "I'm Tammy, and this here's my husband, Tommy. We saw your lights on and thought we'd come say hi."

Sam blinked. "Uh, yeah—we're just winding down. Couldn't sleep."

"Mind if we join you?" Tommy asked, already stepping up into Bertha like it was his own home. "We brought snacks! A little chuckuterrie board for late-night munchin'."

Haylee looked over at David, who gave her a classic we're doing this now? look. She just shrugged.

Sam, being polite, offered them sodas. "Sorry, we don't really have anything stronger."

"No worries, hon." Tammy pulled a mason jar out of her massive purse. "I always carry my moonshine."

"How'd you get that across the border?" David asked, genuinely curious.

Tammy leaned in and stage-whispered, "We stashed it in the crapper. Don't worry, never used."

"Y'all want some?" she asked, waving the jar.

David politely declined. "We've got an early start. Best not."

Tammy shrugged. "Suit yourselves—more for us!"

She set down the so-called *charcuterie* board on the table. It was mostly summer sausage, cheese cubes, grapes, and a suspicious-looking pack of crackers.

"So, where y'all from?" Tommy asked as he made himself a grape-meat roll-up. "Can't place the accent."

"We're from out west—Oregon," David replied. "I'm David. This is my daughter, Haylee, her fiancé Sam. Josie's the snoring dog on the couch, and Bella's the sink queen."

153

"We're from Orangeburg, South Carolina," Tammy beamed.

"What do you do, Sam?" Tommy asked, clapping him hard on the back, nearly knocking him into the dinette.

"I'm... taking a break from work. Customer service." He rubbed his shoulder. "And you, Haylee?"

"I'm a writer. I used to be a bookkeeper."

Tammy's eyes lit up. "Oh, how exciting! Have we read anything of yours?"

"I write mostly travel stuff. Magazines, blogs, that kind of thing. Nomadic lifestyle kind of work."

"That's so cute! You're like a little wanderin' poet," Tammy cooed.

"What about you two?" David asked, trying to steer things back.

"I did hair for thirty years, and Tommy here's a war vet. Hurt his back, so now we just roam when the road calls."

"Oh, speaking of hair," Tammy added, "I could do yours, Haylee—no charge. Consider it a weddin' gift from the road!"

Haylee hesitated. "Uh... sure. That'd be nice."

Before anyone could intervene, Tammy zipped out to her rig and came back with an entire salon kit. Sam and David, now herded to the couch with Tommy, exchanged glances as Haylee was whisked off to the back of Bertha.

"Ever heard of Kristen Stewart?" Tammy asked while brushing. "She was in that vampire-werewolf movie."

"Twilight?" Haylee guessed.

"Yes! That's it. Thought I'd give you a Kristen vibe—real classy." She winked. "You got pretty hair. Real soft."

Haylee smiled nervously. "Just—please don't cut it."

"Wouldn't dream of it," Tammy said, already teasing it sky high. "Gonna do an updo that'll make Sam weak in the knees."

Forty-five minutes later, Tammy spun her around with a proud flourish. "Ta-da!"

Haylee blinked at the reflection. Her hair was piled into a gravity-defying beehive, sprayed so stiff it looked bulletproof.

"Wow, Tammy. This is... really something. Thank you." She choked back a laugh.

"Sam's gonna love it," Tammy winked. "Alright, Tommy—let's hit the hay."

They packed up, said their goodbyes, and even exchanged numbers just to be polite.

As the door clicked shut, Sam and David turned to Haylee in perfect unison: "Wow."

They all burst into laughter.

By the time the clock struck 3:50 a.m., everyone tried to sleep again. Haylee sat upright, unable to lie down without crushing her new 'do.

Sam rolled over, resting his head on her lap. "You smell like Aqua Net and anxiety."

She smiled and stroked his hair. "Welcome to the road."

Butterflies and False Alarms

Haylee eased herself out from under Sam's arm just after 9:00 a.m., careful not to wake him. His head was still heavy against the crumpled pillow, arms splayed like a content dog in the sun. She tiptoed across the warm floor and put on the coffee. The scent alone made the RV feel more alive.

Catching her reflection in the microwave door, she nearly jumped. Between the truck stop snacks from last night and the hardened beehive hairstyle sculpted to her skull, she hardly recognized herself.

"Oh no," she muttered with a laugh, smoothing a crusted section near her temple. "Who even are you?"

Josie stirred first, hopping off the couch with a low whine and stretching long. Haylee clipped on her leash and guided her out for a quiet stroll in the morning light. The geese were still loitering nearby, acting like unpaid security. They gave her side-eye from the grass, and she made sure to steer Josie in a wide arc around them.

When she returned, Bertha was still hushed. She scribbled a quick note:
"Went for a shower. Back soon. — H"

She propped it on the small dinette table and headed inside the truck stop once more.

The private shower stall was a small sanctuary—cleaner than she expected and warm from earlier use. The beehive came out in stages, like unspooling ancient secrets. She washed her hair three times to fully reclaim her scalp, each rinse loosening more of the hairspray spell Tammy had cast. By the end of it, she stood in the fogged mirror, towel around her shoulders, smiling faintly at the version of herself she recognized.

No makeup. No disguise. No chaos. Just her.

Back at Bertha, David and Sam were stretching outside in the bright morning sun when she returned. Her damp hair bounced gently as she walked up.

"Got your note," Sam said, grinning as he took her in.

"Glad to see Haylee's back and not Ma Kettle," David added with a smirk.

"Trust me," Haylee said, adjusting the travel mug lid on her fresh coffee. "She fought me on the way out. But I won."

They loaded up for the short ride ahead, fueling themselves with a truck stop breakfast and refilling their travel mugs with extra caffeine for good measure. David took the wheel this time, giving the "lovebirds" permission to "go be disgustingly sweet in the back."

Not one to argue, Haylee and Sam settled into the bench seat as Bertha rolled out of the lot.

About an hour into the drive, they spotted a roadside farm with bright flags and a small crowd gathering out front. It was a local farmer's market with lush planters, wind chimes made of repurposed tools, and a butterfly conservatory attached to one side. Sam pulled out his phone to check the reviews, but Haylee was already out the door with a gleam in her eye.

The plants were bursting with life—wildflowers, vegetables, herbs in cracked pottery, and decorative garden gnomes that looked a bit too lifelike. Butterflies swirled above in the conservatory space, thousands of wings glittering in the filtered light. They hovered around visitors, resting on ball caps and shoulders like tiny omens.

Josie wasn't allowed in, but she didn't seem to mind. David found a shaded bench with his baguette and a small espresso from the farm café.

Haylee and Sam walked Josie to a riverside park just a few minutes down the road.

It was peaceful. Just the three of them—well, four counting Josie—moving through the quiet air.

Haylee kicked off her shoes for a moment and wiggled her toes in the grass while Sam traced a lazy path beside her, Josie leading the way with her tongue hanging out, proud of every stick she found.

159They weren't in a hurry. And for once, that felt okay.

When they returned to Bertha, the windshield had something stuck under the wiper. Haylee stopped mid-step, pulse skipping.

David was still happily munching his baguette, completely unaware.

"No…" Haylee muttered, picking up her pace. Sam followed her gaze and froze.

It was a flyer. Something printed and glossy with colors too bright for a threat. But for one small breath, Haylee's chest tightened like a fist. She reached for it cautiously.

False alarm.

"It's just a flyer," she said aloud, laughing to herself as she handed it to Sam.

It was for a local art exhibit in Montreal—dates, times, and a watercolor skyline. Completely harmless. She turned it over just to be sure.

Everyone let out a slow exhale at the same time.

Josie, tail wagging and panting happily, waited by the RV door like nothing had happened.

And maybe… nothing had.

Calm Before the Curve

The trio returned to Bertha with sun-kissed cheeks and the kind of breathless satisfaction only a slow morning could bring. The stop at the butterfly farm had worked some sort of magic on them. Spirits lifted, they picked up groceries, a fresh tank of propane "just in case," and a couple of questionable pastries from a roadside shop near the truck stop before making their way to the campground.

They pulled into Camping Mont-Saint-Anne around 2:38 p.m.

After checking in at the office, a kind-faced man met them in a golf cart to guide them to their site. He spoke a blend of Quebecois and broken English, but despite the language barrier, they managed to communicate just fine—through nods, smiles, and a shared understanding that kindness travels fluently.

Their site wasn't paved, but it was shaded, spacious, and came with 30- and 50-amp hookups. A clean bathhouse stood not far off, and a path trailed behind them into the woods.

While Sam leashed up Josie for a walk, Haylee repacked Bertha with the gentle assertiveness of someone finally finding rhythm in the chaos. The fridge shelves got a reset, the pantry was reshuffled, and one of the overhead cabinets surrendered a long-forgotten secret.

A small note fluttered out and landed on the floor.

Haylee blinked, recognizing the handwriting before she even picked it up.
"It's been inside you the whole time. You just need to trust your path will lead you true."
No name, but she didn't need one.
Aggie.

A warm breeze filtered through the open door. Haylee smiled softly, tucking the note into the edge of the mirror above the sink. She didn't need to figure it all out. Not today.

Outside, David had the hood open. He muttered something under his breath that was lost in the hum of the campground, but the tone said enough.

"Shit. It's a wonder we made it here," he said louder this time, spotting Sam and Josie making their way back toward the site.

David gave a sharp whistle. "Hey, Sam."

Sam jogged over, "What's up?"

"There's a hole in the radiator hose. Not huge, but bad enough."

Sam leaned in for a closer look. "You want me to see if someone at the office knows a shop or can give us a ride into town?"

David nodded. "Yeah, but let's not tell Haylee yet. She's happy—for once. Let her have it. We'll fix the hose and then loop her in."

Sam raised a brow but didn't argue. "Got it."

At the campground office, he approached the front desk with a hopeful smile. "Uh, hi. Sorry, I don't speak French…"

The clerk chuckled. "That's okay. I speak English. What do you need?"

Sam exhaled in relief. "Thank you. Our radiator hose's cracked, and our friends haven't caught up with us yet. Any chance someone could give me a lift to the truck stop about ten kilometers back? Might be able to find a replacement part there."

The clerk thought for a moment, then smiled. "I get off in twenty minutes. Which lot are you at?"

"Lot 345. I'm Sam, by the way."

"Dan. Enchanté."

Sam blinked.

Dan grinned. "Habit—means 'nice to meet you.' I'll swing by 345 after my shift."

Back at the site, David had already removed the damaged hose and pulled up a photo of the part on his phone. Sam studied it, committing the details to memory.

"It should work," David said, wiping his hands on a rag.

Sam glanced toward Bertha's open door, where Haylee was dancing a little, humming something off-key as she wiped down dishes in the kitchen. Light spilled in from the window and caught her hair just right. For a second, the world felt soft.

She looked up, catching him staring. Haylee waved with a grin, completely unaware of the little crisis being handled just outside her field of view.

Sam waved back, his own grin forming slowly. Then he turned to David. "Let's get that hose."

Chapter Twenty-Four:
The Things That Keep Us Going

Just after 5:00 p.m., a small green pickup rumbled into lot 345, crunching gravel as it rolled to a stop. Sam and David were out front, sipping sodas like nothing was amiss. The hood of Bertha had been closed strategically to keep Haylee from noticing the earlier issue. They both greeted Dan with a wave.

"Thanks again, man," Sam said as he hopped in the truck with a small cardboard box and a satisfied grin.

"No problem," Dan replied with a nod. "Glad I could help."

As Dan drove off, David glanced over at Bertha and exhaled. "Alright," he said, stretching his back. "Time to distract our girl."

He wandered back inside and found Haylee reorganizing the snack cabinet.

"Wanna go for a walk around the campground?" he asked casually, though there was a nervous lilt to his voice.

Haylee looked up, curious. "Sure," she said with a soft smile. "Let's take Josie and Bella. They could use a little adventure too."

David clipped the leash back onto Josie's harness while Haylee called out, "Bella, come on girl!" The cat blinked slowly from her perch and stretched before hopping down with feline grace.

"Where's Sam? Wasn't he with you and Josie?" she asked, grabbing her hoodie from the bench.

"Yeah, but he rode into town with a local guy to grab something I forgot earlier. Nothing major," David said, avoiding eye contact. "Come on. You'll love the view out this way."

The air outside carried that distinctly northern scent—cleaner, softer. Crisper than what they were used to back in California. Haylee took a deep breath, grounding herself in the unfamiliar yet comforting newness.

Bella batted lazily at a butterfly drifting by, while Josie led the group with eager sniffs and tail wags, her energy contagious.

They wandered through winding gravel paths and passed rows of modest campers and colorful tents. Children's laughter echoed from a distant playground, blending with the breeze rustling through the evergreens. Eventually, Josie tugged them toward a scenic overlook framed by tall trees and wildflowers. A glassy lake shimmered below, hidden just enough to feel like a secret.

They stood quietly for a moment, taking it all in.

Bella had climbed onto a nearby stump and curled up, nose tucked into her tail. Josie chased a new scent with relentless excitement, never straying too far.

By the time they made it back around to the campground office, the light had softened into a golden hue.

"I want to pop in here real quick," Haylee said, nodding toward the shop entrance. "Do you mind taking them back to Bertha?"

David waved her off with a grin. "Have your fun. When Sam gets back, we'll figure out dinner."

"Thanks," she said, already opening the door. "C'mon girls, time to rest those legs," David called, and like seasoned travel companions, Josie and Bella followed him without hesitation.

Inside the shop, Haylee was greeted by the scent of cedar and campfire. The little store had trinkets stacked in cozy disarray—handmade candles, local honey, postcards, and snacks. A small freezer hummed in the corner filled with bags of ice, and a rotating rack held camping stickers. She ran her fingers along the edges of a sticker featuring the campground's name and an old RV under the northern lights.

She smiled and picked it up.

It hit her all at once—where she was, what they'd overcome to get here, and the quiet fact that she was engaged to Sam. She had crossed state lines and borders, both literal and emotional. Bertha wasn't just a vehicle anymore. She was home. And home was a moving target, a moment-to-moment kind of magic.

Maybe she wouldn't collect stickers from every single stop—but the ones that mattered, the ones that made her heart pause and say "this," she'd remember those.

Carefully, she walked to the counter and bought the sticker.

As she stepped back outside, the crisp Quebec air met her skin, and she smiled.

Home on the road.

Pas de Problème (No problem)

Sam climbed into the passenger seat of Dan's faded green pickup and gave a grateful wave to David, who leaned casually against Bertha, sipping a soda. The late afternoon sun filtered through the tall pines, casting a soft gold over the gravel lot.

Dan adjusted his ball cap and glanced over. "You ready?"

"Ready as I'll ever be," Sam replied, tugging on his seatbelt.

"We'll head to the store first. If they don't have it, I've got a few other places in mind."

They drove in companionable silence, the hum of the engine and the occasional birdsong filling the space. The rural roads were lined with dense forest and weathered wooden signs, many in French. Sam didn't understand much beyond the basics, but Dan was a local.

When they arrived at the store—a modest garage-style place with a hardware section and a narrow automotive aisle—Sam followed Dan inside, clutching the old hose box like a golden ticket.

"Hi, I'm looking for this type of hose for a radiator," he said, holding it up and offering a hopeful smile to the older man behind the counter.

Dan quickly translated: "Je cherche ce genre de tuyau pour le radiateur. T'aurais du temps pour m'aider?"

The clerk nodded without hesitation. "Ben sûr monsieur, pas de problème. J'te regarde ce que t'as là, s'il te plaît." He took the box and vanished into the back. Sam tried to decipher their conversation by tone alone. "That sounded promising," he said.

Dan chuckled. "He said he'll take a look—give him a sec."

Moments later, the man returned and slapped a box onto the counter. "Ici."

Dan translated the price. "Ça coûte 35 dollars américains ou 47,69 $ canadiens."

Sam nodded and pulled out a crumpled $50 bill. "I'll go with American."

"Pas de problème," the man replied with a small smile, ringing him up.

The man handed Sam two crisp ten-dollar bills in return.

Sam blinked at the colorful notes. "Well, this is a first."

Dan peeked over his shoulder and grinned. "Welcome to the world of maple money."

Sam held one up, inspecting the translucent window in the corner. "It looks like Monopoly cash—but fancier."

"You'll get used to it. If you buy something at the next place, you might even get some toonies or loonies in your change."

"Toonies and loonies?" Sam laughed. "That sounds like a cartoon duo."

Dan chuckled. "Almost. Two-dollar coins and one-dollar coins. We don't really use paper bills under five anymore. You'll see."

Feeling the win, Sam texted David immediately:

"Got the part. On our way back soon."

Before they left, David replied:

"Good—grab a few groceries. If Haylee asks, make it look like a regular errand run."

Sam sighed. He didn't like lying to her—well, not lying, just omitting… to protect her peace. He tucked the radiator hose safely behind the seat and grabbed a hand basket.

Dan stuck close to help translate as Sam collected a few extras—some snacks, a couple cans of soup, apples, and granola bars.

From there, Dan detoured to a roadside farm stand nearby, where rows of vibrant produce glowed under string lights. Sam picked up two crusty baguettes, a wedge of soft cheese, and a container of fresh strawberries.

"Can't go wrong with good bread and cheese," Dan said. "You guys are really making the most of this trip, huh?"

"Trying to," Sam replied. "Thanks again for helping. I'd have been completely lost in that store without you."

They exchanged numbers before pulling back onto the road. "I'll text you if we get some downtime," Sam said. "Would love to check out some local spots if you're up to it. You seem like the unofficial tour guide around here."

"Ha! You got it," Dan grinned.

Back at lot 345, Bertha gleamed in the golden light. Haylee and David were sitting at the picnic table when Sam stepped out of the truck holding the bagged hose in one hand and a baguette like a prize in the other.

"Honey, I'm home," he said with a grin.

David smirked. "You get the goods?" Heading towards Sam.

"Yup. Here's your part," Sam whispered, handing it off. "And I may have picked up some snacks from a roadside stand. Hope you're hungry."

Haylee perked up at the mention of food. "What kind of snacks?"

"Baguettes, cheese, some fruit. I figured it might buy me forgiveness for sneaking off."

"Hmm… tempting." She raised an eyebrow. "What's the dinner plan?"

Sam shrugged. "You tell me. Though... maybe no charcuterie boards tonight?"

David stifled a laugh and Haylee blushed, recalling Tammy and Tommy's infamous road snack. "Yeah, fair. Too soon."

They settled on burgers, fries, and a simple salad instead. While David got to work on replacing the radiator hose, Sam and Haylee prepped dinner together. The mood was light, the energy easy.

Later that night, the trio sat around the fire pit: David in his camp chair with Bella curled in his lap, Sam and Haylee on a blanket with Josie flopped between them. The stars were bright, the air carried that clean Canadian coolness, and all felt—at least for now—peaceful.

Just before turning in, Haylee looked up at the moon and whispered, mostly to herself, "This... this feels right."

Sam heard her, but didn't say a word. He just took her hand and gave it a gentle squeeze.

Inside Bertha, the air felt still in the best kind of way. Dinner had been simple but satisfying. The small campfire outside had dwindled to a glow, and Josie now lay curled on the rug by the door, belly full and content. Bella was asleep in the front seat again, tail twitching every so often in her dreams.

Haylee stood at the little kitchen counter, slowly rinsing a few dishes and stacking them to dry. The hum of Bertha's systems was steady and familiar, like an old friend quietly keeping time. She wiped her hands on a towel, then moved to the back table where her journal sat closed beneath a tangle of postcards, paper scraps, and a camp store receipt folded in half.

She let her fingers drift across them.

A sticker from the truck stop. A little hand-drawn card from a roadside vendor in upstate New York. That ridiculous flyer that gave her a heart attack. Each item told a different piece of the story they'd been living—just a week on the road, and yet it felt like months had passed since they left the cabin.

She glanced around at Bertha. The walls no longer looked like they belonged to someone else. The soft clutter that had once belonged to Aggie was now blended with their own—a sweater tossed over the couch back, a coffee mug she couldn't seem to part with, Bella's hair in every possible crevice. Somehow, it all belonged here now.

Haylee opened her journal and flipped to a blank page. She didn't write a lot, just a few lines—more feeling than fact.

"Friday night. The air here smells cleaner than I remembered. Not just this campground—but life. It smells like hope. Like rest. We made it to Canada. We're here, somehow."

She paused, then added:

"Tomorrow might change everything again, but tonight—we earned this."

She closed the journal and stood up, reaching for the small pouch of stickers she'd picked out earlier. With a soft hum under her breath, she peeled the backing from one with a tiny cartoon RV and the name *Camping Mont-Saint-Anne* beneath it. She pressed it to the back wall near the door—her first sticker in what might become a whole collection.

Sam appeared at the doorway, silhouetted in the dim glow from the fire pit. He gave her a sleepy smile.

"Hey," he said gently. "You coming out for a bit?"

Haylee nodded, brushing her hands on her jeans. "Yeah, I just wanted to finish something in here."

He stepped inside, his presence easy and familiar. "What's that?" he asked, eyeing the journal and stickers.

"Just… a moment. Just taking it all in." She reached out and squeezed his hand. "We've come a long way."

He kissed her forehead and didn't say anything more. They stood like that for a beat, letting the quiet wrap around them.

Outside, the fire was nearly out, but the sky was clear, stars thick and bright above the tree line. Sam tossed a blanket over the two chairs and held it open for her. They sat down together, legs tucked in, fingers still intertwined.

Neither of them said much.

There was nothing that needed saying.

Sunrise Agreements

The next morning came like a dream they all shared.

Sunlight crawled slow and golden over Bertha's hood, nudging away the last threads of morning mist that clung to the ground. It was the kind of sunrise you didn't want to talk through. Just sit in it. Breathe it in.

Haylee stirred first, then Sam. They didn't say much—just reached for each other's hands and their mugs of coffee, then stepped quietly outside. The air was crisp but not cold, the kind that made your lungs feel fresh and your skin feel real. They settled into the camping chairs just outside the RV, wrapped in the stillness.

Haylee thought briefly about Riles and Ray, wondering if they'd arrived safely wherever they were now.

David lay still on the couch inside, snoring softly.

Josie stretched from her spot at the foot of the bed, then trotted down with a sleepy yawn, letting out a soft ruff as she made her way toward the screen door —her version of "good morning." Bella was still curled into the sink, completely unbothered by the hour or the bustle. She'd moved in and had no plans to vacate.

David eventually emerged, drawn by the scent of coffee and the cool whisper of the morning. His hair was a mess, shirt wrinkled, but he looked content. "Morning," he offered, grabbing the mug Haylee had already set aside for him.

"Josie's ready," he said, nodding toward the dog already wagging her tail expectantly. "I'll take her so you two can enjoy the view."

Sam gave him a grateful nod. "Thanks, man."

Haylee and Sam sat a while longer, their mugs warm between their hands, the silence easy between them.

It felt like their own private corner of the world. A soft pause before the day spun back up.

"Something we didn't think of before," Sam said, glancing toward her. "We should probably get some local currency."

Haylee blinked. "Oh. Yeah. That's true. Everything's been so... I don't know, just moving so fast, I didn't even consider it. No one's mentioned it."

"Dan said the same," Sam added. "He offered to show us some places around town next week. Local stuff. Food, shops. He seems like a good guy."

Haylee smiled into her coffee. "I like that. We could use a little local color."

Just then, David and Josie returned from their walk. Josie's tail was wagging wildly—whatever she'd sniffed had been a good time.

"We'll talk about it over breakfast," Haylee said, standing and stretching. "Sounds good to me," Sam said, following her inside.

David lingered outside for another breath of quiet, watching the last wisps of mist disappear behind the rising sun.

Chapter Twenty-Five:
Sharp Stops and Folded Maps

Wednesday night came quick and quiet, as Ray and Riles rolled into Albert Lea, Minnesota just before midnight, headlights cutting through the small-town quiet like a warm knife through butter. They'd been driving for hours, pushing past exhaustion and replaying every turn, every exit, every shadow in the rearview mirror. Riles's knuckles were white on the wheel by the time they saw the glowing vacancy sign of a modest roadside inn.

Riles stretched as he stepped out of the Jeep. "Place looks halfway decent."

"Better than sleeping in the damn car again," Ray muttered, scanning the parking lot. He didn't spot the black SUV—or anything remotely suspicious—but habits from special ops died hard.

Inside the lobby, Riles checked them in under his old alias, Lieutenant Mark Sharp, just in case. The clerk, barely awake and too tired to question anything, handed him a key without a second glance. Room 6.

They didn't unpack. Just dropped their duffels and headed down the road to a small, neon-lit 24-hour diner that looked like it hadn't changed since 1985—and smelled like it hadn't cleaned the fryer since then either.

A bell jingled overhead as they walked in. A waitress with tired eyes and a silver bob waved them toward a booth. "Kitchen's still open. What'll it be, boys?"

Ray ordered first, "Country fried steak, extra gravy. Mixed veggies. And a Pepsi."

"Same," Riles said, folding his hands on the table.

Their booth was sticky, and the overhead light flickered every now and then. But it was warm, and they hadn't eaten anything real since that dessert sampler in Casper.

Ray pulled out the semi-folded paper map from his coat pocket and flattened it between the salt and pepper shakers.

"We keep this pace, we should hit South Bend by Thursday afternoon. Syracuse by late Friday. Then early start Saturday and cross into Canada by mid-day—give or take a couple hours."

Riles nodded, rubbing his jaw. "No black SUV since Casper. You think we lost 'em?"

"I think they're either gone or watching from farther back. But I'm not relaxing until we're over the border and well past Montreal."

Their food arrived. Steam rolled off the plates, gravy thick as glue. They dug in without another word, the clink of forks and soft hum of an old rock song filling the silence. Neither of them told a story. No laughs. Just food and caution.

After dinner, they walked back to the inn. The cold air sobered them a bit. Sleep came quickly once they hit the beds—gravy-heavy sleep, dreamless and deep.

In the morning, Riles woke early and sent a quick text to David.

"Making good time. Should hit the border Saturday afternoon. Call you when we're North."

The reply came less than a minute later.

"Good to know. We'll update you with our location later."

Riles looked out the window, sipping a bad cup of motel coffee.

They were still in the game. Still moving. Still careful.

And for now, that was enough.

Miles to Go, Maps to Fold

The morning came early and brisk in Albert Lea, Minnesota. Riles and Ray each took turns under the questionable motel showerhead, steam fogging the small mirror, water pressure a far cry from luxury but good enough to wash off the road. They didn't linger. There were still too many miles ahead and too many questions chasing their rearview.

After packing up, they walked to the 24-hour diner they'd eaten at the night before. The same waitress greeted them with a tired smile. She didn't ask for names—just nodded, poured the coffee, and let them be. Breakfast was quick and hearty: eggs, hash browns, bacon, and toast with more butter than necessary. Neither man talked much, but it wasn't from tension. It was just the quiet that came from understanding each other without words.

Back in the Jeep, Ray took the first shift. He adjusted the seat, and set the GPS. Their planned route looked something like this: South Bend by Thursday afternoon, Syracuse by late Friday, and with an early start Saturday, they'd hit the Canadian border by midday—give or take a few hours.

They cruised through southern Minnesota and into Wisconsin, passing half-frozen lakes and long stretches of pine. Roadside billboards promised everything from world-famous cheese curds to oversized fiberglass statues, but they didn't stop. The mission was clear: make time, stay unseen, and keep the Jeep moving. "Still no sign of a tail," Riles noted, scanning the rearview mirror with trained eyes.

"Either we lost them back in Casper, or they were never real," Ray replied, cracking his knuckles. "But let's not get soft just yet."

By the time they hit Madison, they switched drivers. Riles took the wheel, Ray climbed into the passenger seat with a fresh cup of gas station coffee, and the Jeep pressed on like a steel arrow across the map.

The highways bent and curved around Lake Erie like a slow dance. Truck headlights sliced through the night as they passed mile after mile. Riles and Ray talked in short bursts—old stories from old wars, whispered theories about who might be pulling the strings behind this whole mess. But mostly, they rode in comfortable silence.

At 10:45 p.m. Friday night, they rolled past the glowing lights of Erie, the lake dark and vast on their right, stretching endlessly under the stars. They were close now. One last push to Syracuse and then the border.

Ray leaned back in the passenger seat, arms crossed.

"We're almost there," he muttered.

Riles nodded. "Almost."

But almost never meant safe.

What You Can't See

They woke up more tired than either of them expected. Sleep hadn't done much to recharge them—not with their bodies aching from the miles and their minds pacing with a quiet edge of paranoia.

Riles had been up since 3:42 a.m., unable to shake the sense that something was… off. He kept watch from the motel window, arms crossed, eyes narrowed as he scanned the parking lot and the adjacent highway through a rip in the aging curtain.

Ray stirred just after 4:15, sitting up groggily and rubbing his eyes. "Any sign of trouble?" he asked, voice still thick with sleep.

"No. And that's what's bugging me." Riles didn't move from his post.

Ray leaned back against the headboard, still trying to fully wake up. "We haven't seen that black SUV since Casper. You think they gave up?"

Riles turned toward him, jaw tense. "I don't know, and I don't want to find out."

Ray didn't push it further. He knew better. Riles wasn't the kind to speak unless the gears were grinding under the surface.

"I want to leave early," Riles continued, stepping into the bathroom. "If they're watching from a distance, maybe we throw off their pattern. They won't expect us to head out before dawn."

The bathroom door clicked shut.

By 4:52 a.m., they were packed and quietly slipping out of the motel. The air was damp with the kind of morning chill that bit into your sleeves and made your knuckles stiff. Riles drove while Ray nodded off again in the passenger seat, arms crossed over his chest like a grumpy grandpa.

A few exits down the road, they pulled into a truck stop glowing in pre-dawn orange. Riles fueled up the Jeep, eyes still darting now and then to the road behind them.

When the nozzle clicked, he parked the Jeep close to the entrance and gently shook Ray's shoulder.

"Hey. You hungry? I'm grabbing grub and coffee."

Ray blinked, confused by the brightness of the overhead lights. "Yeah, yeah. Grab me one of those sausage biscuit things. And a coffee. Black."

Inside, the truck stop was surprisingly lively—night drivers finishing their hauls, early birds grumbling into foam cups. The coffee was burnt but hot. Riles grabbed two breakfast sandwiches, two large coffees, and a sleeve of mints. He paid in cash, habit more than necessity.

Back in the Jeep, Ray grunted his thanks and tore into the sandwich like it might vanish. "You sure we're still on track for the border by mid-day?"

"If traffic cooperates, yeah." Riles took a long sip of his coffee, then added, "Let's keep the burner off until we're close. I don't want anyone pinging us until it's too late to stop us."

Ray gave a small nod and chewed slowly, thinking. "I still can't believe this is where we ended up. Running like hell, waiting to exhale."
Riles didn't respond. He didn't have to.

They got back on the highway just after 5:30 a.m., the sun still shy behind the horizon. Every mile felt like a countdown now—not just to the border, but to the moment they'd know for sure if they were still being followed, or if the ghosts had finally fallen behind.

In the silence, Ray eventually muttered, "You know what's worse than being hunted?" "What?"

"Not knowing if you're being hunted."

Riles gave a dry nod. "Yeah," he said. "That's the part that'll get you."

Chapter Twenty-Six:
Coffee, Coins, and Conversations

The scent of cinnamon and bacon filled the campground lot like a soft wake-up call. Sam stood at the tiny stove in Bertha, flipping slices of golden French toast with the kind of practiced ease that made it look almost graceful. On the counter beside him, crispy bacon sizzled on a paper towel-lined plate, and a small bowl of cottage cheese waited for anyone who wanted it. The morning felt unhurried, like the universe had hit pause for a while just to let them breathe.

Haylee sat at the small dinette with her coffee in hand, her smile lazy and content. "I still can't believe you cook like this in a moving house."

"It's a gift," Sam said, sliding a steaming slice of French toast onto her plate. "Don't question it."

David accepted his plate with a chuckle, settling into the bench opposite Haylee. "I've got to admit, it's nice having a cook in the family. Better than my old field meals by a long shot."

They dug in, the mood easy and full-bellied. Between bites, Sam broke the casual quiet.

"You know," he said, glancing at Haylee, "we probably ought to think about getting some local currency. I mean, it couldn't hurt. Although the exchange rate could mess up our budget a little."

He reached into his pocket and pulled out a few coins, letting them clink onto the table—two large, gold-and-silver-colored coins and three smaller ones.

"These little guys came back as change at the roadside stand. No bills, just these."

Haylee leaned closer, picking one up. "What is this?"

"Dan called it a 'loonie.' One dollar," Sam explained. "The two-tone one's a 'toonie.' That's worth two bucks."

David chuckled. "Loonies and toonies? That's adorable. Sounds like cartoon money."

Sam smirked. "It's kinda fun, honestly. Feels like Monopoly until you remember it buys real bread and cheese."

Haylee grinned, turning the coin over in her hand. "I don't know… feels like the kind of currency you'd use in a magical vending machine. Insert one loonie for answers from the universe."

They all laughed.

Haylee nodded slowly, her fork halfway to her mouth. "True. We've been lucky so far, but if we're going to be here more than a few days, we should probably be prepared."

David leaned back with a smirk, chewing the last of his toast before chiming in. "Don't worry about it. Everything's on me now per our little cover story, remember? Can't go around making me a liar now, can we?"

Haylee shot him a mock-glare, her lips curling up. "Dad, I didn't expect you to pick up the bill for everything."

He waved her off. "It's your engagement present. Besides, what else am I gonna spend it on? I'm retired. Let me play Mr. Money Bags for a bit."

That earned a laugh from all three of them. Sam raised his coffee mug. "To Mr. Money Bags."

"To baguettes and balanced budgets," Haylee added.

"Okay, okay," David said, laughing. "But we don't need to go overboard. Just the essentials. And maybe the occasional baguette. Or smoked cheese. Or both."

After breakfast, they cleaned up together in a rhythm they'd somehow developed without ever discussing. Sam dried the dishes, Haylee wiped down counters, and David disappeared outside for a bit with Josie padding after him.

They hadn't heard from Riles or Ray yet, but David expected they'd reach out sometime today—assuming things were still on track. He kept that worry to himself.

Back inside, Haylee moved on to cleaning the small shower stall, humming a quiet tune to herself. Sam helped where he could, mostly to keep her distracted. The less she asked about what David was doing outside, the better.

About thirty minutes later, David came back in, dirt smudged on his arms and hands, a few grease marks trailing along his shirt. He tried to slip past unnoticed, but Haylee caught him.

"Dad, what have you been doing?" she asked, eyebrow raised as she spotted the grime.

David glanced down at his hands like he'd forgotten. "Uh—just had to check on something under the hood. Nothing major. Guess I got a little messy," he said with a shrug, squeezing past her toward the bathroom.

Sam caught the exchange and felt a pang in his gut. The guilt sat sharp and low, like something unspoken between them all. He hated lying by omission, but David had insisted. It was just a hose. Just a small fix. No need to worry Haylee about every tiny thing.

Still, watching her go back to wiping down the RV, unaware of the truth, made him swallow harder than he liked.

Outside, the breeze carried the soft smell of pine and firewood. Inside, the quiet buzz of their tiny domestic scene tried to settle back in.

Missing Gear and a Hail Mary

Ray took over driving near Rutland, Vermont. The road curved northward in long quiet stretches, and for the first time in a while, the Jeep felt like it had a rhythm again. Riles reclined his seat and stared out the window, mentally rehearsing the story one more time: a property dispute, an ex-wife, a Montreal address, fishing gear at the cabin. It all sounded reasonable. Not airtight, but reasonable.

They planned to switch again at Swanton, just before the border. That way Riles would be driving and could take the lead on the story, should questions come up. It was a subtle detail, but one they hoped would help their cover feel more believable. By 2:45 p.m., they pulled into the Jolly Shell Wagon Wheel—a truck stop that looked like it hadn't changed since the '80s. Perfect.

While Riles filled the tank and checked the oil, Ray headed inside to splash some water on his face and grab snacks. Thirty minutes later, they were both refreshed and back on the road.

Traffic thickened as they neared the border. By the time they hit the line of cars, it was a full stop.

"Saturday," Riles muttered. "Of course."

The stretch ahead was clogged with RVs, commercial trucks, family vans, and vacationers with kayaks strapped to the roof. Weekend warriors, retirees, and tired truckers all funneling through one set of lanes. It would be a while. Riles shut off the Jeep to keep it from overheating, and they rolled down the windows to let in the breeze. The air was sticky, but it beat burning gas.

Ray watched the clock, then the cars, then the clock again.

"I've never seen this many people in one place for so long, and *everyone's* sitting still," he said, shaking his head.

"Welcome to border crossing during peak season," Riles replied, arms folded.

An hour and forty-five minutes crawled by. Inch by inch, they advanced, barely. When they finally approached the booth, they spotted a uniformed agent walking toward the small building, exchanging places with the officer inside.

"Shift change," Riles whispered.

The female agent stepped up to the window with a neutral smile. "Good afternoon, gentlemen. What brings you to Canada today?" she asked, reaching for their documents.

Riles handed over the passports and answered smoothly. "We're headed to Montreal. My ex-wife and I have property to settle up there, and Mr. Harper's tagging along so we can also do some fishing out west."

She looked over the paperwork, then tilted her head to peer into the back seat of the Jeep.

"Sir, I don't see any fishing supplies in your vehicle."

Ray stiffened slightly. Riles blinked once.

"Ah, yes, ma'am. My gear's already up at the place in Montreal. Figured there was no point hauling it across the country and back again."

A pause.

Then the agent nodded, handed back the passports, and waved them through. As they cleared the last checkpoint and reentered motion, both men exhaled deeply.

"Whew," Ray muttered. "I thought we were cooked for sure just then."

"Yeah," Riles said, adjusting the rearview mirror. "That one almost got us. Forgot the damn rods."

"Missing gear, saved by a Hail Mary," Ray chuckled, stretching his legs out.

Riles kept his eyes forward. "Let's not push our luck. Montreal by sundown, yeah?"

"Let's roll."

Winged Reminders

The dishes were clean. The breeze had softened. Bertha's lot exhaled a kind of hush—like the world was pausing to let something unspoken settle.

Haylee stepped outside with her journal tucked beneath one arm, a pen looped behind her ear. Josie padded beside her, ears perked, nose twitching at invisible scents in the air. The path behind their campsite curved toward a narrow stream, lined with low brush and dandelions that had already gone to seed.

They followed it in companionable silence, the only sounds the occasional birdcall and the soft crunch of gravel under Haylee's boots. She found a flat patch of grass near the water and settled down, legs crossed, notebook resting on her lap. Josie circled once before curling beside her.

Haylee didn't open the journal right away.

Instead, she just... listened.

The water whispered. A crow called out in the distance. Somewhere behind her, wind stirred the leaves like secrets being traded between branches.

Then it came—soft as a sigh.

A yellow and black butterfly floated into view.

Haylee's breath caught, just for a moment. Not out of surprise—she'd seen it twice already this week—but out of recognition. This time, it didn't just flutter past. It hovered directly in front of her, almost unnaturally still, as if the air held it in place. The wings moved in a slow, deliberate rhythm. One, two... pause. One, two... pause.

It circled once, dipping low to the stream, then rose—drifting toward the treetops and vanishing in the sun.

A quiet tingle danced along her skin.

She added a tiny sketch of the butterfly near the margin, its wings slightly askew like it was mid-flight. Then she paused, the pen hovering over the page.

Something was coming. She didn't know what shape it would take—but the world felt thinner this morning. As if the veil between moments—between logic and intuition, seen and unseen—was barely there at all.

Haylee closed the journal slowly and stood. "C'mon, Jo," she said softly. "Let's go home."

Josie wagged her tail and rose, sticking close as they made their way back to Bertha.

The trees whispered behind them, as if echoing the butterfly's silent message: You're not lost. You're close. Keep going.

When We're Not Looking

The golden haze of late afternoon melted into soft evening light as the campground quieted around them. Sam clipped Josie's leash gently to her collar, and Haylee slipped on her hoodie, her coffee now long gone and her heart full of the kind of peace she hadn't known in months.

"Wanna walk with us?" Sam asked with a tilt of his head.

Haylee nodded. "Yeah. Let's stretch out some of that French toast."

They strolled the gravel path that looped behind the campground, Josie trotting ahead with her nose to the ground, tail swishing like a metronome of curiosity. The trees whispered overhead, filtering soft beams of amber light through the canopy. Birds rustled but didn't flee, as if even they respected the quiet spell cast on the land.

"Feels like the world hit pause for a minute," Sam said, brushing his hand against hers as they walked.

Haylee smiled, lacing her fingers through his. "It does. I'm trying not to question it."

He glanced over. "Isn't that what you've been learning? To stop pushing so hard?"

Haylee exhaled, her gaze catching on the subtle dance of a monarch butterfly floating ahead of them. "Yeah. That whole law of detachment thing... it used to feel impossible. But lately?"

She didn't finish the sentence, but she didn't have to.

"It's like when we stopped trying to control everything, things just... worked," Sam added. "Not always how we expected. But maybe better."

Josie paused at a fork in the trail and looked back, waiting for them.

188

"I didn't think I'd find this," Haylee said softly. "You. Us. This life."

He squeezed her hand. "You didn't find it. You created it."

They walked in silence for a while longer, passing a quiet stream where dandelions and wild asters grew in patches like forgotten blessings. The butterfly returned, flitting near Haylee's shoulder before vanishing into the dusk.

She turned her head slightly, eyes glimmering. "Maybe that's the universe's way of saying we're on the right path."

Sam nodded.

Back at the campsite, David sat in a faded camp chair by the firepit, a tin bowl of trail mix in his lap. His phone had no new messages. He thumbed Ray's contact again and hit send—straight to voicemail. He remembered they'd powered down the burner after the last check-in, but he'd hoped maybe they'd turned it back on. He sighed and leaned back, letting the sounds of the campground wash over him —kids riding bikes, someone playing soft guitar two lots down, a nearby fire crackling to life.

The RV door creaked open behind him. Bella stretched and leapt down with deliberate feline grace, then wandered over to a second camping chair. With no ceremony, she climbed in, turned once, and curled into a loaf-like shape.

David smirked and tipped his trail mix bowl toward her. "Didn't think so," he muttered.

Together, they sat—man and cat, both watchful in their own way—until the phone finally buzzed.

As the sky deepened into lavender, Haylee and Sam returned from their walk, Josie trotting faithfully behind them with a satisfied tail wag. The campground was quiet now, a gentle hush settling over the trees like a promise of rest.

David was waiting near the steps of Bertha, hands tucked in his jacket pockets, his expression calm but unreadable.

"They made it," he said, easing into the booth with a quiet smile. "Everything's on track for tomorrow."

Haylee nodded, exhaling as if she'd been holding something in. No questions. Just trust.

Sam gave her hand a gentle squeeze.

The trio slipped inside. Bella had already returned to the sink, curled in her odd little crescent of comfort. Outside, the firepit hissed in its last embers.

Tomorrow could bring whatever it wanted.

Tonight, they rested.

A Side of Poutine, S'il vous plaît

Ray pulled off the highway and into the same truck stop at Saint-Jean-sur-Richelieu that the Bertha crew had stopped at a few days earlier. The sky was just beginning to tint toward dusk, casting a coppery glow over the lot. Riles reached into the glovebox and grabbed the burner phone, dialed quickly, and waited.

David picked up on the second ring.
"Yeah?"

"We're at the truck stop just inside the border," Riles said, adjusting the volume and glancing at Ray. "We should hit my old place in Montreal in about 45 minutes, give or take, depending on traffic. I'll text you when we get there. My ex is gone, so it should be secure."

David let out a low breath. "Okay. Everyone's across the border—mission one accomplished. We made it to the campground. Tomorrow, swing by and pick us up for the next mission."

"Will do." Riles hung up.

They topped off the gas tank before hitting the road again, not wanting to leave anything to chance. The ride to Montreal was a quiet one—low traffic and steady roads. The city's skyline slowly came into view, welcoming them with its layered mix of old stone buildings and modern towers.

At the apartment, they unpacked quickly. Riles opened a few windows to air the place out. It wasn't bad, but it still carried that faint scent of dust and memories. Ray flopped onto the couch and let out a long groan.

"Food?" Riles asked.

"Hell yes."

They wandered the stalls at Time Out Market until the neon glow of Chez Simon Cantine Urbaine caught Riles' eye. He approached the counter confidently, glancing at the overhead menu.

"Deux Big Time Burgers, un avec une grosse portion de poutine, s'il vous plaît," he said with ease. "À emporter."

The cashier nodded and handed over the ticket.

Ray blinked. "Okay, show-off."

"You want food or not?" Riles smirked.

A few minutes later, they found a spot near the back with a view of the market's buzz and bustle. Ray looked at his plate and froze. His burger was impressive—but it was the chaotic mountain of fries, cheese curds, and rich brown gravy beside it that stole the spotlight.

"What is this heavenly mess?" he asked, fork already in hand.

"Poutine," Riles replied, biting into his burger. "That's poutine. Fries, cheese curds, gravy—looks like chaos, tastes like gold."

Ray didn't wait. One bite, and his eyes rolled back in bliss.

"Oh, this is dangerous," he mumbled through a mouthful. "Where has this been all my life?"

"Careful," Riles warned. "Next thing you know, you'll be buying flannel and cheering for the Canadiens."

After eating, Ray pulled a wad of American bills from his wallet and paid. The cashier handed back a mix of Canadian coins and a ten-dollar bill.

Ray stared down at the change like it was puzzle pieces from a different game.

"Uh, Riles? Why is there a bird on this coin? And this one's got... is that a polar bear?"

Riles grinned. "That's a loonie. One dollar. And the polar bear's a toonie—worth two."

Ray held up the coins like they might chirp. "I just tipped with wildlife tokens."

"Better than Monopoly money," Riles said with a shrug. "Welcome to Quebec."

Ray dropped them in his pocket, shaking his head. "Man, I'm gonna wake up bilingual with a moose in my bed."

Riles stood and clapped him on the shoulder. "Then we'll know you've fully assimilated."

"Slow down, man. It's not going anywhere," Riles laughed, watching Ray absolutely demolish the plate.

Ray didn't care. He was in carb-loaded heaven, and for a moment, the tension of border crossings, burner phones, and black SUVs melted away.

Chapter Twenty-Seven:
Sunrise Over Montreal

The sun filtered softly through the wide bay windows of the old apartment, painting long golden stripes across the hardwood floor. It was barely 5:45 a.m., but the light had that unmistakable hush of a Sunday morning—a quiet promise that the day would unfold gently, if only for a little while.

Ray stirred, blinking at the unfamiliar ceiling. It took a moment to remember where he was. The spare room was small but warm, full of soft textures and quiet corners. He'd kicked the blanket off during the night, too warm from sleep and a full belly. The meal from Chez Simon still lingered in his memory like a good dream.

In the kitchen, Riles moved slowly, measuring out coarse coffee grounds with a kind of reverence. The kettle whistled low, and soon the rich aroma of French press filled the space like a grounding spell.

Ray shuffled out a few minutes later, barefoot and rumpled. "Something smells illegal," he mumbled, stretching his arms overhead.

"Mornin'," Riles said, offering him a steaming mug. "French press. Things are more sophisticated up here."

Ray took a sip, eyebrows lifting in surprise. "Mmm. This isn't the usual sludge I drink."

Riles smirked. "It's Quebec, man. We're not savages."

Ray settled into one of the mismatched kitchen chairs, letting the mug warm his hands. "Dude, you're like an onion. So many layers."

"I'll take that as a compliment," Riles chuckled, taking his own mug to the couch
.

The apartment was still quiet, save for the occasional creak of the old building adjusting to the morning. Outside, the city was just waking up—early joggers, the distant clang of a recycling truck, the whisper of a church bell a few blocks away.

By 7:30 a.m., Riles' phone buzzed on the counter. He checked it briefly, then gave a small nod.

"David," he said. "They're up at the campground and sent directions. Told us to come whenever we're ready."

Ray glanced at the window, sunlight now stronger against the glass. "We gonna head out soon?"

Riles typed a reply. "Told him we'd be there around one. I want to check out a couple of things first."

David's reply came back in the form of a simple thumbs-up emoji.

Ray leaned back, sipping his coffee slowly. "I gotta say, this part of the mission doesn't suck."

Riles gave a quiet laugh. "Enjoy it while it lasts."

The morning stretched on in calm silence, the kind that only comes when the worst feels like it might actually be behind you. But neither of them said that aloud.

Campground Chronicles

The soft hum of morning in the Quebec campground was broken by... something not soft.

It was 7:15 a.m. when a blast of play-by-play sports commentary rattled down the gravel lanes like a rogue PA system at a pep rally. David blinked and lowered his mug of coffee. Somewhere nearby, a television was way too awake.

He stepped out of Bertha and followed the noise to its source: a fifth-wheel camper a few sites down, clearly a late-night arrival. The kind of arrival that leaves behind a lawn chair tipped over, a cooler forgotten under the hitch, and an ambitious number of extension cords.

From an open side bay, a large flat-screen TV was mounted and turned up to full volume, replaying a sports highlight reel—baseball, maybe football, hard to tell over the echo. A man in a well-worn hoodie and cargo shorts stood beside the rig, sipping coffee like it was his front porch and the rest of the campground was just lucky to be part of his Saturday morning routine.

David raised a hand in greeting, polite but firm. "Morning, neighbor."

The man turned and grinned. "Hey! Didn't think we'd see many folks from back home up here."

David returned the smile, still easy. "Well, it's a big country. We get around."

Back inside Bertha, Sam cracked the door and peeked out, drawn by the noise. "What's going on?"

"New arrivals," David said with a glance back. "And they brought surround sound."

Just then, Haylee returned from walking Josie, the dog already grumbling at the new chaos. Haylee stopped short, saw the TV setup, the cluttered site, and her dad standing calmly in the middle of it all.

She raised her hands in an exaggerated *what the hell?* motion.

197

David responded with a subtle wave that said I'm on it.

She sighed and headed back inside with Josie.

"Can you believe this?" she said as the door shut behind her. "We were just starting to enjoy the quiet."

"Some people just travel loud," Sam said, handing her a cup of coffee. "Not everyone got the memo on campground etiquette."

"I don't care where you're from, turning up a TV at sunrise should be illegal," she muttered.

Sam smirked. "Maybe they think they're improving the ambiance."

Haylee laughed lightly. "Yeah. Nothing says peaceful pine forest like shouting sports commentators and the faint scent of cold hot dogs."

They sipped their coffee while Josie flopped dramatically onto the rug, ears flat. Outside, David's voice floated in again, still friendly. "Hey, any chance you could turn it down a notch? Sound carries pretty far out here in the mornings."

"Ah, sorry about that," the man replied with a sheepish smile. "Didn't realize the volume was so high."

"Appreciate it," David said, nodding once.

The TV quieted. A few birds dared to chirp again.

Haylee glanced at Sam. "Crisis averted?"

"For now."

She lifted her mug. "To quiet mornings that actually stay quiet."

Sam clinked his cup to hers. "Cheers to that."

By 7:30 a.m., the campground was fully awake—whether people liked it or not.

David stepped back into Bertha, brushing some pine needles off his socks. "Well, I said good morning to the neighbors. Not sure it made a difference, but at least we tried."

Haylee rolled her eyes and took a sip of her now lukewarm coffee. "I guess it wouldn't be a true campground experience without at least one loud family next door."

Sam peeked through the blinds at the other RV, now quieting down ever so slightly. "Still. I vote we head out for a walk later and shake it off."

David nodded. "Yeah, but first I'm gonna let Riles know we're up." He pulled out his phone and typed quickly:

"We're up and at the campground. No rush. Come when you're ready. Directions are pinned."

He hit send and got a reply a few minutes later:

"We'll be there around 1:00 p.m. Got a couple things to check out first."

David gave a short nod to no one in particular and tucked the phone away. He grabbed a banana from the counter and settled outside by the fire pit to enjoy a few rare minutes of quiet—Josie laying at his feet, Bella sunning herself on the nearby picnic table like she owned the place.

Everything was in motion. The reunion was near.

Where Shadows Leave Traces

The sun had barely climbed above the Montreal skyline when Riles tucked a folded photo into the inside pocket of his jacket. "Come on," he said to Ray, already reaching for the keys. "I've got one more thing to check out before we meet the others."

Ray didn't ask questions—he'd learned by now that when Riles moved with that quiet conviction, it was best to follow. They drove through narrow streets, past stone facades and shaded cafés, until they reached a side alley where the pavement buckled and graffiti clung to the brick like stories trying to escape.

"This is the place?" Ray asked, eyeing the building with its dark windows and barely visible sign above the door.

"Doesn't show up on Yelp," Riles muttered, stepping inside.

The bell above the narrow door chimed once as Riles pushed it open. The building didn't look like much from the outside—just another brick-walled storefront tucked between a closed bakery and a boarded-up laundromat. The kind of place you only found if someone told you where to look. Or if you were desperate enough to stumble into it.

Ray followed him in and blinked as his eyes adjusted. The interior looked like an old speakeasy—dim lighting, deep wood, red-leather booths, and a long bar that hadn't seen a crowd in years. The bottles behind it were dusty, but someone had bothered to keep the counter clean. Soft jazz played from a record player behind the bar, warbling faintly.

It smelled like old wood, pipe tobacco, and secrets.

A man appeared from a side door that looked like it led to a coat closet. Tall, lean, and sharp-eyed, he looked at Riles with the kind of recognition you didn't get from being a tourist.

«T'es revenu. Je me demandais quand tu repopperais.»
(You came back. I was wondering when you'd pop in again.)

«J'avais besoin de tes oreilles. Et peut-être de tes yeux.»
(I needed your ears. And maybe your eyes.)

They shook hands, an old code passing between them. Ray watched quietly, standing a little behind Riles. He could tell this wasn't a place where strangers were usually welcome—but Riles had vouched for him by bringing him in at all. The man looked to Ray for a beat and nodded politely, not expecting him to speak.

Riles pulled a folded photo from his wallet and laid it on the bar. "His name is Elliot. That's all I've got for certain. The photo's a few years old. He's… connected to a girl I know. Deeply connected. I think he's hiding. Or being hidden."

The man picked up the photo, studied it under the low pendant light, and let out a thoughtful hum. Then he shifted into French again, clearly feeling more at home there.

«C'est pas un visage que j'vois souvent, mais y'a un truc là… J'vais fouiller. Il laisse une impression, ce gars. Même si c'est pour disparaître.»
(It's not a face I see often, but there's something there… I'll dig around. He leaves an impression, this guy. Even if it's to vanish.)

Ray glanced between them, trying to piece things together from their expressions. The man's tone wasn't dismissive. He looked intrigued. Like a detective smelling smoke.

«Il a une façon de se glisser entre les craques, hein?»
(He has a way of slipping through the cracks, huh?)

«Ouais. Trop bien pour être normal.»
(Yeah. Too well, for it to be normal.)

Ray didn't speak the language, but he didn't need to. He caught the way Riles leaned forward, his shoulders tense, voice low. The way the man tilted his head just slightly, considering the possibilities. The way his eyes flicked back to the photo like it had unsettled something.

He got it.

This wasn't just information gathering. This was a warning shot.

Riles added softly, in English for Ray's sake, "He said if this guy doesn't turn up in his usual channels, then he's wiped his existence clean. And that's not something amateurs can do."

Ray whistled quietly. "So what does that make him?"

The man didn't need a translator for that one. He gave a sharp half-smile and answered in English, his accent thick but clear: "It makes him very interesting." Riles nodded once.

«D'ici demain. Peut-être ce soir.»
(By tomorrow. Maybe tonight.)

They shook hands again. This time with weight behind it.

As they stepped out into the sunlight, Ray exhaled hard. "That place felt like a goddamn portal."

"It kind of is," Riles said. "Only shows up when you're looking for something real."

Ray glanced over his shoulder once more. The door was closed now. The speakeasy vibe gone. Just a quiet brick building on a side street in Montreal. You'd never know what lived inside unless you'd been invited in.

"Well?" Ray finally asked.

"He'll look into it," Riles said, eyes straight ahead. "If anyone can find a man who doesn't want to be found, it's Émile."

"And if he can't?"

Riles hesitated. "Then Elliot doesn't just know how to disappear. He knows how to erase."

They pulled away from the curb in silence, the city rolling out ahead of them like a map half-drawn—roads they'd follow, and others they hadn't even seen yet.

Chapter Twenty-Eight:
Static on a Sunday

"Well," Sam said, nudging Bella off his lap to pour his own coffee, "we might get our peace back soon. David just texted Riles the campground location and said we're up."

"Good," she said. "I miss the Jeep duo's chaos. At least theirs comes with better storytelling and less commentary."

As if on cue, Dan—the campground host—appeared outside their window in his neon green polo and khaki shorts. Clipboard in hand, he was shaking his head at the noise two lots down.

"Someone made the call," Sam said.

"Finally," Haylee muttered, taking a sip. "Let the peace be restored."

Dan ambled down toward the fifth wheel, waving politely before leaning in to talk to the bacon-spatula guy. The conversation was brief but effective. By the time Haylee looked back out the window, the TV volume had been cut in half and the speaker unplugged entirely.

"That man's got campground diplomacy down to a science," Sam said.

Haylee raised her mug. "To Dan. Keeper of the quiet. Bringer of boundaries."

They toasted their mugs with a clink and watched as Josie curled back up on the rug, sensing the return of stillness.

Outside, the hum of Sunday settled in once more—soft footsteps on gravel, birds returning to the trees, the distant chime of wind through leaves. They didn't know what the day ahead would bring, but for the moment, the static had quieted.

A gentle breeze stirred the curtains by the window. Sam set his coffee aside and wandered over to the sink, rinsing a few plates from breakfast. Haylee watched him for a moment—just quiet, thoughtful movement—and smiled to herself.

"You ever think," she said softly, "that peace feels weirder than chaos?"

He glanced over his shoulder, playful. "You mean like... suspicious?"

"Exactly. Like something's about to happen the second you relax."

Sam wiped his hands on a towel and came back to the table, where Bella had reclaimed his seat. He scooted her gently, and she gave a small annoyed meow before curling up beside Haylee instead.

"I used to feel that all the time," he admitted. "But lately? I'm learning to lean into the quiet. Even if it doesn't last, I want to enjoy it while it's here."

Haylee nodded, looking down at her chipped coffee mug. "Same."

They both looked toward the window again, almost on instinct, as if the stillness itself might be interrupted at any second.

And yet it wasn't.

Instead, the morning stretched out gently. David returned from a walk with Josie and handed over a small brown paper bag with two muffins he'd grabbed from the camp store. Haylee lit a candle and cracked the window open wider to let in the smell of damp pine and earth. Sam pulled out one of the folding chairs to sit outside in the shade while Haylee doodled a map of their route so far in her journal, marking odd detours and silly roadside attractions.

It was the kind of lull that didn't ask for anything.

The kind you only noticed once you realized how long it had been since you had one.

Haylee jotted a few notes in her journal, mostly random thoughts about the butterflies yesterday, a dream she'd had the night before that was already slipping away, and how something about Bertha felt a little different that morning.

Not in a bad way—just… lighter. Like the RV herself knew they were getting closer to something.

Just before one, a soft ping vibrated from David's phone. He read the screen, smiled to himself, and stood.

"Jeep crew's five minutes out," he said, pocketing his phone. "Time to put on the coffee and pretend we didn't miss them."

Sam looked up from his coffee. "Too late. Haylee already said it."

Haylee laughed. "I admitted nothing. But I might've saved them the last muffin."

Outside, a lone dragonfly zipped past the open window, catching a ray of sunlight as it disappeared down the path.

Bertha was quiet again. But not the kind of quiet that felt empty.

It was the kind that hummed with anticipation.

Under the Surface

The familiar dust that trailed behind the Jeep was a dead giveaway. Everyone was outside as they arrived, even Bella, who had stretched out on the picnic table in a tight curl, her tail flicking lazily in the shade. Josie lay between David and Sam, ears perked at the approaching rumble.

When the dust settled and the engine cut, two men who looked like they'd wrestled with every mile since Wyoming stepped out of the Jeep Wrangler. Ray gave a dramatic stretch and a yawn, while Riles squinted at the campground like it might personally offend him.

"Nice place," Ray said first, hands on hips. "Even comes with your own entertainment, I see." He motioned toward the oversized fifth wheel a few lots down.

Sam, David, and Haylee looked at each other—and then erupted into laughter. The kind of laugh that bubbles up out of a shared experience you don't even have to explain. It rolled through them like a wave. Riles just raised one eyebrow and waited.

"Care to share with the group?" he asked finally.

"Just had a bit of an incident with our new neighbors there this morning is all," David said, brushing it off with a wave.

"Oh?" Riles glanced sideways at the trailer.

"They're harmless," Haylee added quickly, "Just... noisy first thing in the morning."

Ray smirked, but Riles stayed quiet a beat longer, still reading the trio's expressions like there might be more. Eventually, he let it drop. "So," he said, "how was your trip across this big wide country of ours and into the big wide North?"

The trio looked at each other again—but this time it was different.

"Big news," David said, his voice shifting tone. "These two took the literal meaning of our story to heart and got engaged."

Ray's face lit up. "Ah, that's great!"

"Congrats," Riles added, his tone gruff but genuine.

Sam slid his hand into Haylee's, fingers curling with comfort and certainty. "However," David added, "we had a bit of a situation crossing the border."

Riles' brow arched again. "What kind of situation?"

"The kind that had our rig torn apart by border agents and one with a drug-sniffing K-9," Sam replied, the irritation still in his voice.

"What do you mean? What happened exactly?" Riles asked, his face sharpening with concern.

The trio filled them in—how they'd been pulled into secondary inspection, how the RV had been searched from top to bottom, and how someone had called in an anonymous tip about a vehicle matching Bertha's description smuggling drugs across the U.S.–Canada border.

Haylee's voice faltered at the end. "I knew it was personal. It had Elliot's fingerprints all over it."

"What the fuck?" Ray barked, pacing a small circle. "That's a serious setup. That's not just intimidation—that's framing."

"Yeah," David said grimly. "And what we can't figure out is how they even knew we were crossing into Canada."

"We checked at every stop," Sam added. "Every time. We looked for trackers, bugs, cameras—nothing."

Riles stood quiet, arms folded, lips pressed in a line. His eyes narrowed as his thoughts churned behind them.

"There's gotta be something you missed," he said finally, voice low and sure. Ray disappeared back into the Jeep without a word. A few moments later, he returned holding a small black scanner.

"Bought this after the whole Casper thing," he muttered, flicking it on. "Never trust a clean sweep with dirty hands."

He walked slowly around Bertha, the device humming quietly until it neared the rear bumper. Then—beep beep beep.

"There's something here," Ray called out, crouching low. The others gathered around him.

"We checked under everything," Sam said, frustration mounting. "Literally everything."

Ray's eyes narrowed. He ran a hand along the edge of the bumper, then paused. "Here."

There were faint scratch marks around a small plastic cap—barely visible. Ray took out his knife and popped it loose with a satisfying click. Inside was a tiny black disc, no larger than a bottle cap.

"Son of a bitch," Sam whispered, tightening his grip on Haylee's hand.

Haylee's stomach dropped. It was like all the breath she'd taken that morning had been a lie. "How long has that been there?"

"Hard to say," Ray answered, holding the device up to the light. "But my guess? Long enough."

Riles took the tracker from him and turned it over in his hand. "We need to get this analyzed. See if it's transmitting live or just recording location data."

209

Josie let out a soft growl from her spot under the picnic table.

Haylee crouched down and put a calming hand on her back. "Yeah, girl. I feel it too."

Riles looked up at David. "You said you cleared the RV. Did you ever take off the bumper?"

David blinked. "No. Didn't seem necessary."

Ray gave a low whistle. "That's how they got you. These things are small, and this one's smart. Hidden inside the cap means less likelihood of getting snagged or noticed. Someone knew what they were doing."

Haylee looked toward Bertha like she didn't know her anymore. "I hate that they violated her like that."

"She's clean now," Sam said, pulling her close. "They don't win."

Riles pocketed the tracker carefully. "No, but they're trying harder. Which means we're getting closer to something they really don't want us to find."

The group stood in silence, the hum of insects and the rustle of leaves filling the stillness. In the distance, a car door slammed. The world kept moving.

But inside their circle, the stakes had just been raised.

Just for Today

With the group finally back together, something in Haylee's chest unclenched. The tension that had been twisting inside her since they left the cabin began to soften, like a tightly wound spring easing back into place. The road didn't feel like it was closing in on her anymore. For the first time in days, she felt like she could take a full breath.

After the emotional fallout of the tracker discovery, the group settled around the picnic table with plates of cold sandwiches, kettle chips, and lemonade. Bella circled once on her shaded perch before curling back up in her usual regal loaf. Josie laid with her head on Haylee's foot, finally dozing in the midday quiet.

Riles looked across the table, eyes scanning the group. "Alright, so what's the next step?"

David was the first to respond, but not with a plan. "We regroup. We breathe. We've been running for a week. One day to just exist might do more good than rushing."

Haylee nodded. "I checked. The spiritual shop's open today if we want to ease in, but I don't want us all splitting up right away. Not after everything."

There was a shared look—agreement, maybe even relief.

"We don't know how much time we have before we're running again," Haylee added. "But I think we should just take today. Reset. Let things settle."

Riles, never one to sit still for long, leaned back and crossed his arms. "How about a compromise? I'll take everyone around. Just a short trip—show you the apartment, a couple key spots. Keeps us moving but in a good way."

Ray smirked. "Look at you. Mr. Scenic Detour."

"It's a vibe shift," Riles shot back, eyes twinkling.

They laughed, and just like that, it was settled. A day to breathe, together.

Haylee and Sam secured the pets in Bertha, leaving the fans and soft music on while Bella claimed her sunbeam and Josie flopped across her favorite blanket near the door. Then they all climbed into the Jeep—Riles at the wheel, Ray up front, the rest packed into the backseat with light hearts and open windows.

Their first stop was the campground office. Dan stood behind the desk, sipping from a stainless mug and chatting with a couple checking out. When he looked up and saw the whole group walk in, his eyes crinkled at the corners.

"Salut, ça va?" he said out of habit, the warmth in his voice unmistakable.

Riles stepped forward without missing a beat. "Ah, salut! C'est bien beau de te rencontrer, on va bien merci. Et toi?"

Dan's eyebrows shot up in delighted surprise. "Oho! Un homme qui parle français! J'aime ça!"

They shook hands like old friends who hadn't seen each other in years, and the rest of the group stood back, smiling quietly at the easy flow between them. Riles explained their plans for the day, and Dan shared that he'd been thinking of giving the group a proper tour of Quebec later that week.

"There's a local festival on Thursday," he said, handing Riles a flyer. "Live music, street vendors, the whole deal."

Haylee's eyes lit up. The word festival always gave her a certain peace, a reminder that even in chaos, joy could still be found. "That sounds… perfect."

"Then it's settled," Dan said, clapping Riles on the back. "Meet here around 5:30. You'll love it."

Back in the Jeep, the mood had shifted again—lighter now, buoyed by something simple and hopeful. Riles took the long way out, letting the gravel crunch beneath the tires as they pulled onto the main road, sunlight glinting off the windshield.

No one said much for a while. They didn't need to.

For now, there was no timeline to race, no fear breathing down their necks. Just winding roads, the breeze through open windows, and the gentle knowledge that —for today—they could simply be.

Just for today, they could live.

Four Walls and a Shift

The drive into Montreal took just under an hour, winding past open fields, sleepy roadside towns, and the occasional billboard that reminded them they weren't in the U.S. anymore. Haylee sat in the backseat of the Jeep, her head resting lightly against the window. The quiet hum of the engine, the familiar scent of Sam beside her, and the soft bump of the road lulled her into a rare moment of calm. It wasn't just about reaching the city.

It was about realizing they'd made it—crossed the invisible boundary of possibility. Montreal shimmered ahead like a promise. And for the first time in weeks, Haylee wasn't looking over her shoulder. She looked out the window and saw art murals instead of omens, strangers instead of suspects.

They stopped for fuel just outside the city limits, stretching their legs and grabbing coffee from a little corner café that served espresso with a side of sass. Riles insisted on fueling up the Jeep one last time before parking it in the underground garage below the apartment building. "Walking's easier," he said, "but I'm not about to leave the getaway vehicle behind."

No one argued.

The garage smelled like warm pavement and motor oil, but as they rode the elevator up, a quiet shift took place inside Haylee. The elevator dinged. Her breath caught.

This was really happening.

They stepped into the apartment, and the space unfolded like a sigh of relief. Open, modern, and soaked in afternoon light. Tall windows framed the skyline, casting shadows on polished floors and sleek furniture that looked barely lived in.

"Well," Riles said, unlocking the front door and stepping aside, "here we are."

"Whoa," Haylee whispered, the word slipping out before she could catch it.

Even Sam blinked in surprise. "This is... not what I expected."

Ray walked in like he'd done it a hundred times. "My room's back here," he said casually, disappearing down the hall. Riles chuckled and shook his head.

"He's not wrong," he said. "He claimed that one the minute we arrived. Said he had seniority."

Haylee wandered toward the windows. They looked out over a street lined with boutiques, bakeries, and art galleries. It was the kind of place she'd always seen in indie films and daydreams, not somewhere she thought her feet would ever land.

Sam joined her, slipping his hand into hers. "You okay?"

She nodded, eyes still on the view. "Yeah. Just… wow. This city's alive in a way I didn't expect."

Behind them, David and Riles were taking in the rest of the apartment—three smaller bedrooms branching off a central hallway, a fully stocked kitchen that gleamed like a magazine ad, and a lounge space filled with oversized cushions and local art.

"How does your ex afford all this?" David asked, not trying to pry but still curious.

Riles gave a half-smile. "She's got her hands in half the real estate in Montreal. Properties, investments, a little of everything. This is just one of her places."

"She has fantastic taste," Haylee added from the living room, trailing her fingers along the edge of a bookshelf. "Does she stay here often?"

"When she's not hosting some kind of fundraiser or art party," Riles replied. "This place is more social hub than home. Always someone coming and going. She never did like the quiet."

David lingered behind, his gaze flicking to where Haylee and Sam stood side by side, their fingers still intertwined as they whispered to each other by the windows. He sighed—not out of sadness, but out of realization.

215

They needed room to breathe. To settle. To build something of their own.

David stepped aside with Riles near the hallway.

"Mind if I stick around here for a while?" he asked quietly. "Give them some space? I think it's time."

Riles glanced past him, toward the young couple silhouetted in the light, then clapped a hand on David's shoulder.

"Of course," he said. "We've got the room. And to be honest, Ray and I were getting tired of ordering for two anyway."

David chuckled. "I'll take over dinner duty then."

"It's a deal," Riles said. "Welcome to the Montreal chapter."

Haylee turned just as they rejoined the group, her smile soft, but her eyes sharp. She didn't need to hear the conversation to know something had shifted—something unspoken but understood.

"Ready to explore?" she asked.

"Always," David replied, grabbing his jacket. "But I'm not climbing any more steep staircases today."

Laughter echoed as they headed for the door again, the weight of the past week still in their bones, but lightened now by possibility.

And beneath it all, something deeper settled into place—space for growth, for peace, and for whatever came next.

Small Joys, Big City

The streets of Montreal pulsed with life as twilight settled over the old stone buildings and sleek glass storefronts. Neon signs flickered on as the last of the sunlight caught the corners of wrought-iron balconies and weathered murals. It was the kind of place that carried stories in every brick, every alley, every footstep.

Haylee walked a little slower than the others, letting her senses stretch. The buzz of sidewalk chatter, the perfume of sizzling meats from street vendors, the melodic French lilt of passing conversations—it was all a symphony of somewhere new. Somewhere unexpected.

Riles led them through a short stroll in the touristy part of downtown—cute but polished. Then he smirked, motioned with his head, and said, "C'mon, let's see the real Montréal."

They followed him into a wilder side of the city. The buildings were closer together, their walls kissed with spray-painted stories and wild colors. Even the graffiti felt intentional here—chaotic but honest, like emotional hieroglyphs.

Haylee and Sam broke off to wander through a narrow row of artisan shops. She picked up a handmade necklace carved from driftwood and turned it over in her hands. Sam smiled, nudging her gently with his shoulder. "See anything you like?"

"Everything," she whispered, half to herself. "I didn't expect to feel... this light."

"That's the real magic of a good city," he replied. "It sneaks in when you're not looking."

Ray and David stayed on the food trail, of course. They dipped into bakeries and stalls with plastic tablecloths and barely translated menus, ordering meat pies and skewers, pausing only long enough to laugh and chew. When Haylee spotted David coming out of a boulangerie with a full-sized baguette under his arm, she laughed out loud.

He looked over and grinned. "This thing is an edible sword."

"You're not allowed to joust with carbs," Riles called back.

David just raised the baguette in mock salute. "Challenge accepted."

They meandered through the next street, the five of them moving more like friends than fugitives. It was the first time in days the undercurrent of urgency had dimmed. No one brought up Elliot. No one talked about the Veil or shadows or trackers. For now, it was just this—the smell of grilled onions, the feel of stone beneath their shoes, the cool night promising something good.

Haylee walked beside Sam and took his hand without thinking. "This is what I needed," she said quietly.

"Me too."

They paused in front of a mural painted across the entire side of a building—two hands holding a cracked compass, the cracks filled with stars. Haylee stared for a long moment.

"Lost doesn't always mean wrong," she said softly.

Sam squeezed her hand. "And sometimes it means you're about to find something better."

Around 8 p.m., Ray patted his stomach and looked around dramatically. "Alright, I've been patient long enough. Riles, tell me we're getting poutine again."

"You read my mind," Riles grinned. "There's a spot just a few blocks over. Best one in the city, if you ask me."

"I'll believe it when I see it," David challenged, twirling the baguette like a baton. They ended up at a no-frills local diner with neon lights in the windows and mismatched chairs. Riles ordered for everyone without hesitation—Burgers, extra poutine, and sodas all around. The server brought out the dishes with a wink and a "Bon appétit," and the table fell into the kind of silence only good food could earn.

Haylee and Sam shared a plate, stealing crispy, gravy-soaked fries from opposite sides. Riles watched as everyone enjoyed their meals. David used his baguette to mop up the remnants of his, and Ray finished his entire plate like a man who hadn't eaten in weeks.

"You weren't kidding," David said, wiping his mouth. "That was... spiritual."

Haylee smiled around a forkful. "This might be the best part of the trip so far."

Outside, the city continued without them—horns, music, life. But inside that diner, with bellies full and hearts lighter, everything felt just right.

Afterglow

The group piled into the Jeep with full bellies and a quiet sense of wonder. Something about the night air wrapping around them as they pulled away from the glowing streets of Montreal felt different. Lighter. As if the city had dusted off something old and made room for something new.

No one felt like talking on the ride back. The comfort of silence, shared between people who had made it through chaos and come out the other side, was enough. Riles drove without rush, letting the hum of the road carry them gently back to the campground. Ray leaned against the window, eyes half-lidded. David sat up front, staring at the road, lost in thought.

Haylee curled into Sam's side in the back seat, her hand tucked under his. The glow from streetlights streaked across the windshield, fading to shadows as they left the city behind. Every once in a while, someone sighed—not out of boredom, but the kind that said yeah, this is enough.

When they pulled into the gravel lot near Bertha, the hum of the engine faded and silence settled in again, but this time it felt like closure rather than pause. The kind of silence earned after a good day.

Sam opened the RV door and Josie barreled out gladly to him, tail wagging like a windmill. Bella stretched in a luxurious arc from her perch atop the dash, blinking slowly before hopping down to wind around Haylee's ankles and greet them both.

Haylee crouched to rub Josie's ears, laughing softly as the pup wriggled with joy. "Missed us that much, huh?"

Sam stood nearby, giving Bella a gentle scratch on her head when she brushed past him. For a moment, the little family just soaked in the comfort of being reunited, the chaos of the past few days fading briefly into the background.

From inside Bertha came the faint sounds of a zipper and footsteps shifting. David was up to something, but neither Sam nor Haylee paid it much mind— after everything, it was nice just to stand there together, letting the evening settle around them.

A moment later, Ray broke the quiet with a crooked grin. "Well, this is where we leave you lovebirds," he said. "Try not to miss us too much."

"You'll be back before Josie starts to forget your scent," Haylee teased lightly.

As if on cue, David stepped out from inside Bertha, duffle bag in hand.

"Going somewhere, Dad?" Haylee asked, her brows lifting.

David gave her a sheepish smile. "Yeah… I think I want to try a Canadian bed. Just so I can say I did. You know—get the full experience."

Haylee gave him a long look, one corner of her mouth tugging up. "Right. The 'experience.'"

Sam smirked beside her, folding his arms. "Sure has nothing to do with giving us some space, huh?"

David gave an exaggerated shrug, his smile easy. "You'll never know."

"Well," Haylee said gently, "the couch will be waiting for you when you're ready. Josie might pout for a night or two, though."

At her name, Josie thumped her tail and gave David a look that could only be described as betrayed. He knelt to rub her ears. "It's not forever, girl. Just a couple nights. You hold down the fort."

They all laughed. There were no heavy goodbyes—just quiet nods, subtle thanks in the glances exchanged. Riles and David climbed back into the Jeep while Ray called, "Same time tomorrow?"

"Unless something explodes," Sam answered with a wink.

As the Jeep pulled away, its taillights dimming into the distance, Haylee stood still for a moment, watching it fade into the night.

"This was a great day," she said softly.

"It sure was," Sam replied, wrapping his arms around her from behind.

They stayed like that for a while, just listening. Crickets in the grass, the rustle of wind through pine, the distant hum of a camper door closing somewhere.

Josie waited patiently beside them, leash dangling loosely in Haylee's hand.

"Come on, girl," she said. "Last walk of the night."

They made their way along the gravel path. The campground had settled. Most lights were out. A few flickered dimly from porch bulbs or hanging lanterns, but the stars—tonight, the stars did most of the work. They stretched overhead in a blanket of silver and hush, brighter than Haylee remembered seeing in a long time. Or maybe, she thought, they had always been this bright—she just hadn't noticed them lately.

She reached for Sam's hand again, and he gave it a quiet squeeze.

For now, they were here. Together. And it was enough.

Chapter Twenty-Nine:
Detours After Dark

The ride back to the Montreal apartment was wrapped in a kind of quiet none of them had felt in days. The city lights flickered past in long, sleepy streaks on the highway, and for once, nothing felt urgent. David leaned against the back seat, staring absently out the window, his thoughts drifting toward Haylee and the relief of knowing Sam was there with her. It had been a long time since he'd let himself feel that kind of calm.

Ray sat slouched in the passenger seat, rubbing his belly with exaggerated satisfaction. "Man," he mumbled dreamily, "When's the next time we're grabbing poutine and burgers again. Quebec knows how to feed a man right."

Riles gave a half-smirk but said nothing, eyes fixed on the dark road ahead. His hands gripped the wheel loosely, but there was a way he drove like the Jeep already knew the path home, his mind wandering miles ahead of them.

The sudden buzz of his phone shattered the quiet. It lit up on the console, vibrating insistently. Riles snatched it up, eyes narrowing at the caller ID before pressing it to his ear.

"Ben là, quoi? Là, là? Pourquoi? Bon, OK, j'dis plus rien. On s'en vient, deux heures max." The words were sharp, quick, his tone clipped with urgency before he hung up without waiting for a reply.

The abruptness jolted Ray from his poutine daydream, making him blink and sit up. "Late night booty call, Riles?" he said, voice thick with sleep but tinged with amusement.

"No," Riles muttered, tossing the phone into the cupholder and tightening his grip on the wheel. "We have to go see Émile."

Ray squinted at him. "What? Now? It's nearly midnight."

Riles glanced at him, jaw tight, no hint of humor in his eyes. "Émile's not the kind of man you keep waiting. Or question when he calls."

The Jeep fell silent again, tension settling over the trio like a heavy blanket as the night stretched long ahead of them.

As the Jeep hummed along the quiet road, tires ate up the dark miles between them and Montreal. The sudden urgency from Riles' phone call had wiped away whatever easy silence they'd found earlier. David sat forward now, forearms resting on his knees, eyes flicking between Riles and the road as the minutes stretched on.

Finally, he broke the quiet. His voice was calm but edged with curiosity. "Alright, I have to ask… who is this Émile? And why are we meeting him in the middle of the night?"

Riles' jaw flexed. He kept his eyes on the road, weighing whether to answer or not. Part of him wanted to tell David nothing—not until he had the full story in hand. No sense stirring up more questions when they were already knee-deep in them.

"Actually…" Riles began slowly, "I was gonna drop you two off at the apartment and see Émile alone."

"The fuck you are," Ray said, turning sharply in his seat. There was no bite to his tone, just raw concern under the words. "Not happening, man."

David frowned, glancing between the two of them. "We've come too far to start splitting up now," he said firmly. "If this guy's important enough to drag us out at midnight, we're going with you."

Riles exhaled hard through his nose, one hand gripping the wheel tighter as he thought it over. He didn't like it. He didn't like dragging them into this, but he also knew Ray was stubborn as hell and David wasn't the type to sit back while answers were dangling just out of reach.

"Fine," he said finally, voice low and rough. "But you do exactly what I say. No hero crap, no stupid questions."

"You might not speak a lick of Quebecois, but trust me—Émile and his boys know English just fine. I don't want any snide remarks or sideways comments coming out of your mouths. Understood?"

Ray held his hands up in mock surrender. "Scout's honor."

David gave a single nod, serious. "Understood."

Riles glanced at them both briefly, making sure the point landed, before fixing his eyes on the road again. "Good," he muttered. "Let's keep it that way."

The Jeep rolled on through the dark, the city lights growing closer, but the weight of the meeting ahead settled over all three men like a heavy fog.

The Weight of Urgency

The drive back to the apartment was a quiet one, headlights cutting through Montreal's dark, damp streets. The city was still awake in pockets, late-night bars and corner diners glowing like islands in the night, but their little trio barely noticed. The earlier calm from their drive out had been replaced with something heavier, something that made every passing mile feel tighter in Riles' chest.

He pulled into the dim garage below the apartment building, parking close to the stairwell. "Two minutes," he muttered, grabbing his keys. "Gotta pick up that envelope from my guy before we head to Émile."

David and Ray stayed behind, the Jeep still humming softly. David shifted in his seat, glancing toward the stairwell as if expecting trouble to come spilling down it. The quiet between them felt like it was holding its breath.

Finally, David leaned toward Ray, his voice low, like he was sharing a secret neither of them wanted Riles to overhear. "You've got a look at this Émile guy, right? What's he like?"

Ray sighed, drumming his fingers on his thigh. "Your typical low-life type," he admitted. "But smart. Tactful. The kind of guy who's survived this long 'cause he knows where the lines are." He paused, glancing toward the stairwell. "Riles went to him earlier today, see if he could dig up info on Elliot we couldn't get anywhere else."

David's brow furrowed, suspicion flickering in his eyes. "You trust him?"

Ray hesitated, his voice dropping even lower. "No. But Riles does. And I trust Riles." He gave a small shrug, but it didn't carry much ease. "That's gotta count for something."

Their conversation died off as footsteps echoed in the stairwell. Riles emerged, envelope in hand, moving fast toward the Jeep. He didn't say a word as he slid back behind the wheel, only the hard line of his jaw betraying what was turning over in his head.

"Alright," he said, voice clipped, "let's not keep Émile waiting."

David and Ray exchanged a quick look but didn't push. The air in the Jeep shifted as Riles pulled out of the garage and back onto the main road. Streetlights streaked over the windshield, flashing across his face, catching the tension carved there.

The closer they got to the bar where Émile waited, the more that tension coiled. Riles could feel it twisting in his gut, that familiar pull of bad news lurking just around the corner. What could be so urgent it couldn't wait until tomorrow? What had Émile found that made him call like this?

Thoughts spiraled fast and sharp, each one worse than the last. The envelope in his jacket pocket suddenly felt like it weighed a hundred pounds. Whatever was in it, whatever Émile had uncovered, it wasn't going to make this mess with Elliot easier. If anything, it was about to blow it wide open.

And there was something else gnawing at him, worse than the weight of the unknown: Émile had sounded... afraid. Riles had known the man a long time, long enough to know fear didn't come easy to him. If Elliot's name could put that edge in Émile's voice, then this wasn't just another job or another shady ghost in the dark.

This was a problem big enough to rattle even the ones who weren't supposed to rattle.

Riles gripped the wheel tighter, the bar's neon sign finally glowing in the distance like a bad omen waiting to be read.

Midnight Doors

The bar Émile called his second home sat wedged between a pawn shop and a shuttered laundromat, its neon sign flickering like a heartbeat against the dark Montreal night. Inside, the air was thick with cigarette smoke and the faint smell of spilled beer that never quite washed out of the old wood floors. A single overhead bulb lit the back corner where Émile always claimed his table, half in shadow, half in smoke.

As they stepped in, Émile spotted Riles first, giving a slow nod and motioning him over with two fingers curled like a hook. His voice cut across the low hum of the bar as they approached.

"Tabarnak, Riles, t'étais dû pour arriver." (Damn, Riles, it's about time.) His tone was sharp but not unfriendly, like a man who had better things to do than wait, yet waited anyway.

Riles grinned faintly, sliding into the seat across from him. "Traffic," he muttered, all excuse and no apology.

Émile's gaze shifted to the two men standing just behind Riles, sizing them up like a poker hand he wasn't sure he wanted to play.

"Pis eux autres?" (And these two?) He jabbed a finger toward David, then Ray. "C'est qui le nouveau? New faces make me nervous." His English wove in and out of the French, rough around the edges.

Before David could answer, Riles leaned back, voice calm but carrying weight. "They're good. The tall one's Ray, he was with me here earlier. The other..." Riles glanced toward David, his tone softening just a fraction, "...he's Haylee's dad."

Émile's eyes flickered, understanding passing over his face. He leaned back, exhaling smoke in a lazy curl toward the ceiling.

"Ahhh… la fille," he said, his accent thick, "la petite who's in deep without knowing it." He muttered something fast in Quebecois under his breath, too low for Ray or David to catch, and Riles' jaw tightened.

Ray looked between them, eyebrows up. "We catching any of that or are we just standing here for decoration?"

Riles waved him off. "He's just making sure you two aren't trouble. Sit down, listen."

Once the three men settled around the table, Émile leaned forward, his elbows pressing into the scarred wood. The air between them felt suddenly thinner, like his words might choke on their way out.

"I dig on this Elliot, hein? Man like that, il marche dans deux mondes…" (he walks in two worlds). He glanced at Riles for the right phrase, but none came, so he pressed on. "…One foot here, one foot… ailleurs. Otherwhere." His fingers spread apart like doorways opening. "Physical, spirituel… planes you don't mess with unless you've got a death wish."

David's face tightened, but he didn't speak, letting the man talk.

"I never see a man like that," Émile went on, voice low, gravely serious. "Not alive, not this side of the veil. And I thank every saint in heaven I never meet him in person." His eyes darted briefly to Riles, like this was a warning meant as much for him as for Haylee's family. "But even just digging, même juste un peu, it opens doors…" He tapped the table sharply. "…doors I did not know exist, doors I wish stayed closed."

Ray swallowed hard, his usual humor slipping away. "Doors to what?" he asked, cautious.

Émile's eyes flicked toward him, then back to Riles, as if deciding how much to say in English. "Things that don't sleep. Things that don't forgive. This Elliot…" he hesitated, the name tasting wrong in his mouth, "…he's not just some man who disappears. He got power, des connexions—pas juste ici, pas juste là-bas." (connections—not just here, not just over there.) He pointed upward, then downward, like the planes Émile hinted at were stacked all around them.

Then his expression shifted, a glimmer of worry beneath the grit. "And while I was digging, ta fille…" (your daughter). He glanced toward David. "…someone else was sniffing around her name. Asking questions. People I don't know. People I don't want to know."

David shot up from his chair so fast it screeched against the floor, his hands flat on the table, face pale but blazing with anger. "What the hell do you mean her name came up?" His voice carried enough weight that a couple of heads turned from the bar, but he didn't care.

Riles rose halfway out of his seat, a hand braced against David's arm. "Easy," he said low, calm but firm. "Let him talk."

Émile didn't flinch, just dragged on his cigarette and exhaled slowly, eyes never leaving David's. "Exactement comme j'ai dit," (exactly like I said), he replied. "Your daughter's name's in mouths it shouldn't be. If Elliot's a storm, mon chum, she's already in the wind."

David's fists tightened on the table edge. Every part of him screamed to demand names, answers, anything that would keep Haylee safe, but he forced himself to stay standing, jaw locked, listening. He couldn't afford to scare away the one man with information they desperately needed.

Riles' hand stayed firm on his arm, a silent anchor as the weight of Émile's words settled like a stone between them all.

The table went silent, only the dull thrum of the bar around them. Riles broke it first, voice low but sharp enough to cut. "Then we find out who's asking. And we make sure they don't get answers."

Émile leaned back slowly, eyes never leaving Riles'. "Bonne chance avec ça, mon chum." (*Good luck with that, buddy.*) The words were half sympathy, half warning.

Whatever they'd stumbled into, this wasn't just a manhunt anymore.

No Favors Left to Give

Émile stubbed out his cigarette in a scarred ashtray and pulled a thick, weathered envelope from the inside of his jacket. It landed on the table with a muted thump, a weight that felt heavier than paper should. "C'est tout là-dedans," he said simply. (It's all in there.)

Riles reached for it, riffling through the packet just enough to glimpse documents, a handful of grainy photos, and a folded map tucked inside. His eyes narrowed as he flipped one of the pictures toward the lamplight—a blurred shot of Elliot taken from a distance, his face half in shadow.

"Tabarnak... t'as trouvé tout ça en moins de douze heures?" Riles muttered, disbelief threading his Quebecois. (Damn... you got all this in less than twelve hours?)

Émile gave a dry half-smile, one that didn't reach his eyes. "Quand tu sais où regarder, les choses te trouvent." (When you know where to look, the things find you.) He shrugged like it was nothing, but the way his fingers lingered on the packet said otherwise, like this one had cost him more than he wanted to admit.

He leaned closer, his voice dropping as he spoke in a low rush of Quebecois only Riles could follow: "Va voir là-bas," he tapped the folded map, "mais fais gaffe... les gens qui traînent autour de ça? Ils sont pires que le diable que tu cherches." (Go check there, but be careful... the people tied to this are worse than the devil you're hunting.)

Riles' jaw tightened, but he nodded, sliding the map deeper into the envelope. Whatever they were walking into next, it wasn't just Elliot they had to worry about.

Émile sat back, his gaze flicking briefly to Ray and David before settling on Riles again. He took a slow breath, rubbing a hand over his face before saying, voice quiet but deliberate:

"Riles, mon chum... tu sais que j'ferais n'importe quoi pour toi... but this one?"

He tapped the packet like it burned his fingertips. "This is the last favor I've got in me for this, Elliot. Next time, I might not answer the phone."

The weight in his words needed no translation. Riles met his eyes and gave a slow nod. There was no anger there, just understanding. If Émile—a man who thrived in Montreal's undercurrents—was spooked enough to draw the line, they were all standing on something far darker than they realized.

Breaking the tension, Émile reached for a bottle and three glasses, filling them with a sharp, amber liquor. "Allez," he said, tone lighter but not entirely masking the edge in his voice.

"We drink, then you go. Nice to meet you boys," he added with a glance at David and Ray, "and I hope I don't ever see you again… unless it's for better reasons."

They each took a glass. The toast was wordless, the clink of glass on glass sounding like both a promise and a farewell. When Émile drank, his eyes lingered on Riles, and for a moment, there was no mistaking it—the storm Elliot carried wasn't just coming for Haylee anymore. It could find its way to Émile's door too.

Chapter Thirty:
Dark Roast and Darker Secrets

The apartment door clicked softly behind them as the Jeep Trio came in, the weight of Émile's words still clinging to their shoulders like smoke. The city was quiet outside, Montreal settling into its late-night hum, but none of them felt the calm.

Riles dropped the envelope of documents on the glass dining table and left it there, untouched for now. They all needed a moment to just breathe, but even exhaustion wasn't stronger than the unease threading through the room. Sleep, when it finally came, was shallow and restless. By the time morning light crept through the blinds, it felt like they'd only just closed their eyes.

At 9:48 a.m., Riles stood in the kitchen, sleeves pushed up, moving slow but steady as he pressed the plunger on a French press. The rich, earthy scent of dark roast coffee filled the air, cutting through the haze of last night's tension. The packet Émile had given him sat spread out on the table now—photos, photocopied documents, drone stills of a derelict warehouse in Quebec City. Faces stared up at him from the black-and-white images, names scribbled in a hand he didn't recognize, a trail of strangers somehow linked to Elliot long before Aggie had banished him to the other side.

David emerged first, hair still damp from a quick shower. He paused, inhaling the aroma that curled through the air. "What is that heavenly smell?" he asked, voice low but with a hint of relief.

"French press," Riles replied without looking up, eyes scanning another photo.

"Help yourself. There's plenty." He flipped a page, jaw tightening. "And something tells me we're gonna need every drop."

David poured himself a cup, the warmth a small comfort against the chill that had settled in his chest. The morning felt too quiet, like the city outside was holding its breath along with them.

Thirty minutes later, Ray shuffled out, yawning, hair sticking up on one side like a rooster's comb.

He sniffed dramatically at the air. "Ooo, yummy. French coffee."

Finally looking up, Riles gave him a flat stare. "Don't say 'yummy,' man. Makes it sound like a kindergarten snack, not the only thing keeping us alive right now."

Ray grinned lazily, grabbing a mug anyway. "Call it what you want. After last night, this is liquid gold."

Riles didn't argue, just went back to the spread of evidence on the table, the weight of what they'd learned pressing down harder with each photo he turned over.

Riles leaned back in his chair, rubbing a hand over his face as the last photo slid onto the growing pile. "Some of these people…" he muttered, voice low, "…

I've never seen before in my life. But they all circle Elliot somehow. Even before Aggie sent him packing." He tapped the drone image of the warehouse in Quebec City, grim expression set in stone.

"Whatever's in there, it's a piece of his trail. But it's not just his name that came up last night."

David's jaw tightened, the words still echoing in his head from Émile's mouth: *ta fille*. His coffee sat untouched on the table, growing cold between his hands. "And Haylee's caught in the middle of it," he said quietly. "Someone's looking for her."

"Yeah," Riles admitted, his voice sharp. "But we don't know who or why yet. Which means telling her now?" He shook his head. "We'd just be handing her a storm with no umbrella."

Ray, usually quick with a joke, stayed uncharacteristically serious. "So what's the play?" he asked, leaning forward on his elbows. "We keep this to ourselves? Feels wrong not telling her, man."

David's gut twisted at that. He'd promised Haylee, swore to her face that no more secrets would sit between them. But the weight of Émile's warning, the unknown danger circling her, made his next words taste bitter in his mouth.

"It's not about lying," he said finally. "It's about giving her a chance to… breathe. This is her journey. She deserves to feel like she's in control of something for once."

Riles met his eyes across the table, holding the look for a long moment before nodding. "We keep our mouths shut—for now," he said. "When the time's right, when we've got more than half a story and shadows on a map, then we loop her in." His voice carried no debate, just quiet resolve.

Ray sighed, raking a hand through his hair. "Fine. But if this blows up on us, I'm pointing the finger at you two."

Riles cracked the faintest grin, but it didn't reach his eyes. "Wouldn't expect anything less." He gathered up the packet, folding it neatly before sliding it into his bag. "We'll grab them in a few hours, stick to the plan. Metaphysical shop, some local stops. Let her feel normal, just for today."

David only nodded, but guilt sat heavy in his chest, a knot that wouldn't loosen no matter how much he told himself this was the right thing to do.

Later That Morning

David stepped out into the small balcony of the apartment, phone in hand, staring out over the city. He hit Sam's contact and waited for the line to pick up.

"Morning," Sam's voice came, still thick with sleep but warm.

"Morning," David said, trying to sound casual. "We're running a bit late, but the plan hasn't changed. We'll swing by in a few hours, head to that metaphysical shop you wanted to check out."

Haylee's voice came faintly in the background, cheerful but curious.

"Is Dad on the phone?" she asked. A moment later, she was closer, her tone light.
"Morning! Everything okay? You sound… I don't know, different."

David forced a chuckle, the lie sticking in his throat.

"Just tired. Long night. We'll be there soon, don't worry."

"Okay," Haylee said slowly, not fully convinced. "We'll be ready."

When the call ended, David stood there for a long moment, the phone heavy in his hand. He hated the taste of secrets. It reminded him too much of the past, of mistakes he'd sworn not to repeat. But like fixing Bertha's radiator hose before she ever knew it was leaking, this felt like another thing he had to quietly patch up until it was safe to tell her.

Behind him, Riles slid the balcony door open just enough to say, "She buy it?"

David didn't look back, just stared out at the skyline. "For now."

Chapter Thirty-One:
Anything Is Possible

The day had slipped into a comfortable rhythm by the time the crunch of Jeep tires on gravel broke the quiet at the campground. The late morning sun spilled golden light across Bertha's faded paint, the kind that made everything feel just a little softer. At the picnic table outside, Haylee sat curled around a steaming mug of herbal tea, watching Sam squint at the checkerboard between them.

"You're stalling," she teased, one eyebrow arched as she nudged a red piece forward with a decisive tap.

"I'm strategizing," Sam countered, leaning back in mock offense as he popped the tab on his soda. "Big difference."

Josie sprawled at their feet, her nose twitching every time a breeze brought a new scent past. Bella stretched lazily in the open doorway of the RV, half-lidded eyes fixed on a sunbeam like nothing else in the world mattered. It was the kind of moment Haylee wished she could bottle up and save for every time life felt too big, too messy.

David climbed out of the back of the Jeep just as the game reached its peak, his boots crunching on the gravel. Riles and Ray stayed in the front, the soft rumble of the engine idling like a quiet clock ticking them forward.

Haylee glanced at Josie and Bella. "Inside, girls," she said gently, ushering them back into Bertha and locking the door behind them. She cast one last look at the little bubble of peace they'd made at the picnic table, then slid into the Jeep beside Sam.

As they pulled away, the campground faded into the distance, gravel giving way to asphalt, city traffic waiting somewhere ahead. Haylee leaned into Sam's shoulder, the warmth of his presence grounding her as the Jeep picked up speed.

For a fleeting moment, as the sun caught on the horizon and a cool breeze drifted through the window, she let herself believe what the road had been whispering to her all along: *anything was possible.*

But just as that thought settled warm in her chest, something tugged at her awareness—a sudden, sharp ping, like an invisible thread pulling her gaze to the side. She looked out the window as they passed a weathered fifth-wheel trailer a few lots down from Bertha.

An American family sat outside—too loud, too obvious, all twang and beer cans at noon. But the woman… the woman's eyes followed the Jeep too long, lingering not on the group but on her. Haylee's breath hitched, a chill running over her arms.

For a moment, she swore she knew something wasn't right. A strange certainty she couldn't explain curled in her gut, quick as a flash. Then it was gone, leaving only goosebumps and a passing thought she tried to shake off. Just another camper. Just another family on the road. Nothing more… right?

Bertha Bites Back

The campground quieted as the Jeep rolled away, dust settling on the gravel lot. Two minutes later, the American man strolled toward Bertha like he had every right to be there.

Josie's scent lingered on the grass by the RV's door, making his lip curl in distaste. He glanced over his shoulder—no one watching—and pulled a small device from his jacket. Another tracker, sleeker, harder to spot than the last one they'd ripped off. This one would stick.

First, he crouched low by the door, pulling a small leather pouch from his jacket. A couple of thin tools glinted in the dim light as he slid them into the lock, working with practiced ease. Within seconds, he felt the familiar click of the mechanism giving way. A smug grin tugged at his mouth as his hand reached for the handle to swing it open—

—but before he could pull, the door handle twitched under his grip, then slammed tight with a metallic clang that echoed like a gunshot in the quiet lot. The man jolted, eyes wide, jerking his hand back as if the RV had bitten him.

"What the hell…" he muttered, staring at the door, certain he'd unlocked it. He grabbed the handle again, yanking harder this time, but it refused to budge. The lock clicked back into place with a finality that felt almost deliberate, like Bertha herself had decided he wasn't coming in tonight.

From inside, a low *click* echoed, like hidden gears turning, followed by a sharp metallic snap. The man hissed in pain, clutching his palm where a ragged edge of glass had seemingly sliced him. But when he blinked, there was no glass—only smooth metal where it had always been.

"Stupid piece of junk," he growled under his breath, wrapping his bleeding hand in a rag. He ducked lower, moving to the wheel well to check the brakes. That was when a slick puddle of oil appeared beneath the RV, exactly where he crouched, coating his sleeve and dripping down his collar like Bertha herself had spit on him.

By the time he stood up, a faint whirr came from the roof—an antenna violently without wind, pointed straight at him like an accusing finger.

Josie's muffled bark erupted from inside, low and furious, vibrating through the metal walls. It wasn't a "stranger nearby" bark—it was the kind that promised teeth if he tried his luck again.

The man glanced toward the fifth wheel nervously. Too many eyes, too many chances of being caught. With a final glare at Bertha, he muttered, "Fine," retreating toward his own campsite and leaving greasy footprints in his wake.

He'd plant the tracker later. But for now, Bertha had made it perfectly clear: *she wasn't letting him win tonight.*

Distraction Game

Montreal's late afternoon buzzed with life—the kind of city noise that made you feel small and anonymous. Street vendors called out over the hum of traffic, the scent of roasted nuts and fresh bread mingled in the air, and a warm breeze carried music from somewhere around the corner.

Haylee should have been soaking it all in. Instead, her mind kept tugging back to the uneasy feeling from earlier—the fifth wheel at the campground, that woman's stare. She shook it off, reminding herself this was supposed to be fun. Sam's hand found hers as they walked, grounding her back in the moment.

"Metaphysical shop's just a couple blocks this way," Riles said, checking a scribbled set of directions Émile had given him.

Ray was halfway through teasing Riles about his driving when it happened.

The voice carried first—loud, exaggerated, with that grating "tourist drawl" that turned heads for all the wrong reasons.

"Come on, kids, keep up! We ain't got all day!"

The accent was southern, twangy, entirely out of place in the Montreal street. Haylee glanced over instinctively. There she was—the same woman from the fifth wheel, blonde hair piled high, oversized sunglasses hiding her eyes, herding two noisy kids like a drill sergeant in flip-flops. She laughed loud enough to cut through the city chatter, waving a shopping bag in the air like a flag.

And staring.

Haylee tried to laugh it off. Tourists were everywhere. Coincidence, right? But the woman's gaze snagged on her, just a beat too long. Recognition? Curiosity? Something colder? Haylee couldn't tell.

She looked away quickly, focusing on the path ahead, telling herself she was imagining things.

But every few minutes, that grating voice popped up again—closer now, cutting across the street behind them, echoing near a fruit stand when they paused to look at jewelry. Every time Haylee glanced back, there she was—not close enough to be obvious, but never far enough to be chance.

The ping in Haylee's gut wouldn't quit. That same strange flicker of knowing—not sight, not sound, just… something—that had jolted her earlier by Bertha. Her skin prickled as she stepped closer to Sam, lowering her voice.

"Does that woman seem… off to you?"

Sam glanced back casually, then shrugged. "Just a loud tourist with louder kids," he said, squeezing her hand. "Ignore it."

Haylee tried. She wanted to believe him. But as they neared the metaphysical shop, the woman's voice rose again, exaggerated and booming:

"No, you can't have another ice cream, we're late already!" It made Haylee flinch like a slammed door.

When she glanced back this time, the woman wasn't even talking to the kids—she was looking straight at Haylee, a smile that didn't reach her eyes fixed under those ridiculous sunglasses.

Haylee turned quickly, heart thudding. Rude? Maybe. Random? Maybe not. But one thing felt certain—this woman's attention wasn't an accident, and for the life of her, Haylee couldn't figure out why.

She slowed, instinctively scanning the street, but Sam's voice pulled her back. "You good?"

"Yeah," Haylee said quickly, forcing a smile that didn't reach her eyes. She let Sam lead her on, telling herself it was nothing. Just a rude tourist. Just bad vibes. Behind them, the woman kept up her act, louder now, drawing attention away from the Jeep trio entirely. The real show was happening back at the campground, and her job was to make sure no one suspected a thing.

242

Chapter Thirty-Two:
Le Fil du Monde

"There it is—*Le Fil du Monde*," Riles called out, nodding toward a small storefront tucked between a café and a bookstore. "*The Thread of the World.*"

He grabbed the heavy wooden door, a bell chiming softly overhead as he ushered everyone inside.

The air changed immediately—cooler, stiller, with layers of scents drifting through: sandalwood, sage, and something else Riles didn't place right away. Cannabis was legal here, but this didn't smell like a dispensary. More like a thousand dried herbs stacked on a shelf, sharing space with incense and candle wax.

On the outside, the shop had seemed small, just a sliver on the street. Inside, it opened up like a storybook—tall shelves lined with crystals, rows of candle jars, softly glowing lamps in warm amber hues. A few velvet curtains separated sections of the store, hinting at mysteries beyond. It wasn't kitschy, but it wasn't polished either—just that perfect balance between mystical and welcoming.

Haylee's eyes were wide, soaking it all in. It felt alive somehow, like the shop itself was watching.

Riles wrinkled his nose as he passed a hanging bundle of herbs. He'd smelled worse things in his life, but this wasn't his kind of comfort. Behind him, David and Ray exchanged grins, nudging each other as they passed racks of flowing skirts and small carved statues.

"Look at this," Ray muttered, holding up a moon goddess figurine with mock reverence. "Think it grants wishes?"

David smirked. "Maybe it makes you smarter if you rub its head."

Haylee shot them a glare over her shoulder, lips twitching despite herself. "Behave," she warned softly.

Sam had already drifted toward a jewelry case, fingers brushing over strings of crystals and delicate silver pendants. He looked completely at ease, like the shop whispered directly to him.

Then a tall man stepped out from behind a curtain, moving with the kind of unhurried grace that made you feel like he'd been expecting you.

"Bonjour, c'est Jean-Paul," he said warmly, voice carrying a rich Quebecois lilt. "Puis-je vous aider?" (Hello, I'm Jean-Paul. May I help you?)

Everyone turned to Riles automatically.

"He says his name's Jean-Paul and he's asking if he can help us," Riles translated, stepping forward.

"Salut, Jean-Paul," Riles greeted in French, showing him a worn photograph of Aggie. "On est là pour parler à toi et ta femme Mireille. T'as déjà vu cette dame-là? Agnès? Aggie?"

(Hi, Jean-Paul, we're here to speak to you and your wife Mireille. Have you ever seen this woman? Agnes? Aggie?)

Jean-Paul tilted his head, brows furrowing as he studied the picture. "J'sais pas… Aggie, Agnès… mais cette dame, là—elle connaît ma blonde."
(I don't know… Aggie, Agnes… but this woman, she knows my wife.)

He glanced toward the curtain and called out, "Mireille, viens ici, ma chérie!" (Mireille, come here, my love!)

A moment later, a tall, elegant woman stepped out, dark hair falling loose over her shoulders. She took one look at the group and smiled, eyes kind but curious.

"Salut, je suis Mireille," she said softly, voice melodic. "Puis-je vous aider?" (Hello, I'm Mireille. May I help you?)

Riles gave a polite nod. "Yes, ma'am… do you know who this is?" He handed over the photo.

Mireille's face softened instantly, recognition blooming in her expression. "Ah… voici ma bonne amie Margot," she murmured, cradling the picture like it was fragile. "Une amie bien précieuse… comment va-t-elle?"
(Ah… this is my good friend Margot. A very dear friend… how is she?)

Riles hesitated, glancing at Haylee. She swallowed hard and nodded, eyes downcast.

"She's passed," Riles said quietly. "Elle est partie… c'est sa nièce, Haylee."
(She's gone… this is her niece, Haylee.)

Mireille's gaze lifted sharply to Haylee, eyes shining with sudden emotion. She shook her head gently, a tear threatening to spill. "Non, pas nièce," she said, voice trembling, "sa fille… ben, son bébé."
(No, not niece… her daughter… her baby.)

The room seemed to hold its breath. Haylee's chest tightened, a strange ache of truth threading through her heart even though she already knew.

Mireille pressed the photo to her chest for a heartbeat, breathing in like it carried a memory. Then she looked to Jean-Paul, nodding slightly. Whatever passed between them didn't need words.

"Venez, s'il vous plaît," she said, gesturing to a round table near the back of the shop. "Come, come… we talk proper, pas debout comme ça." (…not standing like this.)

The group followed quietly. The noise from the street seemed to vanish as they settled into mismatched chairs around a table draped in deep blue cloth embroidered with golden threads that shimmered in the low light. Shelves loomed above, lined with jars and candles, yet the space felt strangely private, like it had been waiting for them.

Mireille set the photo down in front of her, fingertips brushing over it.

"Margot…" she said softly, switching between French and English as though her thoughts didn't quite fit one language. "Toujours un mystère, that one. Always disappearing, reappearing… mais toujours le cœur grand." (…but always with a big heart.)

She glanced up at Haylee, studying her face for long moments that made Haylee shift uneasily in her chair. "Mon Dieu… the eyes, same as hers." Her voice cracked just slightly.

Haylee swallowed hard, unsure what to say.

Jean-Paul came over with a battered tin tray holding a pot of steaming tea and a handful of chipped mugs. "Pas grand-chose, mais ça réchauffe," he said as he poured. (Not much, but it'll warm you up.) Then, glancing to Riles with a wry half-smile: "Better than the café down the street. Trop cher là-bas." (Too expensive over there.)

Ray muttered under his breath, "Finally someone speaks my language," earning a sharp elbow from David.

Riles cleared his throat. "We came because… Haylee's looking for answers. Aggie —Margot—she left more questions than we can figure out."

Mireille nodded slowly, cupping her mug like it held memories. "Toujours comme ça," she murmured. "Margot never do anything simple." Her gaze flicked to Haylee again, switching to English carefully. "Your maman… she came here often. Quiet, mais… always with a purpose. Elle savait des choses… things most don't see."

Haylee leaned forward, heart racing. "You knew about her… about what she could do?"

Jean-Paul's brows rose, and he exchanged a glance with Mireille. "Oui… we know a little. But Margot, she was… comment dire…" He searched for the English word, then shrugged. "…between worlds. Pas tout à fait ici, pas tout à fait là-bas." (Not fully here, not fully there.)

246

Mireille added softly, "She believed in le fil du monde... the thread that ties everything together. People, places, even time itself. Sometimes... she followed it. Sometimes... it followed her." She looked to Haylee with quiet weight in her eyes. "And now, maybe, it follows you."

A shiver ran down Haylee's spine. She didn't know what to say, but something deep inside whispered that Mireille was right.

The Truth of Birth

Mireille stared at the photo of Aggie, one hand over her mouth, eyes glassy. Finally, her voice broke through the silence, thick with emotion.

"Margot... elle est venue ici, pas juste visiter. Elle est venue... pour toi, ma petite. Pour te donner au monde."
(*Margot came here, not just to visit. She came... for you, little one. To bring you into the world.*)

Haylee blinked hard. "Wait... what do you mean?"

Jean-Paul's low voice rumbled, "Elle a donné naissance ici, à Montréal. Pas aux États-Unis."
(*She gave birth here, in Montreal. Not in the United States.*)

Haylee froze, breath stuck in her throat.

Mireille leaned forward, switching languages like her heart didn't have time to translate. "I was there, chérie... moi, I help her. Petite maison near the river, pas d'hôpital, rien. Just us, safe... quiet night. You were si petite, like a little bird." Her eyes softened with memory. "Je me souviens..." (*I remember...*)

"That night... pendant que ta maman held you, a hummingbird came to the window. Middle of the night, pas normal..." She glanced at Jean-Paul with a watery laugh. "Tiny wings, beating fast, like it knew un miracle was here."

Her gaze drifted back to Haylee, tears glistening. "Margot... she looked at you, she said, 'Mon petit colibri.'" (*My little hummingbird.*) Mireille's voice cracked. "She said you would always be free... always find the flowers in life, même dans les endroits sombres." (*...even in the dark places.*)

She reached under the counter, pulling out a battered envelope, fingers trembling as she slid out old photos. "Regarde..." (*Look...*) A swaddled newborn. Aggie smiling through exhaustion. Jean-Paul holding a chipped mug in the background.

Haylee's throat tightened. "This… this can't be." Her voice wavered. "I was born in the U.S.—my birth certificate says—"

"Non, ma belle." Mireille's warm, firm hand closed over hers. "Your maman… elle avait peur, comprends? Too many questions… trop de portes fermées. Elle… she make American papers après, later, pour que personne ne cherche trop."
(*She was scared, you understand? Too many questions, too many doors closed. She made American papers later, so no one would look too hard.*)

She glanced at Riles, whispering fast in French. "Elle voulait pas qu'on la trouve. Les papiers US, c'était plus sûr."

Riles' jaw tightened as he translated gently, "She says Aggie didn't want to be found. American papers… were safer."

Jean-Paul's voice was soft but steady. "Mais ici… tu es canadienne aussi, p'tite. Deux patries… deux maisons dans ton sang."
(*But here… you're Canadian too, little one. Two homelands, two homes in your blood.*)

Haylee's hands trembled as she clutched the photo. Tears blurred her vision. "All this time… I didn't even know," she whispered.

Mireille smiled through her own tears. "Margot… elle t'aimait fort," (*she loved you so much*) she said softly, words falling like a promise. "And she knew un jour… one day… le fil du monde would pull you back here. To truth. To us."

The shop seemed to hold its breath, even the candles flickering softer, as if listening to a secret finally set free.

Threads That Bind

Mireille sat quiet for a moment, the weight of old memories pressing down like a heavy storm cloud. Her eyes lingered on Haylee, soft but sharp, as if they saw past the young woman sitting at the table and straight into something older, something deeper.

"Ta maman… elle avait des pouvoirs magiques," Mireille said gently, voice low, almost reverent. (*Your mama… she had magical powers.*) She switched to broken English, words halting but true. "Big gift… strong. Pas juste feeling, pas juste visions. Real magic, qui touche les deux mondes." (*That touches both worlds.*)

Haylee blinked, her heart tripping over itself. "Two worlds?" she asked.

Mireille nodded slowly, eyes never leaving Haylee's. "Oui… like doorways. Open… close. Margot… she walk between, sometimes." She hesitated, tilting her head just slightly, as if listening to something only she could hear. "And you… chérie… you carry same fil… same thread."

A strange warmth stirred under Haylee's skin, the same uncanny hum she'd felt before, only stronger now under Mireille's gaze. Their eyes locked for a long moment, neither speaking, but something passed between them, like two flames recognizing the same fire.

Without another word, Mireille stood and crossed to a shelf near the back. Her hands hovered over a wooden box, worn smooth with time, before she lifted it carefully, holding it as though it could break or burn her at once.

The second the box left its resting place, the air in the shop shifted. A faint vibration seemed to hum through the table, through Haylee's chest, like a heartbeat that wasn't her own.

"C'est pas juste un bijou…" Mireille murmured, voice trembling. (*This is not just jewelry.*) She looked at Haylee, a sad smile tugging at her lips. "Your maman… she give me this, après ta naissance. Said one day, when le fil du monde brings you here… it must be yours."

She set the box down, sliding the lid open with slow, careful hands. Inside lay a delicate pendant on a tarnished silver chain, its stone faintly pulsing with a soft light, as if alive. The glow wasn't bright, but it whispered power, old and waiting. Mireille held it out, and even before Haylee touched it, a warmth curled up her arm, tingling like a memory waking in her blood.

"It feels you, chérie," Mireille said softly, her French weaving through broken English. "Protection, oui… mais plus. It listen only to heart it belongs to. It waited… all this time… for you."

Haylee's fingers brushed the pendant, and a wave of energy shivered up her spine. It wasn't scary, but heavy, like a thousand unseen threads pulling tight around her, weaving her into something bigger than herself.

Jean-Paul shifted uneasily in his seat, glancing at Mireille. "Toujours pareil," he muttered under his breath. (*Always the same…*) She gave him a knowing look before turning back to Haylee.

Mireille's voice dropped, darkening with an old fear. "Margot… she trust me with this because Elliot Pascal was near. Cet homme…" She shook her head sharply, words tumbling out in a mix of languages. "Trop sombre. Pas juste magie noire… worse. Something pas humain, pas d'ici. The kind of shadow you can't wash away."

She reached for her tea, hand trembling slightly. "I tell her to run. Told her… never let that man hold a thread of your life." Mireille's gaze drifted to Haylee, sorrow heavy in her eyes. "But some threads… they follow, peu importe la distance. No matter how far you go."

The pendant sat in Haylee's hand now, warm and alive, a weight that felt like love, fear, and destiny all braided together. She clutched it close to her chest, heart pounding as if it knew—this wasn't just a keepsake.

It was a key. And one day, she'd have to use it.

Chapter Thirty-Three:
Unwelcome Guest

The shop was calm, thick with incense and the quiet murmur of conversation. The pendant rested in Haylee's palm, its weight strange but comforting. She hadn't put it on yet—part of her wasn't sure she was ready.

The bell above the door jingled.

Instantly, a ripple ran through her chest, sharp and electric. Her breath hitched as the air shifted, the warmth of the shop thinning like a draft slipping under the door.

"Afternoon!" A woman's voice cut through the calm, loud and drawling.

"What is this place, some kinda crystal shack or what?" The laugh that followed was brittle, fake. Two kids trailed behind her, one whining about being hungry, the other clattering a toy car along the floor.

Jean-Paul stepped out front with his usual calm but raised brows, switching effortlessly to English.

"Bonjour, madame, bienvenue. May I help you?" His polite tone didn't hide his confusion.

"Nah," the woman said, waving him off dramatically. "Just looking. Doubt there's anything in here for me." She plucked up a carved stone, turned it over, then tossed it back on the shelf like junk.

From the back, Haylee froze. That ping inside her tightened into a pull, like an invisible thread tugging her forward. Without thinking, her fingers unclasped the pendant and slipped it over her head. The chain was cool against her skin, but the stone warmed instantly, humming faintly like it had been waiting for her all this time.

Sam caught the motion out of the corner of his eye. "You okay?" he whispered. Haylee's eyes stayed locked on the front of the shop, shoulders tense.

"Not sure," she murmured. But the pendant settled against her chest like a shield, steadying her heartbeat.

The woman didn't linger. The bell chimed again as she left, muttering about "weird smells" and "hippie junk." Through the slightly open door, Haylee caught the woman's voice, sharp and low, just enough to make her skin prickle: *"Yeah, I followed them here. No clue where they went. Must've slipped out the back."*

She strained to hear more but only caught the sound of the woman's flip-flops moving further away.

Outside, the woman tightened her grip on the phone, irritation lacing her words .A man's voice crackled faintly on the other end, low and heated. *"You useless or somethin'? I told you, keep eyes on her. I nearly had my shot today—that damn RV nearly bit my hand off."*

She snorted, rolling her eyes. *"Dumbass. Can't even do a simple break-in job without my help."*

There was a tense pause before the man's tone sharpened, commanding. *"Don't lose her again. Whatever she's got, it's important. Boss wants it. I don't care how loud you gotta be, just make sure she doesn't disappear."*

"Yeah, yeah," the woman muttered, venom slipping into her voice. *"I'll handle it."* She hung up, tugging her kids roughly toward the side of the shop.

They followed her into a narrow alley, searching for a back door. No luck. A crowd from a sidewalk clothing sale had spilled over, blocking her way out. Muttering curses under her breath, she tried to double back, only to find herself stuck between racks of cheap T-shirts and bargain hunters.

By the time she broke free of the crowd, the shop door stayed firmly shut. She huffed in frustration, yanking the phone out again, but thought better of calling back. *Not here. Too many eyes.*

For now, she would wait.

Jean-Paul returned to the table, shaking his head with a dry chuckle. "Une Américaine bruyante," he muttered. (*A loud American.*) "No manners... pas d'respect pour la magie."

Mireille glanced toward Haylee, concern flickering in her eyes. "Quelqu'un que tu connais?" (*Someone you know?*)

Haylee's hand curled tight around the pendant, its warmth pulsing like a heartbeat against her palm. She stared at the door, voice quiet but certain.

"Not personally," she said. "But yeah... I know who she was."

Chapter Thirty-Four:
Echoes on the Street

The late afternoon sun dipped lower over Montreal, casting long shadows across the sidewalk as the group stepped out of Le Fil du Monde. The door swung shut behind them, the little bell chiming softly, but the warmth from inside didn't follow.

Haylee adjusted the strap of her bag, the pendant still warm against her chest. Every time it brushed her skin, a faint hum rippled through her, like it had its own pulse. She told herself it was just nerves. She didn't believe it.

Mireille's parting words lingered in her mind: "Quand le fil du monde tire encore, reviens me voir, ma colibri." (*When the thread pulls again, come back to me, little hummingbird.*) There'd been something in Mireille's eyes—a knowing sadness—that made Haylee's chest ache.

They walked in silence for a few moments, the sounds of the city filling in around them: car horns, the distant clang of a streetcar, laughter spilling from a café patio. It should have felt normal, safe even. But Haylee couldn't shake the feeling of being watched.

Her gaze skimmed the storefronts and alleys they passed. Nothing obvious. Just people going about their day. But there, across the street—a flash of blonde hair piled high, kids trailing behind. The loud tourist from the shop.

Haylee slowed, the ping in her gut flaring again. The woman didn't seem to notice them at first, flipping through a rack of scarves outside a boutique. But every few seconds, her sunglasses tilted just enough that Haylee could swear the woman was watching them.

Sam squeezed her hand gently, leaning closer. "Hey," he murmured, voice low enough for just her. "I love you, you know that? And whatever this is, I'm here. Always."

Haylee's breath softened, the weight in her chest easing just a little. She turned to him, a small, grateful smile tugging at her lips. "I know," she whispered, before leaning in to kiss him.

Behind them, Ray let out a mock sigh, clutching his chest dramatically. "Aw, look at them, so in love."

David smacked his arm lightly. "Leave them be," he muttered with a smirk. "You'd be lucky to have what they've got."

Ray chuckled under his breath, holding his hands up in surrender. "Fair enough."

The brief warmth of the moment settled over Haylee like a blanket, a reminder that she wasn't alone. But even as she turned back to the street, the unease lingered. The woman was still there, still watching—or pretending not to. The ping in Haylee's gut warned her this wasn't coincidence.

And deep down, she knew this wouldn't be the last time their paths crossed.

Chapter Thirty-Five:
The Weight of Tomorrow

Montreal's early evening air had shifted by the time they reached the quieter side street where Riles had parked the Jeep. The sun dipped low, casting long gold streaks over the pavement, the city alive but softening into twilight.

The five of them walked in an easy line, Ray cracking some story about bad gas station coffee, Riles tossing in a sarcastic "Better than the swill you make at camp," earning a mock glare from Ray. Haylee almost let herself relax, the pendant warm against her chest like a promise of safety.

Almost.

A sudden blur of motion broke the rhythm. One of the tourist kids darted between them, nearly colliding with Sam and forcing him to grab Haylee's arm as they stumbled.

"Hey—watch it, buddy," Sam said, startled but calm, helping Haylee steady herself.

The boy scampered back toward a familiar figure waiting just a few steps ahead. Blonde hair piled high, oversized sunglasses, that same smug tilt to her chin. The woman.

She stood square in Haylee's path, lips curling in a half-smile that didn't touch her eyes. As the kids tugged at her arms, she leaned just close enough for Haylee to hear the words, sharp and venomous.

"You're not so special," she hissed, voice like poison sugar. "What's he want with you, anyway?"

Haylee froze, the words hitting harder than they should have. She opened her mouth, a retort on her tongue—but the kids yanked at the woman's arms, whining for ice cream. The moment broke, and just like that, the woman was turning away, letting herself be dragged back into the crowd, a smirk lingering on her face.

Sam slipped his hand over hers, voice low but steady. "Ignore her, baby. She doesn't know a damn thing about you."

They caught up to Riles, David, and Ray by the Jeep. Riles was leaning against the hood, arms folded, watching the street with narrowed eyes.

"Something I should know about?" he asked, catching the tension on Haylee's face.

"Nothing worth repeating," Sam said, shooting a quick glance at Haylee as if to say later.

Riles studied them for a beat, then opened the passenger door, jerking his head toward the back.

"Alright then, let's get out of here before this city throws any more surprises at us."

Threads of Tomorrow

The drive back to Bertha was quiet, the city lights fading behind them. Riles kept one hand on the wheel, the other tapping absently on the steering column, his eyes on the road but mind clearly elsewhere.

By the time the Jeep rolled into the gravel lot, the sky was velvet dark, stars spilling overhead.

Haylee stepped out slowly, feeling the earth under her boots, the cool night air washing away some of the day's weight. She glanced at Bertha, sturdy and waiting, and let out a breath she didn't know she'd been holding.

Sam came up beside her, their fingers finding each other in the dark. David and Ray started unloading a few things from the Jeep while Riles walked a slow circle around Bertha, scanning the area with sharp eyes. Old habits. He didn't like the feeling of being followed any more than Haylee did.

Haylee touched the pendant, feeling its quiet hum. "I want to go back," she said softly. "To Mireille. Not now… but when I'm ready."

Sam nodded without hesitation, his hand warm around hers. "Whenever you're ready," he promised. "And you won't face it alone."

She leaned into him, comforted by his steady presence. For the first time all day, the tension in her chest loosened, even as a different kind of weight settled in— the weight of everything she'd learned, everything that still lay ahead.

They joined the others by the RV, where Josie bounded up with a happy bark, tail wagging like nothing in the world could ever be wrong. David chuckled softly, rubbing the dog's ears as Ray started a small campfire. Riles finally joined them, grabbing a seat by the fire with a sigh, scanning the horizon one last time before relaxing.

The five of them sat under the stars, quiet but together, the night air cool and still.

Haylee tilted her head back, staring at the endless sky. Maybe the road had always meant to lead her here, to these people, this moment. But as the pendant warmed against her skin and the distant echo of the woman's voice lingered in her mind, one truth settled heavy in her chest:

The fight ahead… it feels like it's just beginning.

Chapter Thirty-Six:
The Cost of Knowing

Haylee stepped out into the cool morning, stretching her arms over her head as the rising sun lit the gravel in soft gold. The air was crisp, laced with the scent of pine and distant campfire ash. Bertha's windows gleamed in the early light, and Josie trotted down the steps beside her, tail wagging lazily.

She reached for the enamel mug Sam had handed her moments earlier, fingers wrapping around its warmth, and took a slow sip. Everything was still. Peaceful.

Normal.

Until it wasn't.

Haylee's gaze drifted down—and then caught.

Something dark stained the gravel just a few feet from the RV door. Not just a drop or two. A spatter. Her brow furrowed. She stepped closer, crouching slightly.

It was blood.

She turned her head slowly, following the uneven trail—smears along the bottom edge of Bertha's side panel. Not enough to make her panic, but enough to make her gut twist.

"Sam?" she called quietly over her shoulder.

He appeared in the doorway, rubbing sleep from his eyes and holding his own coffee.

"What's up?"

She pointed to the gravel. "Did you cut yourself or something?"

He followed her finger and froze, eyes narrowing.

"No... I didn't." He stepped down beside her and knelt for a better look. "That's dried. Maybe from yesterday. But... that's a lot."

Haylee scanned the RV again. "You don't think Josie—?"

"No way," Sam said immediately, glancing at the dog now sniffing around the picnic table. "She's fine. No limping, no whining. And we'd know."

Haylee nodded, unsettled.

They said nothing for a beat, the silence made louder by the flicker of birdsong overhead.

"Let's take Josie for a walk," Sam offered gently. "Might help clear our heads."

She agreed, and they clipped her leash and began their usual loop around the campground. The fifth wheel—the loud one—came into view around the bend. Two lawn chairs were set up outside, along with a cluttered plastic table covered in beer cans and a pack of cards. One of the Americans stood by the firepit, leaning slightly, a grimy cloth wrapped tightly around one hand.

Josie stopped in her tracks.

She let out a low, guttural growl. Not her usual "I'm-on-guard" bark—this was deeper. Focused. Her ears pinned back and her posture lowered.

The man looked over, cold eyes meeting Haylee's for just a second too long. Sam placed a hand on Josie's collar, steady but firm. "Let's go," he said under his breath.

They walked on.

Back at the RV, Haylee couldn't stop replaying the moment in her head—the cloth on his hand, the way Josie reacted, the uneasy silence between the man and herself.

She set her mug down and turned to Sam.

"You don't think…"

He nodded before she finished. "Yeah. I do."

Haylee exhaled sharply. "That guy tried to break into Bertha while we were out."

Josie lay at the base of the steps now, still alert, tail thumping once against the dirt. Haylee sat beside her, resting a hand on her fur, grounding herself in the truth they'd just uncovered.

And suddenly, the peaceful morning felt like it had teeth.

A Plan Forms

Back inside Bertha, the kettle whistled softly on the stovetop. Sam poured water into their coffee maker while Haylee cracked eggs into a cast iron skillet, the sizzle filling the quiet. Josie hovered nearby, hopeful and watchful.

Haylee had her phone on the counter, screen facing up. She kept glancing at it as the eggs cooked, her mind still on the blood outside.

"Text Riles?" Sam asked quietly, sliding into the booth. "See if they're up?"

Haylee nodded. "Yeah. Might as well loop everyone in."

She sent a quick message:
"We found blood by the RV this morning. Pretty sure someone tried to break in. Can you talk?"

The reply came faster than expected:
Riles: *"On a walk but give me 5. I'll grab David and Ray. We'll call."*

By the time the eggs were on plates and coffee poured, Haylee's phone lit up with the incoming video call. She hit accept and set the phone in the middle of the table.

Riles appeared first, windblown and wearing sunglasses. "Hey, you okay?"

"We're fine," Haylee said. "But something weird happened."

Ray and David came into view behind him, both holding coffee cups and looking concerned.

Sam leaned into the frame. "Someone tried to break into Bertha while we were out yesterday. There's dried blood on the gravel and the side of the rig."

"Shit," Ray muttered.

Haylee added, "Josie growled at that American guy outside one of the fifth wheels this morning. He had his hand wrapped in a bloody cloth. Didn't say anything, but it was… off."

David's expression shifted from concern to quiet focus. "You guys all right now?"

"We are," Sam said. "Locked up. Josie's been on high alert."

Haylee nodded, then looked toward David. "While we've got you—there's something else. I want to go back and see Mireille."

David didn't hesitate. "Good. I think that's a smart move."

"I think she can help us with the Elliot situation," Haylee added.

"And…" She glanced at Sam, who gave her a supportive nod. "I want to look into getting a replacement birth certificate. If I was born in Quebec, it should be on file, right?"

"That's actually perfect timing," Riles jumped in. "I just talked to my friend Julien about that. You can apply in person at the Directeur de l'État Civil office. You'll need your ID, passport, and a signed form. It usually takes about ten business days."

"Will I even be allowed to do that?" she asked.

Riles answered, "Yes. As long as you're the person named on the certificate, you have the right to request a replacement. Especially if it's a Quebec record."

"Riles, can you pick us up to go into Montreal?" Sam added. "Need to exchange currency. Might as well do it all in one trip."

David nodded. "That's smart. By the way, when we crossed the border, we were all stamped with a six-month visitor status. So if you need more time, you've got it. Don't worry about the campground reservation—extend as needed."

"We only booked three weeks," Haylee said.

"You can pay monthly. Most places will give you a discount for that," Riles added.

"Exactly," David said. "I'll cover it. You focus on what you need—Mireille, the certificate, anything Aggie might've left behind."

Haylee felt a strange mix of emotions bubble up—gratitude, relief, and the low hum of anticipation. For once, she didn't have to rush. She could actually stay.

"I guess Bertha's settling in too," Sam said with a small smile.

"Let's not let her grow roots," Haylee joked. "She's got more stories to chase."

Josie barked once, tail thumping, and everyone on the screen smiled.

Haylee looked around their little space, then back to the phone. "Thanks, guys. We'll keep you posted."

"Keep safe," David said. "And keep Josie close."

"Always," Sam replied.

The call ended, but the momentum remained.

Haylee turned to the window and caught her reflection in the glass—older somehow, more grounded.

She wasn't just passing through anymore.

She was here.

And it mattered.

Change of Plans

By late morning, the familiar sound of Riles' Jeep rumbled into the gravel loop near their site. Josie perked up from her spot under the picnic table, tail thumping before she let out a single bark.

Haylee stepped outside with a half-grin. "There they are."

Sam followed behind her, brushing crumbs from his shirt and tossing a water bottle into Bertha's open side compartment. "Right on time."

The Jeep rolled to a stop, and the passenger door opened first. David stepped out, squinting against the sun. "Still standing?" he called with a slight smirk.

"Barely," Sam replied.

Ray and Riles got out next, stretching and exchanging quiet greetings. Riles handed over a to-go bag from a roadside diner. "Breakfast sandwiches, just in case you forgot to feed yourselves."

"We didn't," Haylee said, "but I'm not saying no to hash browns."

Riles grinned. "Didn't think so."

David glanced toward the campground office. "Let's take care of your reservation before we head out."

They crossed the gravel lot together, the office tucked neatly under a weathered awning. A bell jingled as they stepped inside. Dan, the gruff but kind host they'd met on check-in day, looked up from his clipboard.

"Mornin', folks," he greeted. "Everything good?"

"So far," Sam said. "We'd like to extend our stay. Probably for the next few months."

Dan leaned back slightly and tapped at the computer. "Your current site's booked solid after the three weeks—someone snagged it months ago.

"But I've got two other full-service lots opening around the same time. Want me to move your reservation over?"

"Yeah, that works," Haylee said. "We're fine switching spots."

"Monthly rate'll be cheaper," Dan added. "And you'll still be close to the bathrooms and main trail. I'll flag it in the system."

"Appreciate it," David said, pulling out his card. "I'll cover the first month."

Haylee opened her mouth to protest, but David gave her a look that left no room for argument. She closed it again with a nod.

Dan printed out a fresh slip with the new site number and handed it over. "You'll just need to move by the end of the third week. I'll swing by and check in closer to the date."

With the logistics handled, the group piled into the Jeep and started the drive toward Montreal. The roads were wide and tree-lined, sunlight flickering through patches of green and gold as farmland turned into suburban sprawl. Haylee sat in the back, a folded piece of paper in her lap—the new site number Dan had given them.

The ride was quiet but comfortable, each of them wrapped in their own thoughts until Riles pulled into a small local bank.

"Time to swap the funny money," he said, cutting the engine.

Inside, they exchanged their American bills for Canadian cash. The exchange rate was decent, and Haylee tucked the unfamiliar bills into her wallet with a strange sense of finality—like she'd just bought herself into a new chapter.

From there, it was a short drive to the Directeur de l'État Civil office. A low stone building with clear signage and a surprisingly modern lobby.

Haylee hesitated just a second before stepping inside, her fingers brushing over the strap of her crossbody bag.

"You good?" Sam asked gently.

"Yeah," she said, but her voice caught. "Just… weird. I've never had to prove I exist before."

He gave her a soft smile. "You do. Loud and clear."

They arrived at the Directeur de l'État Civil office just after midday. The building was modest, tucked between a boulangerie and a pharmacy, its signage printed in both French and English. Inside, the air was clean and cool, and the quiet hum of a copier played beneath soft overhead lights.

A woman behind the counter glanced up as they stepped in. She wore a fitted blazer and thin-framed glasses, her expression politely neutral.

"Bonjour, vous avez un rendez-vous ou c'est une demande sans rendez-vous?" she asked, voice quick but not unfriendly.

Riles stepped forward, slipping into French. "Sans rendez-vous. Elle veut faire une demande de certificat de naissance. Elle est née ici, au Québec."

The woman nodded, glancing toward Haylee. Then, still in French, she said, "D'accord. Elle devra remplir ce formulaire, fournir une pièce d'identité valide, et signer ici en bas. Le coût est de cinquante dollars et cinquante sous."

Riles turned toward Haylee. "She says you'll need to fill out this form, show a valid ID, and sign at the bottom. It's $50.50 CAD."

Haylee gave a small nod, already reaching for her ID and the pen on the counter. The woman slid the form across. "Elle peut inscrire une adresse canadienne si elle souhaite recevoir le certificat ici, sinon on peut envoyer aux États-Unis mais ça prendra plus de temps."

Riles translated again. "You can use a Canadian address if you want it mailed here. Otherwise, they can send it to the U.S., but it'll take longer."

Haylee looked up. "Can I use the campground's address?"

David, who had already stepped forward with his wallet ready.

"I'll clear it with the office. We'll check the mailbox regularly." Riles added.

Once the form was completed and signed, Haylee carefully handed it back along with the fee. The woman reviewed the information, gave a small nod, then stamped a confirmation slip and handed it to her.

"Le traitement prend environ dix jours ouvrables. Elle recevra une copie officielle par la poste."

Riles translated without being asked this time. "It'll take about ten business days. You'll get the official copy by mail."

"Merci," Haylee said softly, and the woman gave her the slightest smile in return.

Haylee exhaled as she stepped back from the counter, clutching the stamped form like a fragile relic.

"That's it?" she said, half-laughing.

"Paperwork always feels underwhelming," David said from behind her. "Until it changes everything."

They stepped outside into the sunlight, the air warmer now, the wind carrying a hint of city smells—coffee, exhaust, a bakery down the block.

Haylee looked down at the receipt, then up at the sky.

She had no idea what was coming next.

But for the first time, she felt like she might actually be allowed to find out.

Sam leaned in. "You okay?"

She nodded. "Yeah. It's just... kind of surreal."

David clapped her gently on the shoulder. "That's because you just made yourself real on paper."

Haylee held the stamped receipt between her fingers, looking down at it, then back toward the road ahead.

For once, the road wasn't just something to run from the past.

It was a place to stand and face it.

Chapter Thirty-Seven:
Stamped and Seen

Back in the Jeep, with the stamped receipt tucked safely in Haylee's bag, the group made their way out of the city.

As they passed the green welcome sign for their campground's exit, Riles tapped his phone and held it to his ear. "I'm calling Dan," he said to Haylee.

"Need to make sure we can use the office address for your birth certificate."

Haylee nodded, still a little dazed from the weight of the morning.

Riles spoke casually but clearly when Dan picked up.

"Salut Dan, c'est Riles. J'ai une petite question pour toi… On attend un document officiel pour Haylee. Est-ce qu'elle peut recevoir du courrier ici, au bureau du camping?"

A pause.

Haylee could hear Dan's voice faintly through the speaker, his usual no-nonsense gruffness softened just a bit.

"Yeah, that's no problem," Riles relayed. "He says they hold guest mail behind the desk. We can check in once or twice a week."

"Thank you," Haylee said quietly.

"Don't thank me," Riles said, grinning. "You're the one becoming legal."

The Bell Above the Door

The shop smelled of sage and stories.

Haylee stepped inside first, the bell above the door giving a soft chime. Sam followed close behind, with David and Ray just behind him. Riles stayed beside Haylee, alert but relaxed as he led them deeper into the cozy, candlelit shop tucked between a boulangerie and an apothecary.

Mireille looked up from behind the counter. Her dark eyes lit with recognition.

"Ah, là voilà," she said softly, stepping out from behind the counter. "La fille avec les yeux d'orage."

Haylee didn't catch all the words, but she felt them. The tone was warm, familiar, and a little reverent.

"She said you've got storm eyes," Riles whispered with a faint grin. "And that you came back."

Mireille approached and took Haylee's hands gently, then stepped back and gestured to the round table near the back. "Venez. We talk."

The others fanned out quietly through the space. David hovered near a shelf of incense, Ray leaned on the edge of a windowsill, and Sam sat on a bench near the wall—but all kept their focus on the conversation unfolding.

Mireille settled into one of the chairs and motioned for Haylee and Riles to sit opposite her. She lit a cone of incense in a small dish and murmured something under her breath.

Riles translated in a low tone, "She's asking the space to hold what's true."

Once the smoke began to curl, Mireille folded her hands and looked at Haylee.

"You feel it now, oui?" she asked in her lilting accent. "Il est proche. Le voile... c'est fragile."

"She says you can feel Elliot," Riles explained. "The Veil is thin again."

Haylee nodded, her voice quiet. "Yeah. We do."

"On dirait qu'il revient," Riles added. "Ou ben, il essaie."
("We think he's coming back—or trying to.")

Mireille gave a slow, grave nod. "La cérémonie n'a pas tenu," she said. "Parce que Margot... elle m'a laissé ça." She pointed to the pendant Haylee was wearing.

Mireille touched it reverently. "Non. C'est plus vieux que Margot. Mais elle le portait. Elle savait ce qu'il était."

"She said it's older than Aggie. But Aggie wore it—and knew exactly what it was," Riles translated.

Mireille continued, "Le médaillon... et le pendentif. Ensemble, ils gardent le sceau. Séparés... le sort est faible."

"The pendant and the medallion have to be together," Riles said. "That's why the banishment failed."

Haylee stared at the pendant, heart racing. "She left it with you on purpose."

Mireille nodded solemnly. "Pour te protéger. Trop tôt... le pouvoir attire l'ombre. Elle a attendu."

"She did it to protect you," Riles explained. "If she'd given you both too soon, it would've drawn Elliot back faster."

From the bench, Sam finally spoke. "Then what do we do now?"

Mireille looked at Haylee, then at the pendant. "Tu choisis. You begin. C'est le moment."

Haylee hesitated. "I don't know where to start. Any of this. I don't know how."

"Alors tu apprends," Mireille said simply. "Je vais t'aider. Margot voulait ça. Elle m'a laissé d'autres choses."

"She said: 'Then you learn.' And she'll help," Riles translated. "Aggie left more behind for you."

Mireille reached beneath the table and returned with a small key and a folded paper. "Une maison. En dehors de la ville. Elle l'a achetée avec Elliot. Avant... tout ça."

"She says there's a house. Outside the city. Aggie bought it with Elliot—before things went dark."

Haylee stared at the key in her hand, then opened the folded paper. It was a map. Hand-drawn. The ink faded but still legible.

"She left me a house?" Haylee whispered.

"She left you something safe," Riles said. "Maybe more."

Mireille's voice softened. "Ce lieu... te parlera. Va. Écoute. Reviens."

"She says: Go. Listen. Come back."

"Les ombres n'aiment pas la lumière," she said with a faint smile. "Mais toi... tu brilles déjà."

"She said the shadows don't like the light," Riles murmured. "But you? You're already shining."

Grease and Grace

The familiar neon glow of the restaurant flickered against the dusky sky, just as it had the last time they'd stopped here. The savory smell hit them as soon as they stepped inside—fried onions, rich gravy, and a hint of malt vinegar in the air.

Ray clapped his hands together as they approached the counter. "Oh yeah. This is the place. I've been dreaming about that poutine."

"You've had it twice," Riles said, smirking.

"Exactly," Ray shot back. "And once was all it took."

They slid into a booth near the window while Riles ordered at the counter. Within minutes, the table was full—stacked burgers, bottles of cold soda, and four large trays of poutine. One sat between Haylee and Sam, already steaming, the gravy soaking into the fries in perfect proportions. Ray, Riles, and David each had their own—because, as Ray declared, "Some things are too sacred to share."

Haylee forked a cheese curd and passed it to Sam, who caught it with a grin.

"Mmm-hmm," Haylee said, already going back in for another bite. "I get why Ray wouldn't want to share."

Across the booth, Ray was in poutine heaven. "Look, I'm not saying I'm an expert or anything, but this? This could convert a man."

David chuckled. "Let's not get ahead of ourselves. You still called it 'gravy fries' yesterday."

"Out loud?" Ray asked, suddenly alarmed. "I thought that was an inside thought."

Riles leaned back in his chair, sipping a soda.

Haylee and Sam exchanged a look, their laughter easy and warm. For a moment, everything felt normal. Not simple—but grounded. Like the weight of the day had been temporarily lifted by the magic of good food and old habits.

But Sam's gaze lingered on her a beat longer than usual, and she knew what was coming.

"You really want to do this?" he asked softly, his voice low enough to stay between them.

Haylee nodded. "I do. Mireille made it clear—it's not just about Elliot. It's about finishing what Aggie started."

Sam's eyes held hers. "I'm with you. Just… be careful, okay? I know what you're stepping into is bigger than either of us."

"I'm not alone," she reminded him, brushing her foot lightly against his under the table.

"No," he said, squeezing her hand. "You're not."

David looked over just then and raised his glass. "To unexpected second chances —and second helpings."

They all lifted their drinks, clinking the glasses together in a casual, unspoken agreement.

Outside, the sky had shifted to twilight, painted in soft streaks of blue and pink. The restaurant buzzed with quiet conversation and the sound of cutlery against ceramic.

Haylee glanced down at the half-finished tray between her and Sam, then out the window toward the road ahead.

But tonight, there was still room for one more bite.

The House That Waited

The road narrowed as they drove farther from the city, weaving through thick forest where the trees leaned in close, their branches arching overhead like a canopy. Even the GPS seemed unsure, blinking twice before rerouting with a stubborn "recalculating."

"This place better be real," Ray muttered from the back seat, craning his neck to peer out the window.

"It's real," Haylee said quietly, staring down at the faded map Mireille had handed her earlier. The curves and marks on the paper were too intentional to be fiction. The Jeep hit a gravel turnoff with a jolt, dust swirling behind them. As they rounded a bend, the trees suddenly parted—and there it was.

The house sat half-hidden under a blanket of moss and wildflowers, vines curling up its outer walls like nature had tried to reclaim it but thought better of it. A crooked chimney leaned slightly to one side. The windows, though old, were intact. Shutters hung like quiet sentinels.

It looked like no one had touched it in decades.

But as they stepped out of the Jeep, something shifted—just like it had at the cabin.

Haylee paused near the steps, her boots crunching over gravel. The air felt different—denser, maybe, but calm. Like the house had been waiting for her.

Riles walked slowly around the front, then stopped. "Huh."

"What is it?" Sam asked.

"I can't go any further," he said. "Something's blocking me."

"She made it so nothing could break in?" Haylee asked.

Riles nodded. "Or break out. Either way, you're the one with the key."

Haylee reached into her pocket and pulled it out. The brass was worn smooth, but it still glinted in the filtered sunlight. She stepped onto the first stair— nothing stopped her. No warning hum. No resistance. The lock clicked easily.

Inside, it was still.

Dust floated like fine snowflakes in the filtered beams of light cutting through thick curtains. A faint herbal scent lingered—sage, lavender, something earthy and grounding. The furniture was old but in perfect order: a floral armchair with a folded quilt, a tall bookshelf filled with worn spines, and a stone hearth with neatly stacked logs beside it.

Everything was clean.

Untouched, yet lived-in. Like someone had only just stepped out for tea.

"Did someone... keep this up?" Sam asked, his voice hushed.

"No," Riles said slowly. "I think... this place keeps itself."

"Magic," Haylee whispered.

Sam whistled softly. "She's not wrong." He looked around. "I can feel something."

In the small kitchen, Haylee ran her fingers over the countertop. Glass jars lined the shelves, labeled in flowing script—herbs, dried flowers, salts.

"She was preparing this for me," Haylee said. "Even if she didn't know how or when."

Sam came up behind her and wrapped his arms around her waist. "It's yours now."

"You mean *ours*," she said, smiling at him. "I don't even know what to do with it."

"Then take your time figuring it out."

Behind them, Riles had found a wooden box on the mantel. He tapped the lid. "You'll want to look through this later. Looks like journal pages. Some in Aggie's handwriting."

Haylee's breath caught. "Add it to the stack."

David exhaled and stepped back toward the door. "Let's give the house a minute. Let Haylee sit with it."

They trickled outside one by one.

Haylee remained behind, standing in the center of the room.

The house held stillness like a secret.

And for the first time, she didn't feel like she was trespassing in Aggie's life.

She felt like she was being welcomed into her own.

Haylee moved quietly through the rooms, letting the house guide her. Each step brought a new discovery: a narrow hallway lined with candleholders; a pantry with perfectly stacked jars and tins; a closet stuffed full of candles, bundles of dried herbs, and woven cloths dyed in deep indigos and rust.

She found bookshelves tucked into nearly every corner, their titles scrawled in French or Quebecois—topics ranging from energy work and herbal remedies to journals with no title at all. A few were dog-eared. Others had slips of paper peeking out like breadcrumbs.

In one small bedroom, she paused at a dresser where a series of framed photos stood in a neat row. Haylee reached out, fingertips brushing the edge of the wood. One photo showed Aggie—Margot—smiling in a way Haylee hadn't seen before. Unburdened. Younger. Another showed Elliot beside her, arm slung casually over her shoulders. The early years. Before Haylee. Before everything broke.

She let the house reveal itself.

Every now and then, that familiar buzzing sensation rose—small pings in the air, like static in her chest. Some were faint, like distant echoes. Others bloomed stronger, curling around her ribs and lighting up her senses like tiny sparks. But by now, she was used to them.

She didn't flinch. She didn't panic. She felt alive when it happened.

She crouched near a worn trunk in one of the smaller rooms and lifted the lid. Inside were boxes labeled in French, contents unknown. Something told her this place would keep giving, if she let it. If she was patient.

Standing again, she turned slowly, letting the energy of the house settle around her like a blanket. It wasn't just a building. It was a memory. A talisman. A piece of Aggie that hadn't been taken by the Veil.

And maybe, a piece of Haylee too.

She wasn't ready to give up the road, not yet. Bertha was still home. This house didn't change that. But it gave her something else—something rooted. Something waiting.

She didn't know how to make sense of it, not yet.

There was training ahead. Hard truths. Elliot.

But right now, she let herself exhale. Deeply. Fully.

The house wasn't asking her to figure it all out.

It was just asking her to be here.

Smoke before the Fire

Haylee walked out the house, locking the door behind her - an action that quietly reset the wards surrounding it.

The Jeep pulled into the campground just as the sky shifted from golden to gray. No one spoke during the ride back—not out of tension, but out of reverence. There were too many thoughts to sort through and not enough words to shape them.

Haylee sat in the passenger seat, turning the brass key over in her hand. Its hum had quieted now that the door was sealed, the wards resetting with a near-audible thrum. Sam kept glancing at her—not out of worry, but because something had changed. Was changing. He could feel it like a new current in the air. Magic didn't just buzz around Haylee anymore. It resonated through her.

She wasn't the only one shifting. Sam was starting to recognize the feeling too— that subtle tug in his gut, like being nudged by an unseen wind. It made sense now. Why Bertha felt alive. Why Bella always seemed to know what no one else did.

As they pulled up beside the RV, Ray climbed out and immediately began scanning the perimeter. Haylee unlocked the RV, and Josie jumped down to greet them, tail wagging. But as Ray passed under the steps with his handheld scanner, a sharp beep pierced the quiet.

"Another one," he muttered, crouching. "Under the damn steps this time. Nearly missed it."

The others gathered around as he pulled the tiny device loose from the undercarriage.

"That explains the blood," David said. "He probably cut himself planting it."

"We still can't prove it," Riles added, scanning the rest of the frame.

"Not yet," Ray replied, holding up the device like a trophy. "But we're not waiting for another visit."

He and Riles got to work installing the magnetized security cameras on all four sides of the RV. By the time the last one clicked into place, the group had gathered around the firepit—though no flames danced there yet.

Sam grilled pork chops and hotdogs while Haylee prepped a quick salad and baked beans inside. Josie lay beside Sam on a blanket they'd spread on the gravel, nose twitching as the aroma drifted through the evening air.

The peaceful moment didn't last.

A few lots down, the American man emerged from the fifth wheel, strolling up with a smile that never reached his eyes.

"Hey there, guy," he called, too casually.

Sam looked up, jaw tightening. "Hey."

As the man drew closer, Josie let out a low growl. Her body stiffened, fur rising.

"Josie, what's the matter, girl?" Sam asked. But she didn't settle. Instead, she started barking—loud, sharp, and unrelenting.

The others stepped out of the RV, drawn by the noise. Haylee came outside just as Sam grabbed Josie's collar to keep her from lunging.

"Maybe you otta put that mutt in the rig," the man said, tone turning sharper.

Sam's glare darkened. "She didn't start barking until you walked up. Something you want to tell me?"

"Whoa, what you mean? I just walked up here and your dog wants to take my head off!"

"There's probably a good reason for that," Sam replied flatly. "What happened to your hand?"

284

The man glanced down, then quickly tucked his hand behind his back.

Dan pulled up on his golf cart just then, clipboard in hand. "T'as vu tout le bruit?" he asked, raising an eyebrow. "The barking and yelling?"

"I just came to be neighborly," the man insisted, raising his hands. "And this mutt started barking like it was gonna attack me."

Josie continued to go wild. Ray slipped past and gently ushered her back into the RV. From inside, she kept barking. Bella's low hiss echoed from the window.

Haylee's gaze narrowed as the woman from Montreal appeared beside the man.

Her stomach dropped. "Why were you following me?" she asked, voice cold.

The woman blinked. "Honey, I don't know what you're talking about."

"Lady," Riles cut in, "we all heard you. In the shop in Montreal. Rude as hell. And your brat barreled into me."

Haylee turned to Dan. "I want to report that this man tried to break into our RV yesterday. There's blood on the doorframe. He cut himself doing it."

"Prove it," the man sneered.

"Look at the stain on my rig," Haylee said, pointing. "That's not ours. And look at his hand. He's hiding it because he knows we're right."

Dan's eyes narrowed. "That could be from an animal. Maybe that dog of yours."

"What happened to your hand, sir?" Dan asked.

"I… uh… cut it cleaning fish I caught for supper," the man stammered.

"You have a permit to fish here?" Dan pressed.

"No, but… I uh…"

"We ain't stayin' where we ain't wanted," the woman interrupted, voice sharp as flint.

Dan raised a brow, shifting in his seat. "C'est ça? Not wanted, you say?"

The man shot her a glare, but the damage was done. The group stood in silence, the weight of her words thick in the air like humidity before a storm.

Sam stepped forward slightly, voice calm but clear. "You're right about one thing. You're not wanted here—not near our rig. And not after yesterday."

"You got no proof," the man growled. "No cameras. No witnesses."

"Not yet," Ray said coolly. "But next time you try anything, there'll be more than blood left behind."

"You folks are paranoid," the man spat.

"No," Haylee said. "We're prepared."

Dan tapped his clipboard and looked between the RV sites. "You want to test how long you stay? Be my guest. But you won't like the outcome. I'll be filing this as a formal incident. Campground misconduct. You're on watch. One more complaint, and you'll be removed—no refund."

The man opened his mouth to argue, but the woman tugged at his arm. "Forget it," she muttered. "They ain't worth the trouble."

"You'll regret pokin' around," the man called over his shoulder.

"No," Haylee replied. "You will."

Josie barked again from the RV window. Bella let out a low, guttural hiss—neither one backing down.

Dan gave them one last nod. "I'll check in later. Let me know if they come back near your site."

With that, the cart rolled away, the dust rising behind it like punctuation.

The group stood in silence a beat longer before Ray broke it with a low whistle. "Well. That escalated."

"No kidding," David said. "But Josie knew. She always knows."

Sam nodded slowly, glancing toward the RV. "Good girl," he murmured. "We've got you."

Inside, the air felt heavier—but also protected. The red light on the camera blinked steadily. The tracker was gone.

And for now… the house stood, the rig stood, and so did they.

Eyes in the Dark

The firepit had burned down to faint embers, the pork chops and hotdogs long gone, and the salad bowl picked clean save for a few stray leaves. The group lingered in their camp chairs, eyes scanning the lot every so often, but mostly they just talked. Low conversation. The kind that came after conflict. The kind that said: We're still here.

Riles stood, stretching with a quiet groan. "I'm gonna have a look into our neighbors."

"Which neighbors?" Ray asked, dryly. "The delightful ones who think bleeding on our rig is an icebreaker?"

"Exactly." Riles cracked his neck and headed toward the campground office. "Back in a bit."

Dan was closing up, flipping through a stack of reservation slips behind the desk when the door opened.

Riles walked in, casual but firm. "Got a minute?"

Dan looked up, eyes narrowing just slightly, though he didn't seem surprised. "Pour quoi?"

"I need names," Riles said. "Of the couple in Lot 342. It's official business now."

Dan didn't hesitate. "Bon. I never liked them. Told them too many times about picking up after themselves. Always leave trash by the firepit. And after today?" He grabbed the clipboard and flipped a few pages. "I'll help however I can— especially if it means getting rid of them."

He jotted the names on a sticky note and slid it across the desk.

"Merci," Riles said, folding it and tucking it into his jacket. "Quiet look into their background. Just making sure they are who they say they are."

Dan gave a tight nod. "Let me know if you need anything else. I'll keep an eye on them."

Back at the RV, the others were winding down. Sam and Haylee were cleaning up the last of the dishes inside while David hovered near the front, watching Ray do one final sweep of the camera feeds.

"You sure the signal's solid?" David asked.

Ray nodded. "Crystal. I've got alerts set up for motion after ten. Plus, I synced Sam's phone so he can watch the feed even when we're not here."

"Good." David exhaled. "That helps me sleep a little easier."

Sam stepped out of the RV and double-checked the lock before pulling his phone from his pocket. The app blinked to life with four camera angles, each one clear and steady.

"Nice," he said, impressed. "I've got eyes on Bertha now."

"Which means I don't have to babysit both properties," Ray added. "Still got the cabin on mine."

Riles returned not long after, flipping the sticky note over in his hand before pocketing it again. "Got what I needed," he said quietly, then looked around at the group. "Let's give it until midnight. Just in case."

No one argued.

The Jeep crew stayed up, watching and waiting. The Americans didn't make a move, but that didn't mean they weren't watching, too. The campground settled into stillness, frogs calling in the distance, and the occasional car crunching over gravel somewhere far off.

Inside the RV, Bella curled up in the dashboard nook, her eyes flicking toward every shadow outside. Josie lay just under the table, ears twitching at every creak.

Eventually, Sam and Haylee turned in and the Jeep crew left for the apartment. The last porch light clicked off.

And outside, in the hush of night, the red lights on the cameras blinked steadily.

Watching.

Waiting.

Prepared.

Chapter Thirty-Eight:
The Morning Knows

Riles stood by the window of the apartment, bathed in the pale hush of early morning. The clock on the stove blinked 4:32 AM. His voice was low, almost a growl, as he spoke into the phone.

"Harry and Mable Combs," he said, fingers resting on the glass as he watched the faint light of the city glow in the distance. "From Dothan, Alabama. Yeah. I need everything. Cross-check aliases too—just in case."

There was a long pause while he listened, nodding silently to no one.

"Got it. Let me know what you find."

He hung up and let the phone drop to the counter beside him. Outside, the faintest shade of blue was beginning to climb up the sky, dissolving the last grip of night.

Behind him, the sound of footsteps shuffled across the floor.

David stepped into the kitchen and started the coffee without saying a word. Ray followed behind, still in a hoodie, rubbing the sleep from his eyes.

"Everything okay?" David asked, voice scratchy with sleep but clear with concern.

Riles nodded once. "Just called in a favor. A buddy of mine owed me one."

"You get anything yet?"

"Names are real. From Dothan. He's checking deeper databases now, looking for records, priors, affiliations. Anything that might explain why they're snooping around here."

David poured two mugs and slid one toward Riles, who accepted it with a grunt of thanks.

Ray leaned against the fridge. "I don't like that guy."

"No one does," Riles muttered. "But we're not just going off vibes anymore."

David sipped his coffee, looking toward the window. "You think they're working for him?"

"I think they're either scouting or stupid. But it's not a coincidence."

They stood in quiet for a moment, listening to the drip of the coffee maker and the occasional creak from the floorboards overhead.

"I didn't know Aggie had property up here," David finally said.

"She probably didn't want anyone to." Riles said.

David nodded slowly. "Makes sense. But it means something. If Haylee was born here, and Aggie left that house behind, it's hers now. All of it."

Ray frowned. "You think they're after the house?"

"I think they're after what's inside it," David said. "Or what it protects."

Riles turned to face him, his expression firm. "You want me to stay close while Haylee is training?"

David nodded. "Yeah. Just in case. Mireille's got a good eye, but Haylee's still finding her footing. I need someone watching the rest while I focus on her."

"You got it," Riles said. "I'll be the shadow in the trees."

David cracked a small, tired smile. "That's exactly what I was counting on."

As the sky outside lightened, the air in the apartment felt sharper—more awake. They didn't need to say more. The day was coming, and with it, whatever truths or trouble waited just beyond the veil.

And the morning…
The morning already knew.

Back at the campground, the light was still soft and blue as Sam eased himself upright in the bed, careful not to wake Haylee. He padded quietly into the front of the RV, the camera feed already open on his phone.

All four corners blinked red on the screen. Still recording. Still steady. Still silent. He flipped through the night's playback. Nothing but shadows, branches swaying, and a few curious raccoons sniffing near the firepit. No signs of the fifth wheel couple—or anyone else.

"You know," came a soft voice behind him, "a watched pot never boils."

Sam nearly dropped his phone. "Jeez—don't sneak up on me like that."

Haylee wrapped her arms around his waist from behind and rested her cheek against his back. "You're not exactly subtle when you sneak out of bed at dawn with security footage on full brightness."

"Yeah, well," he muttered, locking the screen, "I just wanted to see if anything happened."

She peeked over his shoulder at the phone. "And?"

"Couple animals. One squirrel that might've been possessed, based on how long it stared into the camera. But nothing human."

Haylee exhaled, still holding him. "Good."

The silence that followed was a different kind of heavy—anticipation. She could feel it building in her chest like the weather.

"I'm a little nervous," she admitted.

Sam turned in her arms, looking at her closely. "About today?"

She nodded. "I don't know what I'm walking into with Mireille.

294

I know she's powerful… but she told me to bring the medallion and the pendant. That feels like a big deal."

"It is a big deal," he said, brushing a thumb along her cheek. "But so are you."

Haylee smiled faintly. "You're not coming this time."

"Nope. Just you and Riles."

She pulled back slightly, giving him a teasing look. "So what are you guys gonna do while I'm gone? Build a treehouse? Join Dan's Neighborhood Watch?"

"Who knows," Sam said with a smirk. "We might just drink cheap beer and roast hotdogs with Dan until we forget how to pronounce our own names."

Haylee laughed and gave him a playful shove. "Well, don't have too much fun without me."

"No promises."

She walked toward the bedroom to get dressed, tossing a flirty glance over her shoulder—and Sam stood there frozen for a moment before following her. The laughter faded, replaced with something quieter, deeper. Something just theirs. The world would still be there.

Afterward, they lay tangled together in the dim morning light, a shared silence stretching between them. Not awkward. Not uncertain. Just full. And grounding. Eventually, Haylee sat up and pulled her clothes on, reaching for her hoodie and sliding the pendant around her neck. Sam was already up, lacing his boots.

Her phone buzzed on the table.

Riles:
"Be there in an hour."

She read it, nodded, and looked up at Sam. "Guess we've got time for a walk."

Outside, the campground was peaceful again. The mist had burned off, leaving damp grass and crisp edges on the air. Josie trotted ahead of them on her leash, tail swaying, nose twitching at every pine needle and squirrel track.

Haylee's thoughts swirled like leaves in a current, but Sam's hand in hers kept her tethered.

"You've got this," he said as they circled back toward the RV. "Whatever it is."

Haylee looked at him—really looked—and nodded.

She believed him.

Lessons in Stillness

The scent hit her first.

Lavender, cedar, sage, and something almost sweet—like rosewater carried on old wooden beams. The shop had a stillness to it, despite the bustle just outside on the cobblestone street. The moment Haylee crossed the threshold, it felt like the space exhaled around her.

Jean-Paul nodded from behind the front counter, sorting tiny glass vials and dried bundles with practiced ease. When the back room door creaked open, he gave her a knowing smile.

"Elle vous attend," he said softly. "She's waiting for you."

Riles held the curtain aside for Haylee as he grabbed an old French magazine from a basket.

"Elle est à l'arrière. Fais pas attention à elle. Elle est dans l'un de ses coups de gueule," Jean-Paul muttered.

"She's in the back. Don't let her scare you. She's in one of her intense moods," Riles translated.

Haylee raised a brow. "Intense how?"

"Elle a déjà fait bouillir deux cafetières de chicorée et a commencé à chanter avant même que je m'asseye."

"She already brewed two pots of chicory and started chanting before I even sat down," he added.

"Well. That's… comforting," Haylee murmured, brushing the curtain aside.

Mireille stood barefoot in the center of the room, surrounded by soft candlelight and chalk markings on the wooden floor. She looked up sharply, eyes catching the light like glass.

Her energy wasn't harsh—just deeply present. Focused. She gave Haylee a small nod.

"Ferme la porte doucement," she instructed, voice thick with her accent. "Close the door softly."

Haylee obeyed.

The back room was small but sacred. An altar stood in the corner, adorned with faded photos, small stones, flower petals, and incense coils still releasing smoke. A copper bowl of water sat nearby, unmoving despite the draft.

"Viens. Sit," Mireille said, pointing to the cushion across from her. "You bring les objets?"

Haylee reached into her crossbody bag and pulled out the pendant and the medallion. Together, they seemed to pulse faintly in her palm.

"Bon," Mireille whispered, eyes softening. "Ça, c'est bien. We will begin now."

Haylee sat cross-legged on the cushion and placed the objects between them. Riles stayed near the curtain, thumbing through his magazine with one leg crossed over the other—present but distant, her translator and quiet protector when needed.

Mireille took a deep breath and began, slipping seamlessly between languages as if walking between worlds.

"Tu es trop tendue. You must learn... stillness. Magic is not loud. C'est comme le vent—soft... or sharp... but never wasted."

She guided Haylee to close her eyes and began a slow rhythm of breathwork: four counts in, four counts held, four counts out. Mireille's hands never touched her, but Haylee could feel the air shift with each gesture, like she was drawing threads from the space between them.

"Magic is in le silence," Mireille said softly. "In the pause. You do not pull from it. You become it."

Haylee let herself relax. Her body grew heavy, grounded. Her thoughts slowed. With each breath, something shifted—not huge, but real. A small current brushed her skin. A vibration behind her ribs.

Mireille opened her palm and let a single beeswax candle flicker into a larger flame without touching it. She nodded toward it.

"Tu essayes. Try."

Haylee focused, exhaling slowly—not with force, but with presence. She imagined her energy not as fire, but as light, waiting to be invited.

The candle shimmered.

Just a flicker, but real.

Her eyes widened. "Did I—?"

"Oui," Mireille said firmly. "But doucement. You burn too fast if you do not learn to... hold. You are like matchstick." She mimed the gesture of a flare igniting and vanishing. "We teach you to be lantern."

Just then, Haylee tried again but accidentally knocked the candle over.

From the front room, the sound carried—a customer looked to the door. Jean-Paul's voice carried out with calm amusement. "C'est un vieux bâtiment! It's just the building settling!"

Haylee smiled faintly. Riles chuckled behind his magazine.

Mireille picked up the candle and holder, offering Haylee a small, reassuring smile. Baby steps.

After the breathwork, Mireille showed her how to bind a simple ward using herbs, thread, and intention.

It was a charm to hang discreetly near the RV door—one that would vibrate slightly if someone approached with ill intent.

"You feel de hum?" Mireille asked, passing it to her.

Haylee nodded. "Yeah… like a warning bell. Low but steady."

"Good. This one is simple. When you learn more, we do stronger. But this will hold. It listens for you."

Haylee held the charm close, suddenly emotional. Not because of the spell—but because of what it meant.

"I never imagined I'd ever learn this," she whispered.

Mireille's face softened. "Mais tu es née pour ça. You were born for this."

The candle beside her flickered again.

Under Bertha's Belly

By 8:30 a.m., the sun had finally crested high enough to warm the gravel lot outside the RV. Birds chirped lazily from the trees nearby, and a breeze rustled the leaves just enough to keep the mosquitoes guessing.

Sam crouched under Bertha, tugging open the storage compartment with a grunt. "Alright, gentlemen," he called, "today's agenda: cleaning out Bertha's belly."

David groaned but grabbed the edge of a dusty bin anyway. "How'd I get roped into this again?"

"You said—and I quote—'I don't mind helping if you need a hand,'" Sam said, pointing a gloved finger at him.

Ray smirked, already hauling out a tub labeled Cables & Tools – Aggie. "I believe that's legal consent to manual labor."

"I was bribed," David said, brushing a cobweb off his arm. "Beer and pizza. Who can say no to beer and pizza?"

Sam grinned. "Exactly."

They worked their way through bins of mismatched clothes, camping gear, rusted tools, spare parts, and at least two mystery items none of them could confidently identify. Josie lay nearby on a blanket, her head resting on her paws, content to supervise. Bella had claimed her usual perch inside the sink, her tail twitching as if silently judging the entire operation.

Around 9:00 a.m., Dan rolled up in his cart, clipboard under one arm. He stopped short when he saw the small mountain of clutter surrounding Bertha.

"Mon dieu," he said with a whistle. "You guys building a second RV out here?"

"Just liberating the undercarriage," Sam said, wiping sweat from his brow.

"Just liberating the undercarriage," Sam said, wiping sweat from his brow.

"You want to hang out later?" he asked, leaning casually on the cart. "We're thinking pizza and beer this afternoon. I know you get off at two."

Dan lit up. "I do, actually. And I know the best place to order from. Real Quebec-style pies. They even deliver here."

"That's a win," Ray said, pushing a heavy bin toward the firepit.

Dan nodded approvingly at their progress. "I'll swing back after work. Maybe bring a six-pack."

"Deal," Sam said, lifting a bin triumphantly. "It's gonna be the most productive lazy day we've had all week."

Dan chuckled and rolled off, the sound of his tires fading as the group returned to the mess. The sun climbed higher, casting warm light through the open RV door where Bella stretched luxuriously.

Inside and out, Bertha buzzed with motion—but in the way a home does when it's being tended to. Cared for. Reclaimed.

And under her belly, friendships settled deeper into their grooves, the kind only built by sweat, shared grumbles, and the promise of pizza.

Chapter Thirty-Nine
Rewards and Laughter

By the time Dan's golf cart rumbled back into the lot, the bins were stacked neatly by the RV, the dust had been swept away, and Bertha's underbelly looked cleaner than it had in years. Sam wiped his hands on a rag, grinning like they'd just rebuilt her from the frame up.

Dan hopped out of the cart with a cardboard carrier of sweating beer bottles in one hand and two large pizza boxes balanced in the other. "Fresh from town," he announced. "One pepperoni, one all-dressed. Don't make me regret sharing." David leaned against the picnic table, cracking open a beer. "You had me at 'all-dressed.'"

Ray grabbed paper plates from the RV while Sam popped the lids on the boxes, letting the steam curl into the cool afternoon air. "Alright, dig in before Bella decides the pepperoni's hers."

They ate in that easy way friends do when work is behind them and there's nothing pressing ahead. Josie sprawled in the grass, tail thumping whenever someone dropped a crust her way.

Dan took a long pull from his beer and gestured toward the stack of cleaned-out bins. "So, what's the verdict? Find anything worth keeping?"

"Half a roll of duct tape, three mismatched socks, and a wrench older than me," Sam said.

"And a travel mug from a diner in Oregon," Ray added. "No lid, but somehow still full of coffee."

David chuckled. "Aggie was a collector, alright."

"Collector or borderline hoarder?" Sam asked, smirking.

"Potato, potahto," David said, raising his bottle in a mock toast.

The afternoon drifted by on the hum of light conversation—half about nothing, half about stories from the road. Dan told them about a camping couple who once tried to smuggle a goat into their site. Ray countered with the time he and Riles accidentally slept in a parking lot that turned into a farmers' market overnight.

By the time the sun began to dip toward the trees, the pizza was gone, the beer was light, and laughter had settled into a comfortable quiet.

Sam leaned back on the bench, catching the soft gold light on Bertha's side. "Not a bad way to spend a day off."

Dan nodded. "The best kind. Nothing urgent, just good company."

They all sat there a moment longer, content to let the evening come to them.

Seeds of the Work

Haylee stood, stretching her legs after hours cross-legged on the cushion. The small ward charm dangled from her fingers, still warm from her hands and the herbs woven into it.

"Merci, Mireille," she said softly. "I'll keep practicing."

Mireille's eyes softened, though her voice kept its steady weight. "Oui... practice every day. But remember—ce n'est pas juste comment faire... it is not just how to perform. You must know why. You must feel each part of the ritual... here." She tapped her chest, then her temple. "When you understand both... alors tu es prête—then you are ready."

Haylee nodded, absorbing each word. "I'll get there."

"You will," Mireille said firmly. "Ton voyage... your journey... is only beginning."

Riles stepped forward, slipping the magazine under his arm. "Alright, rookie witch," he said with a small smirk, "let's feed you before you faint."

They stepped out into the street, the scents of lavender and cedar trailing faintly from the shop door before it closed. Outside, the air was warmer now, the bustle of the cobblestone street in full swing.

They found a café tucked between two narrow buildings—one of those places with mismatched chairs and chalkboard menus that felt like it had been there forever. Lunch was quiet, both of them eating without much small talk, their thoughts following separate trails. For Haylee, it wasn't worry anymore—it was curiosity, and the strange comfort of knowing she was finally on the right path. The ride back to the campground was the same. No heavy words. No rush. Just the hum of the road and the silent understanding that something had shifted today.

What lay ahead of her was more than any of them could imagine. But Haylee knew this much—she was tougher than she'd ever given herself credit for. And resilient enough to keep going, no matter what waited down the road.

The campground was humming softly when Riles eased the Jeep into the lot. Sam and David were still out by the picnic table with Dan, empty pizza boxes stacked like trophies between them and a cooler resting on the grass. The smell of grilled peppers and charred crust lingered in the air. Josie trotted over immediately, tail wagging like they'd been gone for weeks.

"Hey," Sam called, standing as Haylee climbed out. "You survive your first day of witch school?"

Haylee grinned, holding up the ward charm. "Not only survived—graduated the beginner's class."

They swapped quick stories as the group gathered. Sam recapped the monumental task of clearing out Bertha's belly and the real challenge of not getting buried under a landslide of Aggie's old tools. Dan bragged about picking the perfect pizza order. Haylee told them about Mireille's breathwork, the candle flame exercise, and the way it felt when she finally got that first flicker.

David's eyes softened while she spoke. He'd been against her learning like this at first—thought it should have been Aggie guiding her. But watching her now, hands animated as she described every step, he realized it didn't matter. She wasn't late. She wasn't behind. Whoever taught her, she was meant for this, and he was just glad she had someone skilled and trustworthy to guide her.

"Alright," Haylee said, pulling a candle from the RV. "You wanna see?"

They gathered around the table as she set it down and took a steadying breath. The first try—just a faint spark. The second—a quick shimmer before it fizzled out. Sam leaned in, eyes bright. "That was bigger than last time."

David noticed it too. Each attempt, the spark held just a fraction longer. Not frustration—determination. Every miss was another chance to try again.

Dan leaned back in his chair, watching Haylee with mild curiosity as she cupped her hands over the candle. He didn't say anything—just tilted his head slightly when the wick sparked once, twice, then caught for a split second.

His eyes flicked to Sam, then David, as if silently asking what exactly he'd just witnessed. But no one offered an explanation, and Dan, being the sort who knew when not to push, just cracked open another beer. Whatever it was, it was clearly between them.

"Alright, one more before dinner," she said, and this time, the candle caught for a second—just enough for everyone to see the flame before it went out.

"Not bad," Riles said, impressed despite himself.

"Think I could use this on the grill?" Haylee teased. She walked over, focusing on the ignition, but the second the flame popped up, it flared—fast and hot. She jerked back, laughing.

"Okay, fire-starter," Sam said, grinning as he brushed an imaginary singe from her hair, "time to take a break before we have to explain missing eyebrows."

"Fine, fine," she laughed, raising her hands in surrender.

As the evening settled in, Haylee could still feel it—that hum inside her. The more she practiced, the more awake she felt. And the others could feel it too. Not just in her magic, but in her.

Her training had only just begun. But the spark was already there.

At lot 342, the woman in the neighboring fifth wheel scrubbed at a frying pan in the tiny sink when she heard the burst of laughter. "Harry, some weird shit's going on down there at the lot—you need to come see," Mable called.

Harry emerged from the back, wiping his hands on his jeans, and stepped up beside her at the window. His jaw went slack. "What the fuck?"

"Did you know about this?" Mable asked, her voice sharp with suspicion.

"Hell no. Nobody told me a damn thing about magic." Harry yanked his phone from his pocket and dialed. "Yo, Arnie—what the fuck, man? This bitch is doing magic right here in the goddamn campground. No, you didn't tell me. What do we do now?" He paused, pacing as he listened. "Alright."

Mable crossed her arms. "Well? What'd he say?"

"He said we're on a need-to-know basis, and we didn't need to know yet. He'll get back to us on what to do next. For now, we watch from a distance."

"But how can we?" Mable pressed.

"You follow her back to that shop. I'll see if I can get closer to the RV again. We still haven't found what we came for, and I'm not giving up just because she can light a damn candle."

Grabbing the cooler of beer, Harry stepped outside, his face hard. The late summer evening wrapped around the campground, the air thick with barbecue smoke and cicada song. Somewhere in the distance, Haylee's laughter drifted across the lot, oblivious to the eyes—and intentions—locked on her.

Chapter Forty:
Morning in Motion

The sun broke over the treeline in a pale wash of gold, spilling through Bertha's front window and pooling across the worn kitchen counter. The smell of coffee drifted through the RV, carried by the faint hiss of the percolator on the stove.

Haylee stretched beneath the blankets, Josie's cold nose nudging her leg in a gentle but insistent reminder that morning walks were non-negotiable.

Sam's voice floated in from outside. "Morning, sleepyhead." She stepped out barefoot onto the cool gravel, Bella winding between her ankles like a shadow. Sam was folding a camp chair, tucking it against Bertha's side. His hair was a little messy, his T-shirt rumpled in that way that meant he'd been up since sunrise.

"Thinking we should make it a slow one today," he said, stretching his back. "Go into town for lunch, grab a few things for the weekend. The festival's tonight— no need to burn ourselves out before it starts."

Haylee smiled, but the small knot in her chest from the night before hadn't loosened. She still felt the echo of the candle sparks, the hum under her skin. Restless. Eager to try again. But also aware—though she couldn't have said why —that someone might have seen more than she intended.

Sam pulled his phone from his pocket and put it on speaker.

"Morning," Riles' voice answered groggily.

"Hey," Sam said, "thinking today's a take-it-easy day. We're heading into town for supplies and lunch. You guys still good for the festival tonight?"

"Sounds great. We need a few things too. Yeah, as far as we know," Riles replied. "We'll head your way in about an hour."

"Got it." Sam ended the call.

Haylee and Sam took Josie for her morning walk, Bella tagging along this time.

They were just clearing breakfast plates when Riles pulled up in the Jeep outside Bertha.

Across the lot, the blinds on a nearby fifth wheel twitched. Inside, Mable leaned toward the slat. "Harry—Jeep's back."

Harry stepped up beside her, squinting through the gap. "They weren't here last night?"

"Nope. Came back early this morning."

He watched as Haylee and Sam climbed into the back seat next to David. "So, they stayed here alone last night."

He kept watching as the Jeep rolled toward the exit. "And now they're leaving again..."

Mable's tone was sharp. "You want me to follow 'em?"

"Not yet," he muttered, grabbing a can of beer from the counter. "We'll keep an eye on the place while they're gone. Still think whatever we're looking for is in that RV."

What Harry didn't know was that the moment he stepped outside, two tiny cameras hidden under Bertha's awning and near the rear bumper caught him on record.

Before heading into town, the Jeep stopped at the campground office. Dan was behind the counter sorting papers. "Salut. You folks still up for the festival tonight?" he asked, peering over his glasses.

"Can't wait," Sam said. "Need us to bring anything?"

Dan grinned. "If you see any good local cider in town, grab a couple bottles. Goes fast." His gaze flicked briefly toward Haylee, then away again—curiosity in his eyes, but no questions on his lips.

On the way back to the Jeep, Haylee felt the pull of two different currents—one drawing her toward an ordinary day, the other tugging her toward the strange, electric undercurrent of something much bigger.

The day was just beginning. But somewhere, a plan to shadow her had already begun to unfold.

Lists, Lanterns, and Local Stops

By late morning, the Jeep was rolling down the narrow road into town, windows down, summer air carrying the scent of warm pavement and distant river water. Haylee leaned back against the seat, jotting a short list on the notepad she kept tucked in Bertha's kitchen drawer: bread, fresh vegetables, something sweet for later.

Riles parked outside a small strip of shops where the general store sat between a bakery and a place selling paper lanterns and carved wooden trinkets. "Alright," he said, shutting off the engine, "split up or stick together?"

"Stick together," Sam decided. "Less chance of forgetting something… or someone."

Inside the general store, they wove between narrow aisles stocked with everything from fishing lures to jars of maple cream. Ray found a bin of rubber duck keychains and started lining them up on the shelf by color. "It's an art form," he muttered. Riles shot him a grow up look, to which Ray just grinned and rearranged them into a smiley face before walking away.

Riles made a beeline for the coffee section, grabbing two bags of dark French roast like they were rare treasure. Sam picked out a bag of local kettle chips "for research purposes," while Haylee studied a bin of late-season apples, turning each one in her hand like she was weighing more than just its ripeness. David, meanwhile, hovered near the bakery display until the clerk came out with a fresh tray of baguettes. "I'll take three," he said with a grin, tucking them under his arm like prized souvenirs.

At the register, the clerk—a woman with kind eyes and a nametag that read *Claire* —slipped a flyer into their bag. "Festival tonight," she said with a smile. "Lots of music, dancing. You'll like it."

On the way back to the Jeep, they stopped at the bakery for a paper bag of cinnamon twists still warm from the oven. The little lantern shop next door caught Haylee's attention.

She drifted inside, drawn to a pale blue paper globe painted with swirling stars. The shop owner wrapped it carefully, chatting in a mix of English and French that made Haylee's heart twist with curiosity and something she couldn't quite name.

By the time they loaded the Jeep, the scent of bread, coffee, and cinnamon was filling the air. "Supplies acquired," Riles announced, tapping the paper bag. "And maybe a little extra magic." He nodded toward Haylee's lantern, and she just smiled, tucking it safely between the bags.

The ride to the next stop—lunch—was easy, full of small chatter and the kind of silence that doesn't need to be filled. The day was still bright, the festival hours away, but something about their errands felt like a prelude to whatever the night might bring.

Plates and Promises

The café sat on a corner just off the main street, its front windows thrown open to let the breeze carry in the smell of grilled meat and fresh bread. The five of them—Haylee, Sam, David, Riles, and Ray—claimed a table near the open window where they could watch the slow rhythm of town life drift by.

A waitress in a sunflower-print apron brought water and menus, rattling off the specials in a lilting Quebecois accent. "Trust me," she added, "if you try the smoked meat sandwich, you won't regret it."

They didn't.

When the plates came, they were stacked high—rye bread, layers of peppery smoked meat, and a smear of tangy mustard. Riles gave an approving nod, already halfway through his first bite. Ray, not to be outdone, leaned back dramatically after his first taste.

"If I die right now, at least I've lived."

Riles shot him another grow up look, though the corner of his mouth twitched. David tore into his sandwich like it was a challenge, pausing only to break off pieces of pickle and slide them onto Haylee's plate.

"You need these," he said, like it was a matter of health, not preference. Sam grinned and swiped one for himself before Haylee could protest.

The conversation wove between light teasing and the evening ahead—how long they might stay at the festival, whether they'd dance, if they could find Dan once the music started.

"Think he'll make good on that cider request?" Haylee asked.

"He's probably already got a stash tucked somewhere." Sam chuckled.

By the time the plates were cleared and the coffee refilled, the afternoon had softened into that golden pocket of time when it's too late for more errands but too early to call it a day.

"We head back now," Riles said, glancing toward the door, "we'll have time to unload and maybe relax a bit before we follow Dan to the festival."

The plan was simple—return to the campground, stash their finds, meet Dan when he came by. But as they stepped out into the sun, Haylee caught herself glancing down the quiet street, a flicker of unease sliding through her chest. It passed quickly, replaced by the easy chatter of the group as they made their way back to the Jeep.

Whatever the night held, for now, it was enough to have full bellies, good company, and the promise of music under the stars.

Festival Lights and Faint Shadows

Back at the campground, the Jeep rolled into its spot with the easy rumble of a day well spent. The air was cooler now, the heat of the afternoon giving way to the crisp promise of evening. Bertha sat steady and quiet, her awning catching the last streaks of sunlight.

David unloaded the baguettes first, while Riles carried a brown paper sack that smelled faintly of French roast coffee. Ray, hands free, twirled one of the empty paper cups from lunch like a basketball until Riles snatched it away.

"Dude, really?" Riles muttered—more reflex than reprimand.

Sam and Haylee stashed the groceries inside Bertha, Josie padding behind them, curious about the new scents. Bella hopped onto the counter, eyeing the baguettes as if she had every right to them.

Dan pulled up in his truck forty-five minutes later, window down, elbow hanging casually over the door. "Prêt pour un peu de musique? Ready for some music?" he asked.

"Oh yeah," Riles replied, grabbing his keys off the picnic table.

"Ready for cider," David added, earning a laugh from Dan.

They followed him in the Jeep, winding along back roads as twilight deepened. When they arrived, it was much like other festivals—stretched out like a pocket universe, strings of warm lights draped between poles, the scent of sugar and fried dough in the air. A small stage glowed at the far end, and a trio was tuning instruments—accordion, fiddle, and guitar. The music, when it began, was all French and Quebecois folk, lively enough to keep feet moving without needing to understand a word.

It didn't matter. The vibe was the language.

They sampled cider sharper than expected, swayed with the crowd, and let the rhythm carry them. Haylee caught herself smiling more than once, the hum in her chest still there, but quiet now—tucked into the music like it belonged.

Across town, the campground was still.

The blinds in the fifth wheel shifted, and Harry stepped outside. Mable joined him, arms folded. They waited until the last trace of the Jeep's taillights disappeared down the road before moving. This was their chance.

Harry glanced toward Bertha, calculating. "Let's see what they're hiding," he muttered.

What they didn't know—what they couldn't know—was that the moment they stepped into frame, two tiny cameras under Bertha's awning and near the bumper came to life, sending a silent ping to Sam's phone.

In the middle of the festival, surrounded by music and light, Sam's pocket buzzed. He glanced down, the easy smile fading.

"Uh, guys…" he started, already turning toward Riles.

The night was about to change.

Breaking the Ward

Riles leaned in as Sam showed him the phone screen. The tiny thumbnail from the camera feed left no doubt—Harry and Mable were creeping toward Bertha under the cover of night.

Haylee's expression hardened. "That's our rig," she said flatly, the cider-fueled ease from moments ago already gone.

"They're not just looking," Riles muttered. "They're breaking in."

On the feed, Harry glanced over his shoulder before pulling a small pouch from his jacket. He worked the lock with his good hand, Mable keeping watch as a golf cart passed into a lot on the next lane. A few minutes later—click—the lock gave way.

"They're inside," Sam breathed.

The angle shifted as the rear camera picked them up. Mable tossed two small meatballs just inside the doorway. Josie barked once, sharp and furious, before her voice faltered, dropping to a groggy whimper.

Haylee's stomach dropped. "What did she toss in there?"

"They made sure Josie couldn't get in the way," Riles said quickly, eyes scanning the footage.

"Did they drug her?" Haylee gasped.

"Yeah, pretty much," Sam said, watching Josie lay down.

Inside Bertha, the couple moved with deliberate purpose, pulling open drawers and tossing cushions aside. They searched with a desperate, methodical energy.

The longer they stayed, the more their movements slowed. Mable rubbed her temples, her face paling. Harry coughed—steady at first, then ragged.

"They're getting sick," Sam noted.

Haylee's pulse quickened. "The sachet," she whispered. "The one I hung by the door—it's working."

The two stumbled toward the exit, empty-handed and looking like they'd aged a decade in minutes. Harry muttered something to Mable, who didn't reply, her hand clamped over her mouth. They disappeared into the night.

"That's it," Sam said, already pulling his phone from his pocket. "We're going back—now." He dialed Dan's number.

Dan appeared at their side, his easy grin gone. "I know a guy on the police force," he said. "I'll have him meet us there."

The festival lights blurred into the darkness as they hurried back to the Jeep. No one spoke. The music still played behind them, but the spell of the night had been broken.

When they pulled into the campground, Dan's police friend was already waiting by the office, cruiser lights off but presence unmistakable. The officer met them halfway, listened to Riles' clipped explanation, and reviewed the footage on Sam's phone.

"Merde. That's more than enough," he said, jaw tight.

It didn't take long. The knock on the fifth wheel was firm, the arrest quiet but unmistakable. Harry and Mable were led away in cuffs—burglary, trespassing, and harming an animal. A second police car arrived for the children, who sat wide-eyed and silent in the back seat as the cruiser pulled away.

Haylee knelt beside Josie as soon as they were gone. The dog's eyes fluttered open, groggy but alert. "You're okay," she whispered, stroking her fur. "You're safe now."

In the aftermath, Bertha stood silent but solid, the faint scent of the ward still lingering in the cool night air.

Chapter Forty-One:
Fire in the Veins

Morning came slow, the air outside thick with that damp chill that seeps in after a restless night. Haylee sat at Bertha's table, a half-empty mug of tea cooling in her hands. Josie was sprawled at her feet, still a little groggy but clearly on the mend, tail thumping lazily when Haylee reached down to scratch her ears.

Sam moved quietly in the background, making a point not to hover. The break-in had shaken her—he could see it—but there was also something else in her eyes this morning. Not fear. Not even anger. Determination.

Riles showed up around 9:15, a thin folder tucked under his arm. He gave her a look that said, You good? She gave one back that said, I'm fine, but not really.

"Got some answers," Riles said, dropping the folder on the table. "The Combs? They're small-time thieves—real bottom-feeder stuff. Work freelance for whoever pays."

"Let me guess," Sam said, leaning against the counter, arms crossed. "Whoever's paying now is tied to Elliot."

Riles nodded. "Dummy corporation. Paper trail's a mess, but it all points back to one of his shell companies. My contact says this isn't their first gig like this. They get sent in to poke around, stir the pot, see what they can dig up. Once they find something, it gets handed off to someone higher up the chain."

Haylee's fingers tightened around her mug. "So, they were never here just to annoy us."

"They were here for something specific," Riles confirmed. "And if they couldn't find it, they were supposed to keep looking until they did."

Haylee's gaze flicked to the sachet hanging near Bertha's door, the faint scent of its herbs still in the air. "Well, they can look all they want. They won't find what's mine."

Riles studied her for a moment. "You still going to the shop today?"

"Yeah," Haylee said, sliding her mug into the sink. "If last night proved anything, it's that I'm not just going to wait around for them to make another move. I need to be ready."

Sam gave a small nod. "Then we'll make sure you get there."

Outside, the morning fog clung low to the ground as they climbed into the Jeep. The air was sharp, clean—like the kind of day that dared you to move forward. Haylee didn't look back at Bertha. Her path was pulling her somewhere else now.

By mid-morning, she was standing in front of Mireille's shop again, the little bell on the door chiming as she stepped inside. The space smelled of rosemary and faint woodsmoke, the air warm despite the grey light outside.

"Bonjour, Haylee," Mireille greeted, her voice even softer than usual. "I heard about last night. You are unharmed?"

"I'm fine," Haylee said, but her tone carried an edge. "Bertha's fine. Josie will be okay. But I'm done being caught off guard."

Mireille studied her for a long moment, then nodded. "Bon. Then today, we test your control."

The session began with the breathwork Haylee had practiced before, only now Mireille pushed her further—faster breathing, sharper focus, holding the hum inside her until it felt like her skin was buzzing. A single candle burned on the table between them.

"Again," Mireille instructed. "But this time, you will not chase the spark. You will call it."

Haylee steadied her hands. On the first try, the wick shivered, a small flame catching before it fizzled. On the second, it flared brighter, holding for two heartbeats before dropping to smoke. Mireille's mouth curved in the faintest of smiles.

"Now, your third."

Haylee inhaled deep, letting the air settle low in her belly. She pictured the heat, the pulse of it, curling into her palms. When she exhaled, the flame rose—steady, sharp, and alive. It held until she released it.

The hum inside her swelled, warm and clean, like sunlight breaking through clouds.

Mireille's eyes glinted. "Très bien. You have control now. But control is not the same as power. That will come next."

Haylee didn't answer—she just nodded, but in her chest, the determination burned hotter than the candle. Last night had made one thing clear: she wasn't going to wait for protection. She was going to make her own.

Chapter Forty-Two:
Threads in the Dark

Riles lingered by the Jeep, phone pressed to his ear, the morning sun glinting off the windshield. Sam and Haylee had gone inside Bertha to get Josie settled, but David hung back, loaf of bread under his arm like it was a prized artifact.

"Yeah," Riles said into the phone, voice low. "Got it. Send it to the secure line." He listened, jaw tightening. "No, I'm not surprised. Just… thanks."

He ended the call just as Sam stepped down from Bertha. "That your contact?"

"Yeah," Riles replied, glancing over his shoulder to make sure no one was close enough to hear. "And it's worse than we thought."

They walked toward the picnic table, Ray following with two cups of coffee that smelled like they were brewed for endurance, not taste.

Riles set his phone down. "The Combs weren't freelancing for fun. They're tied to something bigger—a network Elliot's been using for years. My guy says it's layered through dummy corporations, fake charities, shell companies. The Combs are just one pair of hands in a long chain."

"Hands for what?" Haylee asked, reappearing with her tea in hand.

"Finding things," Riles said. "Testing defenses. Seeing how far they can push before someone pushes back." He tapped the table. "They weren't just looking for the medallion or pendant. This was reconnaissance. Someone's setting the stage for something bigger."

David's expression darkened. "And Elliot's behind it?"

Riles nodded once. "All roads lead to him."

From his spot by the next campsite, Dan was half-watching, half-pretending to adjust the hitch on his truck. He caught bits of the conversation, his mind working faster than he let on. But he didn't step in—not yet.

Ray slouched against the picnic table, sipping his coffee. "So what's the play? We just wait for the next batch of creeps to roll in?"

"No," Riles said firmly. "We watch, we prepare, and we tighten every layer of security. And Haylee—" He met her eyes. "You keep working with Mireille. You're the one thing he can't predict."

Haylee's fingers tightened around her mug. "Then we make sure it stays that way."

Somewhere deep in the campground, a golf cart buzzed past, the hum fading into the trees. The air felt still, but Riles knew better. The quiet before a storm always felt this way.

Under Quiet Skies

By the time they rolled back into the campground, the air had shifted—cooler, touched with that faint woodsmoke scent that always seemed to settle in the evenings here. Bertha waited under the soft wash of the security lights, steady and grounded, but Haylee still felt the faint hum of the day's work in her chest.

David was at the picnic table, polishing off the last of a sandwich. Riles leaned against the side of the Jeep, phone in hand, his expression unreadable until he caught Haylee's eye.

"Got that follow-up from my guy," he said, voice low. "You're gonna want to hear this."

They gathered inside Bertha, the coziness of the small space a strange contrast to the weight in his tone. Josie hopped onto the couch beside Haylee, tail wagging once before settling, Bella curling into the crook of her arm.

"The Combs aren't just random small-timers," Riles began, flipping open his notebook.

"They've worked for half a dozen companies in the last few years—all paper ghosts. No real addresses, no legit business, just holding accounts. Every single one traces back to Elliot's network. Different names, different locations, same signatures on the filings."

"Meaning?" Sam asked, though the set of his jaw said he already knew.

"Meaning this wasn't a lucky guess or a personal grudge," Riles replied. "They were here for a reason. And the way my contact tells it, the Combs usually work the early stages. "They poke around, map the place, test defenses." Then, someone else steps in to finish the job."

Haylee felt a ripple of unease, though it was sharper now, less like fear and more like warning. "So last night wasn't the end of it."

"No," Riles said. "If anything, it was just the first pass."

David let out a slow breath. "And we don't know when the second one's coming."

"No," Riles agreed. "But my contact's watching for movement. If anyone tied to Elliot so much as buys a cup of coffee in this province, I'll know about it."

Outside, a golf cart hummed by on the gravel lane, its headlights briefly sweeping through the RV's blinds. Haylee glanced toward the door, feeling the quiet press in around them.

Dan appeared in the doorway a few minutes later, a casual knock against the frame. "Just checking in," he said, but his eyes flicked from Haylee to Riles, like he'd been listening to more than he was letting on. He held up a thick, official-looking envelope. "Also—this came through the office for you. Looks important."

Haylee froze, staring at the plain envelope in his hand. The government seal was stamped in the corner. Her name, bold and strange in both French and English, sat above the campground's address.

Sam rose and took it from Dan, passing it gently to her. "Go on," he said softly.

Everyone was watching now. The small RV, already tight with unspoken worries, seemed to hold its breath as Haylee slid a finger under the flap. Paper rasped. She unfolded the document, the official weight of it trembling in her hands. The faint scent of ink and paper rose up, grounding and dizzying all at once.

Her Canadian birth certificate. Real. Tangible. Proof.

For a moment she couldn't speak. The page blurred until she blinked hard, grounding herself in the familiar warmth of Josie pressed against her knee and Bella's purr vibrating in her arm.

David leaned forward, his voice rough. "You've got it, kiddo."

Haylee managed a small nod, clutching the paper like it might vanish if she let go. It wasn't just documentation—it was a key. To her past, to her future, to the truth they were all still chasing.

"Told you it looked important," Dan said, tipping his cap. He hesitated, then added, "Oh, and one more thing—you won't need to shuffle Bertha after all. The couple who booked your site canceled this morning, so you can stay put as long as you like."

With another nod, quieter this time, Dan left them in the hush that followed.

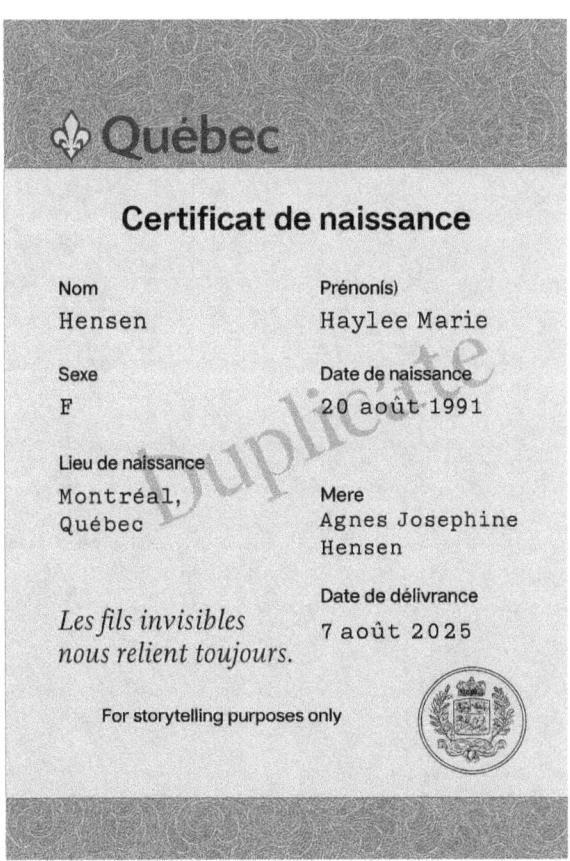

Chapter Forty Three:
The Weeks Between

In the weeks that followed, Haylee's magic wove itself into the rhythm of her days. With Mireille's steady guidance, she practiced whenever she could—sometimes in the quiet hum of Bertha's kitchen, other times beneath the old maple behind the shop. Each lesson felt less like learning and more like remembering, as if she were brushing dust from something she'd carried all her life.

Mireille's voice was a mix of warm Quebecois and fractured English, the syllables rolling like music. "Encore… plus doux, ma chère," she would murmur, guiding Haylee's hands into the right motion. Or, with a smile both proud and wary, "You learn… trop vite. Too fast."

Riles was always there, leaning against a wall or sitting just within reach of the shop's front windows, translating when Mireille's words grew too tangled. He didn't speak much, but his eyes missed nothing. For all he'd seen—war zones, backroom deals gone bad, the worst of what people could do—this was different. The shimmer in the air when Haylee's concentration peaked, the way her breath synced with the slow pulse of whatever force she was calling on—it made something inside him tighten.

One afternoon, while Haylee practiced a ward on the back steps, Riles lingered in the doorway with Mireille. She glanced at him, then at Haylee, lowering her voice. "Elle a du feu… dans le sang. She has fire in the blood. Your friend? She… not easy to stop."

Riles gave a small nod. "That's what worries me."

Because it wasn't just the skill—though that was impressive enough—it was the sheer determination behind every movement. Haylee didn't just want to learn; she meant to master it. And Riles, who'd never been easily shaken, found himself wondering what she'd do—and what lines she'd be willing to cross—when the time came to use it.

Not to Be Underestimated

The quiet rhythm of work, training, and the faint scent of herbs drifting through Mireille's shop. Haylee came every morning, shaking off the chill of the Montreal air, ready to practice. With Riles stationed nearby as her silent shadow, she learned to hold her focus steady while Mireille guided her in a lilting mix of Quebecois and broken English, hands shaping the air around spells as if they were living things.

The progress was fast—faster than Mireille had expected.

"Comme si tu l'avais toujours su," she murmured one afternoon, smiling at Haylee's latest ward. Like you've always known. And in a way, Haylee had. The power didn't feel foreign; it felt like breath—always there, just waiting to be exhaled.

Some moments were perfect: coaxing a wilted plant to bloom on the counter, weaving a shimmer of protection around a jar of dried lavender. Other moments were less controlled. A glass vial cracked mid-incantation one morning, releasing a pop of air that made everyone jump. Mireille's eyes widened, but her tone stayed calm, guiding Haylee through the grounding steps.

Riles watched all of it from the corner, leaning against the doorframe, arms crossed. He wasn't afraid of much—men, guns, the ugly side of people—but this was different. Magic had its own rules, and Haylee seemed to be breaking them in all the right ways. That raw determination in her eyes... it was a kind of fire no bullet could put out. Later, when Haylee stepped outside to breathe in the cold air, Riles spoke low to Mireille.

"She's going to be a problem for him," he said.

"Oui," Mireille agreed without looking up from her herbs. "For Elliot... et pour anyone who underestimates her."

The ward over the shop door flickered—just once—and Riles' gaze snapped to it. Mireille noticed too, pausing mid-stir. Outside, a crow sat on the lamppost, watching through the glass with an unsettling stillness.

Haylee came back in, cheeks flushed from the wind, unaware of the glance Mireille and Riles exchanged. Whatever had just brushed against the edges of their protections, it hadn't crossed the threshold… yet.

Chapter Forty-Four:
Fault Line

The candle flickered again.

Haylee felt it first—like a breeze moving the wrong direction. She stood in the back room of Mireille's shop, palms hovering over the small brass bowl, the candle's flame cupped and steady. The hum inside her settled low and sure, not flashing this time, not burning out. Holding.

"Reste ici," Mireille murmured, circling with slow steps, fingertips grazing the chalk line. "Tu tiens l'espace. You hold the space."

Haylee nodded, exhaling through her nose. The flame answered her breath.

From the front room came the soft chime of the bell as a customer left, Jean-Paul's gentle "Bonne journée" following them out. Riles ghosted the doorway, phone in his hand, eyes scanning without seeming to. He was doing the thing he did when he didn't want to spook anyone—reading a room in layers.

His phone buzzed.

He glanced down. One line from his contact:

"Movement spotted. One asset tied to Elliot crossed into Quebec at dawn."

Another buzz, almost on top of the first:

"Might not be alone. Will confirm."

Riles slid the phone into his pocket like he hadn't read it at all and leaned a shoulder to the frame. "How we doing?"

"Bien," Mireille said, eyes on the circle. Then, to Haylee, softer: "Encore. Plus doux." (Again. Softer.)

Haylee listened. The candle didn't flare this time; it held—precise, obedient, alive.

At the Campground

Outside at the campground, Sam and David lingered near Bertha with takeaway coffees gone lukewarm. The late-morning air had that damp, quiet heaviness that made voices carry farther than you intended.

David picked up a pocketknife he'd been "meaning to clean" for three days and ran the cloth over it like the blade had personally offended him.

"You know," he said finally, "I've seen talent before. This is… something different."

Sam didn't take his eyes off the horizon. "She's still Haylee."

"Power changes people," David said. Not unkind—just honest. "Even the good ones."

Sam's jaw flexed. He swallowed whatever reply wanted to come first. "She's not going to lose herself," he said quietly. "Not after everything it took to find it."

David nodded once, like he wanted to believe him. "Then we make sure the world doesn't try to take it."

Somewhere far off, a breeze shifted through the pines, sharp enough to prickle the skin on both their arms. They exchanged a glance, each silently wondering if Haylee had just done something—or if something had just found her.

When the Veil Trembles

Inside, Mireille's head tilted, listening to something that wasn't sound.

"Le voile…" she said, the words thin as thread. "Il est… fragile, aujourd'hui." (The Veil… it is fragile today.)

Riles stepped farther into the room. "Translate that for the guy with no sixth sense?"

"It means be ready," Haylee said without looking up. The flame answered her, steady as a pulse.

Mireille's mouth curved, proud and wary at once. "Très bien, ma belle. Control… you have it now." Her eyes slid to Riles. "Mais le monde regarde." (But the world is watching.)

As if to underline it, the clear quartz fixed high on the wall—a focus point for the room—cracked down the center with a hairline split. No impact. No heat. Just a soft, decisive tchik that turned every head.

Bella hissed from her shelf perch. Josie, asleep at the threshold, lifted her head and gave a low growl.

Riles' phone buzzed again. He didn't look at it. He already knew.

"Say it," Haylee said, eyes on the candle.

He pulled the phone out anyway.

"Update: Not just one. Multiple signatures. Headed your way."

"Company," he said. "More than one. We need to—"

The bell out front gave the gentlest chime. Not a customer's chime. A draft's.

Jean-Paul called, "Allô?"—then went quiet, as if deciding silence was safer than the answer.

Mireille moved first. "Reste," she told Haylee, no room for argument. "Tu tiens la flamme." (Stay. You hold the flame.) She slipped through the curtain toward the front.

Riles angled to follow, then checked himself, splitting his attention—one eye on the back circle, one on the hall. "You good?"

Haylee didn't blink. "I'm done being anything else."

The air shifted. Not colder—emptier, the way a room feels after someone you love steps out and closes the door. The candle's flame bent, then straightened, refusing to bow.

From the shop, wood creaked—a floorboard taking weight. A shadow slid across the far wall, just beyond the curtain's edge.

The front room looked empty. It wasn't. The empty feeling had shape.

Mireille backed into view, eyes sharp, voice low and rapid in Quebecois. "Ils ne sont pas... comme avant," she told Riles, switching to English only for the part that mattered. "Someone is here... but not how you think."

A strand of incense smoke drifted sideways, pulled by nothing visible. The crack in the quartz widened with a soft, glassy sigh.

Haylee's candle flared—not wild, not out of control, but brighter, as if it had been waiting for this moment.

A voice threaded the air. Low. Almost amused. Close enough to taste.

"Well," it said, not quite from the doorway and not quite from the room. "Took you long enough to find me."

Haylee didn't turn. She didn't need to. The flame stretched toward the sound, steady as a compass needle.

The ward over the door went dark.

And the shop—every window, every corner—exhaled.

About the Author

Kimber Guise is the author of Keys to Wonderlust, a story inspired by her own nomadic lifestyle. She is a full-time traveler, adventurer, and storyteller who explores the open roads of North America in her beloved RV. Accompanied by her loyal pup and curious cats, she embraces a nomadic lifestyle rich with discovery, quiet moments, and scenic detours. From winding mountain passes to tucked-away campgrounds, Kimber finds inspiration in the natural beauty of National and State Parks across the United States and Canada.

A published author and lifelong reader, Kimber believes stories have the power to connect us, heal us, and remind us who we are. When she's not writing, you'll find her chasing sunsets, sipping coffee by a campfire, or browsing the shelves of a local bookstore. She's committed to savoring the journey—wherever the road may lead.

Follow Kimber's adventures and writing life on TikTok and Instagram **@vibing.rvlife**, on Facebook at **Vibing RV Life**, or on YouTube under **Kimber Guise (@vibing.rvlife)**.

www.ingramcontent.com/pod-product-compliance
Lightning Source LLC
Chambersburg PA
CBHW050123030726
47505CB00007B/2006